SATAN'S CHOIR

A JOHN BURKE MYSTERY

SATAN'S CHOIR

TOM HARLEY CAMPBELL

Cayuga Street Press

Cayuga Street Press
Trumansburg, NY USA

Satan's Choir
by Tom Harley Campbell
(tomharleycampbell.com)

First Printing – June 2021
ISBN: 978-1-68111-410-1
Library of Congress Control Number: 2021937600

Author photograph by Jason Koski

Printed in the U.S.A.

0   1   2   3   4   5

For my wife, Annie, and my parents, Molly and Dick
Rest in peace, Pappy

Justice is that virtue which gives everyman his due.
— Saint Augustine

1

Riverside, Ohio
August, 2011

Hot and getting hotter. Ten o'clock on a Monday morning and already eighty-five degrees. The salvage team was sweating as they lowered a home-made diving shot over the steep bank of Eastwood Lake until it broke the surface of the water, about ten feet down. The diving shot was a six-inch thick disc of concrete weighing perhaps seventy pounds, with an eye-bolt imbedded in the center where a nylon rope attached. The diver who was suited up shinnied down the bank holding onto the rope. Once in the water, he adjusted his respirator mask, waved, and the crew began to lower him down with the shot.

He would anchor the heavy shot in the lake bed, and the rope would be used by the divers to move between the surface and the dive site. The lake had once been a huge gravel pit, and the crew already determined that the bottom was about eighty feet down.

In this case, the dive site was the resting place of a beautiful, turquoise and white, 1957 Chevy Bel Air coupe. An unfortunate young man had apparently snuck off with his father's prized car and it somehow ended up at the bottom of Eastwood Lake. The salvage team had been hired out of Cleveland and arrived in Dayton the night before. *Easy money,* they said.

A large crane truck was parked nearby, just off the service road that bordered the lake, and the crane operator stood and watched as the crew slowly lowered the shot. The lone diver held on to the shot line, and although the sunlight dimmed somewhat as he descended,

1

the white top of the car was soon visible. *A lucky break*, he thought – the Chevy had settled right-side-up.

As the shot neared the car, the diver guided it off to one side and let it settle down into the silty bed. He swam free from the rope and inspected the car's position. *This will be a piece of cake*, he thought. There was still some natural light at eighty feet, but the diver turned on a handheld flashlight that had been clipped to his belt. Swimming to the other side of the car, he drew up short when he spotted the ghostly shape of what appeared to be another car, nestled on the silty lake bed maybe four or five feet from the Chevy. The ghost car, too, was sitting right-side-up, buried to the bumpers and covered completely with a blanket of gray-brown silt. Fascinated, the diver moved toward the car and noticed the open windows. He swam to the driver's side and shined the light into the car.

"Jesus Christ!" he garbled into his respirator.

There, perched on the front seat, partially covered with silt but completely recognizable, was a human skull and rib cage.

2

Burke's Law

Around that same time, Police Captain John Burke heard laughter coming from the squad room as he walked down the third-floor hall in the Dayton Police Department headquarters. He wondered what was so goddamn funny. Through the glass wall he could see the other detectives huddled around the coffee maker. When they saw him coming, the group broke up, and the detectives moved off to their desks.

"Grounded for life!" was the last thing he heard, as he opened the door to the squad room.

Burke was the Supervisor of the Homicide/Assault squad for the DPD. Although he was highly regarded by the other detectives, beloved actually, they were never quite sure which Burke they were going to get from day to day. But he was always fair and straight forward with the squad, and happy to advise or help out with their cases. He knew their families, asked about them often, and was even invited over for a meal once in a while.

But Burke's disposition seemed to run hot, cold, or somewhere in between. The squad tended to stay out of his way in the morning, letting him set the tone for the day. At times he would lighten up and smile, maybe even laugh and joke around with the squad, and whenever that happened, they considered it a real coup. No one could quite figure him out, including his own son, Kevin, who had followed in his father's footsteps and was also a detective on the squad. But the person most affected by Burke's mood swings was his wife.

Maggie taught at a public grade school, and they had raised Kevin, their only child, in an old neighborhood in north Dayton, near the school. Burke and Maggie had been living apart for twelve years now, but had never divorced. He knew Maggie still loved him, but she had long ago given up trying to make their marriage work on an everyday basis. She still lived in their house, and made dinner there for Burke maybe once every two weeks. Occasionally, Burke would take Maggie out to eat at Jay's, her favorite restaurant, down in the gentrified Oregon district on the eastside of downtown. Sometimes they would take in a movie or a Dayton Dragons baseball game.

Maggie called him *Johnny*. Kevin called him *Pop*, or *Pops*. The squad and almost everyone else called him either *Cap* or *J.B.*, and despite his unpredictable temperament, the squad was going to miss him when he retired in October.

Burke went to his desk and turned on his computer. Kevin followed him and tossed some papers down in front of his father. Burke was grooming Kevin to be the next head of the homicide squad for the DPD.

"Morning, Pop. These need to be signed by the end of the day."

"Who's grounded for life?" Burke asked, hanging his still crisp summer suit jacket on the back of a chair.

"Oh, that dumbass kid who rolled his old man's '57 Chevy into the lake. You must have heard about it. One of the Metropark cops was telling Danny and Jamal about it last night."

"No. What happened?" Burke asked, sitting down.

"Well, I guess this stupid kid snuck off with the car, and he and his girlfriend somehow got into Eastwood Park after closing time. Anyway, he parked just off a service road, near the edge of the water. Apparently, there's a spot there with a good view up the lake to the city lights. So, they were doing whatever they were doing on a blanket nearby, when the damn car rolled into the lake." Kevin rolled his eyes. "The kid must've put the car in neutral when he parked it, and there was just enough slope."

"Dumbass is right," Burke said, shaking his head in disgust.

"They're going to pull the car out sometime today," said Kevin. "Anyway, Danny and Jamal said it was a quiet night. They're outta here, and Tarisa and Marco are in for today. But she might have to leave for an hour this afternoon to register her daughter for school."

Tarisa Williams was the only female detective on the squad, a single African-American mom who'd come up through the ranks. Everyone on the squad had come up that way. Besides Burke, Marco Renzi was the most senior detective, but he had declined when offered a captaincy to replace Burke. Ten years ago maybe, he said, but he'd be retiring himself in a couple of years. Marco and Tarisa were a good team.

Danny and Jamal checked out, and Burke watched them amble down the hall in their crumpled suits and loosened ties. He was glad it had been a quiet night, a rarity at this sweltering time of year. Dayton could be miserable in August, like any of the low river towns in the Midwest, with high humidity and 90-degree temperatures, maybe a little cooler at night.

Dayton's homicide rate had decreased over the years. It was nothing like it had been when Burke first joined the force in the 1970s, when the title for the highest murder rate in the country was swapped back and forth every year between Dayton and Detroit, or maybe Newark. Back then, the murders were domestic or drug related, and mostly *black-on-black*, a term that Burke had never been quite comfortable with. He was well aware that even now, a high percentage of the homicide victims in Dayton were black, but even if it *was* mostly *black-on-black* he wondered why they didn't they call it *white-on-white* when a white person committed a crime against another white person. More recently, gangs had been thrown into the mix, and a lot of people in town were in denial about the existence of a gang culture in their city.

"How's your Mom?" Burke asked Kevin.

"She's good. She had to get a new compressor for the air conditioner. I'm sure you'll hear about it. When's the last time you talked to her?"

"Oh, probably a week," said Burke. "I pissed her off the last time I was over there. She said I was too negative about everything."

"Yeah, she told me," Kevin said, shaking his head. He'd heard it all before. "Look Pop, you've got to lighten up when you're around her. And stop being such a damn grump. I know you guys get along sometimes, so just talk to her. That's all she wants."

Hot, cold, and somewhere in between. Burke couldn't figure it out either. At Maggie's insistence, he'd been to several counselors and shrinks over the years, but he could never stick with anyone for very long. Kevin had mostly stopped trying to talk to Burke about his moods and his relationship with Maggie.

"I'll call her soon. We should work on these special requests," Burke said, changing the subject. "I'm going to meet with Claire tomorrow to go over this stuff. And we should start looking at the candidate list – not that there's any money for adding staff. But just in case, we ought to have some people in mind."

Major Claire Winston was Burke's boss, head of Special Investigations. She was a few years younger than Burke and his first female superior. Her position – mostly administrative – had been offered to Burke, but he'd turned it down, and Claire was promoted from another division in the department. They got along well – she left his department alone for the most part – and she and Burke trusted and respected each other, something he couldn't say about some of his previous bosses.

"Bones and Pete will be in this afternoon," Kevin said. "Same shifts all week for now. You and I can fill in if need be, if that's OK with you?"

"Fine with me," said Burke. He was going to miss the squad as much as they would miss him – it was the best crew he'd ever put together. Burke ran a pretty tight ship, and the squad rarely complained about his old-school rules, including his dress code. For Tarisa it was slacks, pantsuits, or a skirt, *not too short*, and for the guys it was suits or sport coats, *nothing too flashy*, and slacks, *no jeans*. Khakis and cords were okay. And Burke didn't want to see any tattoos. If you had them, *keep 'em covered*, and *no damned buzz cuts* like a lot of the patrolmen were sporting. Burke said he didn't want his squad looking like a bunch of neo-Nazi skinheads.

"When was the last time you saw a *black* neo-Nazi?" Jamal had cracked. Burke made an exception for Bones, who was prematurely very nearly bald, and let him shave what little was left.

Burke's Law somebody called it, in reference to the TV detective show from the sixties that the younger detectives had never heard of. Burke also banned squad room texting – unless it had something to do with a case. And no *twittering, tweeting,* or *Facebook.* Burke, Marco, and Pete carried the barest-boned phones available. Burke's was at least four years old and the object of much derision. The rest of the squad all had the latest high-end smart phones, and in the lunchroom, they were always bragging and showing off new apps. *Waste of time*, Burke thought.

Burke and Kevin spent the morning going through paperwork, mostly requisition forms and reports from the weekend. They went out to Lucky's for a sandwich at lunchtime, and Burke was back at his desk when the office phone rang. Kevin answered and talked briefly to the caller. He laughed and leaned back in his chair.

"It's for you, Pop," he called across the room. "Gary Stanley from Metro." Stanley was the chief of the Metropark Police, and his district was the area's Five Rivers Metropark system, including Eastwood Lake. Burke picked up.

"Gary, how's it going? I hear you had a little incident at the lake the other night. Something about a '57 Chevy?"

"Yeah, Cap, but more like *in* the lake," Stanley laughed. "Some numbnut kid really fucked up. That's actually what I'm calling about."

"So, what's up?" Burke asked.

"Well, I'm here at the lake right now, and they just craned the car out. It was down about eighty feet. Anyway – and you're not going to believe this – when the divers came up, they said there was *another* car down there, right next to the damn Chevy!"

"You're kidding me!"

"No! I shit you not . . . side by side, just like they're in a Kroger parking lot. They said it was pretty dark down there but they got a good look at the other car before they stirred things up. I guess it's been down there a long time. The reason I'm bothering *you* is that the divers saw what they think are some human bones on the front seat of the second car. A rib cage and a skull."

"Holy shit, Gary!"

"Holy shit is right. That's why I called you. Anyway, the divers and the crane crew said they'd be happy to bring the other car up if we want them to, just as long as they get paid. They said the car looks like it's in pretty good shape, and it shouldn't be a problem. They think they can get it up in one piece using the same strap rig they used on the Chevy. What do you want me to do?"

Burke thought for a second.

"Do you think these guys know what they're doing, Gary?"

"They seem pretty slick to me," Gary said. "We had to go on the Google to find them."

Burke couldn't help grinning. "Go on the Google?"

"Yeah. They're salvage divers. We hired them out of Cleveland. They do a lot of work up on Lake Erie."

"Okay. Ask them to stick around," Burke said, after a moment's thought. "Tell them the DPD will pay for it. And I guess you'd better tape off the area. I'll call the coroner, and then I'll be right down. But leave the car in the water for now, all right?"

"Got it," said Gary. "How much area should I tape off?"

"Hell, I don't know. Whatever you think. If there's a crime involved it probably happened so long ago it's not like we'll find any evidence. Go out maybe two hundred feet all the way around from the edge of the lake. I'll call Catherine's office and then head right down. Where on the lake are you exactly?"

"In Riverside, just off Harshman Road, on the south side of the lake. You'll see the crane."

Marco and Tarisa had walked into the squad room just as Burke hung up. Kevin stood up, gave them a quick wave, and walked to his father's desk.

"What the hell was that all about?" he asked, eyebrows raised.

"They found a second car in the lake, eighty feet down, possibly some human remains," Burke said. "Out near my old stompin' grounds. Can you call Catherine at the coroner's office? Tell her what's up, and tell her they're ready to bring the car up. See if she can send someone to meet us down there right away. It's in Riverside, just off Harshman Road on the south side of the lake. Tell her she'll see the crane."

"You got it, Pop. You sure you want me to come along?"

"Yeah, this could be interesting – and you might learn something. Tarisa and Marco can hold down the fort. Are you guys good?" Burke asked them.

"No problem," replied Marco. "We've got some follow-up to write on that domestic out by the airport. We'll probably be in here till the end of the shift."

"Okay, thanks," said Burke, turning back to Kevin. "I'll give Major Winston a heads up and then meet you at my car. If there really are remains involved, she'll probably have to set up a press conference at some point."

Burke grabbed his jacket and started for the hall.

"Hell, maybe *I'll* learn something," he said to no one in particular.

3

This Very Spot

Burke drove east out of downtown on Third Street and angled left onto Springfield Street. Kevin turned on the car radio. It was tuned to *WYSO*, the local *NPR* station broadcasting from Antioch College in Yellow Springs. Burke liked to listen to the station for the news. Kevin switched to a classic rock station. "Snoopy vs. The Red Baron" was playing.

"Turn that shit off," said Burke. "That song sucked forty years ago."

Kevin laughed and turned the radio off, shaking his head. *Pop's right*, he thought, *the song sucks,* but Burke's reaction reminded him of his father's general dislike for all music. Apparently, it hadn't always been that way. Burke's mother once told Maggie that he sang all the time when he was a kid. Now, he didn't seem to like any of it, and he'd never been able to really explain why.

Through the smoggy afternoon haze, Burke spotted the crane off to the left as they drove along Springfield Street on the south side of Eastwood Lake.

Off to the right, Burke could see rows of vintage aircraft, and the collection of huge hangar-like buildings that make up the National Museum of the United States Air Force, spread out at the edge of Wright Field, the oldest area of Wright-Patterson Air Force Base. It was the largest and oldest aviation museum in the world, and Burke and Kevin had visited the museum together many times over the years. It was one of Burke's favorite places, and had been since he was a kid.

That was back when the original museum was located in an old hanger on a different part of the base out near Fairborn. Then it was simply called the Air Force Museum, and that's what almost everyone still called it.

"Maybe we should go and check out what's new at the museum if we have time later," he said, pointing to his right. "I haven't been there since last year. Remember? We went to see the new paint job on Kennedy's plane."

John Kennedy's Air Force One was one the most popular of all the presidential aircraft on display, including FDR's, Truman's, and Eisenhower's. It was a modified Boeing 707, the jet that had taken Kennedy and Jackie to Dallas on November 22, 1963. It's where the iconic photo was taken of Lyndon Johnson being sworn in – a distraught, disbelieving, and blood-and-brain spattered Jackie Kennedy at his side, as the jet flew Kennedy's body back to Washington.

Burke had grown up just on the other side of Wright Field, a mile and a half away, in a neighborhood surrounding St. Nicholas Catholic Church. Back then, the runway was still in regular use, and the sky was always filled with every sort of jet and airplane imaginable. Burke and his friends, many of whose fathers were Air Force officers, competed to identify all the different aircraft. They cussed and argued, showing off how much they knew about each plane's distinguishing features, but they would shut up and stare in awe when some strange, new experimental jet was spotted for the first time, and cheer for the sonic booms that shook the air on an almost daily basis.

Patterson Field, containing a much longer runway, was located several miles northeast of Wright field, and had once been home to a Strategic Air Command unit. From there, back during the Cold War in the 1950s and 60s, a SAC squadron of nuclear bomb-laden B-52 bombers had rotated in and out of the sky, round the clock, as part of America's nuclear deterrent program. In a strange mixture of braggadocio and fear, young Burke and his friends often boasted that if the Russians ever decided to launch an attack on the United States, WPAFB would be one of their first targets. At St. Nicholas School,

Burke grew up with the *duck and cover* drills that were taught during the Cold War. He remembered a visit to one of his school friends who lived in base housing. The father of his friend was an Air Force colonel, who had scoffed at the idea of *duck and cover*.

"You'd best just bend over, put your head between your legs, and kiss your ass goodbye," the colonel said, laughing and waving the terrified boys away.

"Kiss your ass goodbye," Burke said quietly, watching for the light to change.

"Say what?" asked Kevin, leaning toward his father.

"Duck and cover," Burke said.

"Oh, yeah," Kevin said. He'd heard the story before.

Burke took a left onto Harshman, crossed the bridge over Mad River, and turned into the park. The Five Rivers Metropark system was named for the five waterways that converge in Dayton – the Great Miami River, Mad River, Stillwater River, Wolf Creek and Twin Creek.

He headed for the crane, just beyond a parking lot, not far from the edge of the lake. The '57 Chevy sat nearby, a beautifully restored, two-door, white and turquoise Bel Air, gleaming in the hot sun. The crane and the car were inside a perimeter, taped off with plastic yellow police tape. There were several other cars inside the tape, including two Metropark police vehicles and a Riverside police car. This section of the lake was within the Riverside city limits, and although Riverside was now incorporated, it had once been a hamlet of Mad River Township, just beyond the old Dayton suburbs. Any criminal investigation in Riverside not within the scope of Metropark or the local cops fell to the Dayton police. Five or six more cars, a flatbed wrecker, and several vans – one of them official-looking with an Ohio state seal decal on the door – were parked in the lot nearby.

A small crowd of people, mostly curious onlookers, were standing around or sitting at some picnic tables under a small grove of willow trees outside the perimeter. The crane crew and four or five divers sat together under a small maple tree. One diver was still wearing a wet suit, open and hanging from his waist. The other divers had on Speedos or shorts.

Gary Stanley, looking overheated in his black Metropark uniform, and Scott Kaminsky, the Riverside police chief, broke from the crowd and walked quickly towards Burke and Kevin. As if choreographed, both father and son stepped out of the air-conditioned police cruiser and immediately removed their jackets, tossing them back into the car. The heat in the parking lot was fierce.

"Man, I'm glad to see you guys," Kaminsky said, extending his hand. "Everybody's getting a little cranky."

"Nice car," Burke said, looking toward the Chevy. He shook hands with the two officers.

"Yeah, nice and wet," Kaminsky laughed.

"Is Metro paying for that?" Burke nodded toward the big crane.

"No way." Stanley grinned. "*We* lined up the crane and the divers, but poor Daddy's going to get the bill. That's him in the blue T-shirt. He's kind of pissed off that we wouldn't let him take his car home. He's got that wrecker waiting." Stanley pointed.

Burke gave it a glance and then surveyed the rest of the scene.

"Go ahead and let him take the car," he said, looking again at the group of onlookers.

"I was hoping you'd say that," said Stanley.

"Is that the kid who put the car in the lake?" Kevin asked, pointing to a skinny teenager who was standing off by himself, punching away on a cell phone.

"No, that would be Lisa Fowler's son. You must know Lisa from the *Daily News*. That's her, over there at the picnic table."

"Christ, how the hell did she hear about this?" Burke wondered aloud, spotting the reporter. She threw Burke a quick salute, and he could tell she was laughing.

He liked Lisa Fowler. She was a good reporter, and always got the story right. Lisa wrote for the *Dayton Daily News,* and over the years she'd interviewed Burke many times. She was always happy to cooperate when he asked her to sit on a breaking story, if there was any chance it could hamper an investigation. Lisa was almost always the first reporter at any serious Dayton crime scene. She was tough and flirty and poked fun at Burke for being so serious all the time. She even made him laugh once in a while.

"Total coincidence," Stanley said. "She was here to cover the Chevy being pulled out. Her son is here because it just happens to be Bring Your Kid to Work Week at the paper. Poor kid looks to be bored shitless."

Burke smiled at that.

"Who's in the state car?" Kevin asked.

"Ohio EPA," said Stanley. "Adding insult to injury. Looks like Daddy may have to pay a fine if they determine the car polluted the lake. It's part of the city water system."

"Dumbass kid," Burke said, shaking his head. "Well, hell, I guess we're just waiting for someone from the coroner's office. You called her, right Kevin?"

"Yeah. I told her what we knew. She said she'd pull together a crew and probably have to stop and pick up some equipment."

"Good," said Burke. "Why don't you take a look around inside the perimeter just for grins. And talk to the divers, find out what they saw down there. And ask them and the crane guys if they can invoice the DPD for our share of this. Give them any contact info they might need. I'm going to say hello to Miss Fowler."

Burke wiped his sweaty face with the back of his hand. "*Goddamn* it's hot! Is there anywhere to get a drink of water around here, Gary?"

"I think the divers have a cooler full of bottled water. I'll see what I can do."

"Thanks," said Burke. He headed for the picnic table where Lisa Fowler was sitting.

Lisa stopped writing in a notebook and got up when she saw Burke coming toward her. She was trim, with ash brown hair pulled back in a ponytail, maybe in her mid-forties.

"Hiya, J. B.," she said. "I hear we may have a mystery on our hands."

When he shook her hand, he was surprised at how cool it felt. "We'll see. What have *you* heard so far?"

"Not much. One of the Metro cops tipped me off, and we – my son and I, that's him over there – we just came down to watch them crane that beautiful car out of the lake. Thought I could file a story on the whole mess. I told Jason he'd better never pull a stupid stunt like that."

Lisa caught her son's eye when he looked up from his phone, and waved him over. Burke watched as the boy ambled slowly toward them, barely taking his eyes from the phone.

"Captain Burke, this is my son, Jason," she said. "Jason, this is Captain Burke. He's head of the homicide division for the DPD."

That got the teenager's attention.

"Cool!" he said, shaking Burke's hand. "Mom's told me about you. She says you're a great cop."

Burke would have blushed if he hadn't already been flushed from the heat. Lisa did blush slightly, and smiled.

"It's nice to meet you, Jason. You helping your Mom today?"

"Not really. She thought it would be cool if I just followed her around. Is there really a skeleton down there in another car?"

"I don't know," Burke answered, looking at Lisa. "Sounds like you guys know about as much as I do."

"When will they bring it up?" Jason asked.

"Well, we're waiting to get the OK from the chief coroner. She's on her way."

"*She*? The chief coroner is a *she*?" Jason said. "That is so cool!"

"I have him well trained as you can see," Lisa said, laughing. Stanley approached with a small plastic bottle of water and handed it to Burke. "Compliments of the divers," he said.

"Thanks, Gary." Burke offered the water to Lisa.

"No thanks," she said. "We've got plenty in the car."

The bottle was cold and wet and Burke rubbed it across his forehead. He opened it and drank off half the water. They sat down at the picnic table, and mostly chatted about the heat. Jason wandered off, typing rapidly on his phone.

"My daughter said she wouldn't be caught dead following me around," Lisa said, watching Jason. "They're both pretty good kids, though."

Burke watched his own son walking away from the group of divers, stuffing a notebook and pen into his shirt pocket. Kevin headed for the '57 Chevy, where the wrecker driver was lowering the bed of his truck.

"If you'll excuse me, Lisa," Burke said, standing up, "I'd like to get a look at that car before they take it away."

Kevin was peering in at the waterlogged interior as Burke approached.

"I always thought I'd like to have one of these someday," Burke said. "Exactly this same car. Same model, same color. See this? It's a sport coupe – different than a two-door sedan – no post between the front and rear windows."

Burke glanced over at his drab-gray, four-door Pontiac cookie cutter police cruiser and then back at the beautiful Chevy, shaking his head. Kevin was surprised at his father's familiarity with the vintage car.

"Maybe you should make that poor guy an offer," he said, nodding toward the car's owner who was talking to the wrecker driver. "I'll bet he'd give you a good deal right about now."

The owner looked like he was ready to cry. Burke was about to offer the man some consolation when he saw the coroner's van turn into the parking lot.

"There's Catherine," he said. The van parked, and Dr. Catherine DiMarco, chief coroner and head medical examiner for Dayton and Montgomery County, stepped out from the shotgun seat. Three others, two men and a woman, also piled out, wincing at the sun and the oppressive heat.

"Hi, Catherine," Burke greeted her. "See you brought the crew."

"You *bet* I brought the crew. I don't think any of us have ever done anything quite like this before. Should be interesting. You guys all know each other, right? *Man*, it's hot!"

"The crane operator and the divers are ready to go," Kevin told her. "Maybe you guys should talk to them." Kevin led the forensics team over to where the divers were still lounging about under a tree.

"Nice car," said Catherine, nodding toward the Chevy, which was now being strapped down to the flatbed.

"The other one is still at the bottom of the lake," said Burke. "What do you want to do?"

"Hell, let's pull it up. You think these guys know what they're doing?"

"I guess we'll find out," Burke replied with a wry smile. "Shall we check out the lake?"

The two of them crossed the parking lot and stepped over a low guard rail. A grassy incline, brown now from the summer heat, brought them down to a gravel service road. Another dry, grassy median, maybe forty feet wide, lay between the road and the drop-off at the edge of the lake. The crane was set up just off the road, and a large cargo van, all the doors open and cluttered with diving gear, was parked nearby.

Burke and Catherine walked to the edge and looked ten feet down at the water. The bank was almost vertical. The lake, once a huge gravel pit, had been donated to the city long ago by the gravel company. Fed by the Mad River, it had filled with water and became part of the city's water supply, eventually becoming Eastwood Lake.

Suddenly, Burke looked up from the water. Squinting, he gazed down the lake toward the city skyline, shimmering now in the bright afternoon light, but quite visible. He stared for several seconds, then glanced quickly across the lake, and then to his right. *I've been here before*, Burke thought to himself. *I know this spot.* He turned around and looked back at the parking lot, then again, up, down, and across the lake.

"Jesus, Catherine," he murmured. "I think I used to swim in this very spot."

4

Positively No

"Are you okay?" Kevin asked Burke, walking up to where Burke and Catherine stood with their backs to the lake. Burke looked slightly bewildered.

"Yeah, I'm fine. I was just telling Catherine I *think* this is the very spot where we used to swim sometimes when we were kids. It's quite a bit different now, but I'm pretty sure this is the place. There were a lot more trees along the road back then, and more trees by the shore. Lots of brush, too. We used to bike over from the neighborhood and sneak in, probably right up there by the park entrance." Burke pointed. "We picked a lot of blackberries back in here. You couldn't see this place from the road."

"Very cool," said Kevin. "So, this was kind of a known place?"

"Yeah, it was."

"That could be important," Catherine said, arching her eyebrows.

"Maybe, maybe," said Burke, obviously caught up in the memory. "There was a wooden sign on a tree, next to the cliff. Can you imagine that? We called this a *cliff*. Anyway, the sign read "POSITIVELY NO". That's all it said. The "SWIMMING" part was missing, so that's what we called this spot, "POSITIVELY NO". That's what everybody called it. Man, I haven't thought about this place in years."

"Did you come here a lot?" Kevin asked.

"For two or three summers, I think," Burke nodded his head, still in the moment. "We couldn't afford to join the pool, but I *loved* swimming here. There was a rope tied on a limb that you could swing

18

out on, and another one hung down in the water for climbing out. Man, it was great!"

Burke stared down into the water. "But then poor Vinny Vincent drowned, and I stopped coming here. Vinny was a few years older than us, and those guys were always trying to see if they could touch the bottom. Nobody ever did, and I guess poor Vinny died trying. I was kind of creeped out about the place after that."

Again, Burke peered down into the water. His reverie was broken by the approach of Stanley and Kaminsky. They made their excuses, said they would try to come back later, and Burke watched as they drove off. Catherine's staff stepped over the guardrail and came down to the edge of the lake.

"The car is in silt, halfway up the tires," one of them explained. "The divers said they can dig it out and work the lift straps in, probably by feel once they stir it up."

The divers were fairly certain the car would stay in one piece. They could bring it up with the straps and wouldn't have to use airbags to float it to the surface. The crane crew and the divers huddled near the crane for a few minutes, and then the divers started to suit up. The temperature at eighty feet down was a cold forty-two degrees, they said, and because of this they were donning their warmer, baggier dry suits as opposed to wet suits. The cold temperature also had a lot to do with the old car being in such good shape, they guessed.

Catherine explained to the crane operator what she wanted him to do with the car once it was out of the water. She had one of her staff bring their van down the service road, and they unloaded four or five rolls of six-foot-wide fiberglass window screen, several large plastic containers with lids, a pop-up tent canopy, and a large-size package of paper towels.

"Good ol' Home Depot," said Catherine.

Two of the divers, carrying small, military type trenching spades, climbed down the bank using a rope that had been anchored to the lake bed, and disappeared underwater. Twenty minutes later they resurfaced, clambered up the bank and handed the shovels off to two other divers. They alternated like this for about an hour, with all six divers taking part.

Finally, the divers announced they were ready for the sling rig to be lowered. The crane operator fired up the crane and extended the boom out over the water, lowering the rig. One diver took hold of the rig and disappeared down into the murky water. Three other divers followed the rope down to the submerged car. Fifteen minutes passed before one of the divers surfaced, motioning for the crane to draw up the cable. When it tightened, he motioned for the operator to stop. Diving back down, he reemerged after ten minutes, and once again motioned the operator to start reeling. The crane's motor revved, strained at first, and then suddenly eased. Burke visualized the car breaking free from the mud. The diver in the water motioned the crane operator to stop, and he dove down one more time.

Burke and Kevin had been watching the diving operation, but now turned and walked back to where Catherine and her crew were busy laying out the window screen over a large flat area on the grassy median. One of the divers helped them fill the plastic containers with lake water, using an old spackle bucket tied to a piece of nylon rope.

"Looks like you have a plan," Burke said to Catherine.

"Hell, J.B., I'm just making this shit up," replied Catherine. "We're hoping this screen will catch anything important that drips out of the car."

"What's the water for?" Kevin asked, pointing to the plastic tubs.

"We're going to put any remains – or whatever else we might find – in the containers," she answered. "The stuff may fare better if we keep it in the lake water until we can examine it in the lab."

"I think I saw something like that on one of those Jacques Cousteau specials once," said Burke.

Catherine laughed. "Where the hell do you think I *got* the idea?"

A few minutes later all the divers came to the surface and scrambled up the bank. Everything looked good, they said, and the crane began to reel in the cable. They all moved to the edge of the bank – Burke, Kevin, the divers, Catherine and her crew – and watched, transfixed, as the car finally broke the surface, and the lake gave up its long-time guest.

"It's another Chevy," said Burke. "Looks like a '63."

5

Riverside, Ohio: November, 1963

Mike Donnelly was in his office when he got a call from the school secretary at St. Nick's, informing him that his son, Tim, a sixth grader, had left school at lunchtime and hadn't returned. There was no signed excuse note at the office, and his younger sisters, also students at the school, didn't seem to know why their brother had left. The secretary had tried to call Mike's wife, Eileen, but Mike knew she was away for the day, volunteering at St. Elizabeth hospital.

Mike and Eileen had been worried about Tim. Over the past month, he'd been withdrawing from the family, becoming more sullen and quieter every day. He'd quit pee-wee football and the choir. Sister Roberta, the school principal, had called recently about his falling behind in class. With no official guidance counselor at the school, she'd recommended that Tim talk to Father Nelson, the assistant pastor and director of St. Nicholas Boys' Choir; apparently, the priest had received some counselor training in the seminary. Timmy had refused to talk to him.

Mike spoke with his boss and headed for home. He worked as an electrical engineer at the Delco Products plant in downtown Dayton. As a young man, he'd volunteered for the Army, rising to the rank of sergeant. Not long after D-Day, he was landed in southern France as part of Operation Dragoon. Already battle-hardened from the brutal campaigns in Sicily and Italy, he led his men from village to village, chasing the Germans up the Rhone valley. After the war, thanks to the

GI bill, Mike earned his degree at the University of Dayton, and eventually landed a job at Delco.

It was just a fifteen-minute drive from work to his house. He drove through east Dayton to Belfair Avenue, made the sign of the cross as he passed St. Nicholas Catholic Church, and immediately turned right onto Harvard Drive. The plat of houses – modest clapboard and brick, ranches and capes – surrounded the church and school. His house was the fifth house up from St. Nick's, on the same side of the street.

Mike entered the house through the side door and noticed Timmy's school books, neatly covered in ink-marked brown paper grocery bags, stacked on the kitchen table.

"Timmy?" he called out. No answer. He walked down the hall and pushed open the door to Timmy's room. The boy was lying on his back, cradling his father's twelve-gauge shotgun in his arms, the muzzle tucked under his chin. A box of shotgun shells was open on the bed. Tim was sound asleep.

Horrified, Mike entered the room quietly and carefully lifted the gun from Timmy's arms. He moved the safety to the off position and unloaded the gun, leaning it in the corner of the room. Sitting down on the bed, he gave his son a little shake to wake him. Slowly coming out of his sleep, Timmy sat up, looked around, and burst into tears. He threw his arms around his father and began to sob, quickly moving Mike to tears, and they rocked back and forth as Mike patted and stroked his son's back.

"It's okay, Timmy," he repeated over and over. "It's okay." Tim cried, gasping until he could hardly breathe. Mike continued to rock his son in his arms for a long time, until the sobbing slowly subsided and the boy went limp in his father's hold.

"Timmy, please . . . please tell me what's wrong?" Mike begged, holding Tim away from him and wiping his face with the bed cover. The boy offered no resistance and stared back at his father.

"I can't tell you," he said quietly, starting to cry again. "I can't tell anyone."

Mike held him close and told him that everything would be all right. He let his son cry for several minutes, wiped his face again, and held him even tighter.

"You won't believe me," Timmy sobbed. "No one will believe me."

Mike tipped his son's face up and looked him in the eyes. "Timmy, you know I love you more than anything in the whole world. There's nothing you can't tell me. I'll listen to you and I'll help you, and everything will be okay. I promise. I'll believe you no matter what you say. But I can't help if you won't tell me what's wrong. Please, please, Timmy, tell me what's wrong."

Tim cried softly, pressing his face against his father's shoulder. Finally, he stopped, wiped his own nose with his sleeve, and relaxed into his father's embrace.

"He . . . he . . . p...p . . . put his p . . . p . . . penis in m . . . my mouth," he stuttered, almost whispering. "And in m . . . my b . . . b . . . bottom."

Mike held Timmy tightly and rocked back and forth, patting the boy's head and kissing his tear-stained cheeks.

"Who did, Timmy? Who did this?"

"You can't tell Mom," Timmy sobbed.

Mike promised not to tell. But he would kill the sonofabitch.

6

1963 Impala

Turbid water poured from the half-open windows as the crane operator swung the car toward the shore.

"How do you know it's a '63?" Kevin asked Burke. "Hell, how do you even know it's a *Chevy*?"

"The Chevy part is easy," Burke said, studying the dripping car. "Cars used to be a lot more distinctive. Back when this car was new, me and my friends, we knew every damn car on the road – could name it from a block away."

"But what makes it a '63 then?" Kevin asked.

"See the points in the body shape, in the front and the back?" Burke drew a sideways "V" in the air with his finger. "It's distinctive. It was like that only one year, 1963."

Catherine could only imagine what important evidence was washing back into the lake from the dripping car. Everyone on shore stood back out of the way while the operator maneuvered the car over the area where the forensics team had laid out the rolls of screen. As the car rotated slowly in the air, Burke got a look at the rear end. He noticed a bent license plate still in place – he hadn't seen one on the front.

"It's an Impala," he said with a slight grin, knowing that the observation would rile Kevin.

"All right, how the hell do you know that?"

"See the three taillights on each side?" Burke said, pointing again. "The Bel Air and the Biscayne only had two per side."

"Jesus, Pop!" Kevin said, shaking his head.

"The middle light of the three is the backup light," added Burke, just for good measure. He wasn't a hundred percent sure of this, but he didn't tell Kevin that.

The crane lowered the car slowly, and just before it touched down, Catherine and her crew spotted the skeleton. When the Impala finally thumped to the ground, the skull toppled from atop the rib cage and fell onto the seat.

"Ouch!" one of the crew muttered. "That's gotta hurt," someone else snickered. The car had come to rest more or less in the center of the screen, and water continued to drain out from around the deteriorated door gaskets. A lot of the silt had been washed away from the exterior as the car came up through the lake, and while there was quite a bit of rust and missing chrome, it was evident that the car had been painted black. The tires were all flat and the whitewalls stained, but still recognizable as whitewalls.

Catherine asked the divers to remove the straps, and the crane swung the harness out of the way. She let all the divers look into the car briefly, then asked everyone to stay off the screen, except for her and her team. Burke and Kevin were now part of the team.

They approached the car and peered into the front seat area. Sure enough, there were several bones and what appeared to be a mostly intact rib cage protruding from the remaining silt on the driver's side of the front seat. The skull had nestled near the middle of the seat, face up and missing the jaw bone. The seats themselves were remarkably intact, and one of the team guessed it was most likely because of the synthetic material they were made of. They also noticed what looked like a seat belt mixed in with the bones and the silt, and Burke tried to remember when seat belts had become an option. Looking closer, they spotted more bones on the driver's side floor of the car, below the steering wheel. The back seat seemed to contain nothing but silt.

"Okay then. Let's get the gloves on," Catherine directed, "We'll put the remains into the containers. And let's set up the canopy. It's too goddamn hot to work in this sun."

Burke and Kevin pitched in. They tried to open the doors of the car, but it was hopeless. The team decided it was better to leave them closed anyway for the time being. Instead, they leaned in through the open windows to reach the material. They were careful where they stepped as they began methodically to extricate the bones. What looked to be scraps of clothing were mixed in with the bones, along with some keys and coins. One key was rusted into the ignition. They found a watch, a pair of shoes, and part of a leather belt. They handled things as little as possible; the car and all of the material would be investigated more closely once it was back at the lab.

Burke and Kevin inspected the lone license plate, which appeared to be firmly attached. It was folded over on itself, almost in half, with the metal torn and crunched up at one corner. The plate was rusty, but the embossed surfaces were still evident. They could even make out the small lettering of *OHIO.*

"We'll get that straightened out and give it a good look in the lab," said Catherine, nudging them aside and squatting down for her own inspection.

"Maybe it got bent up like that when the car went over the edge," Kevin said, standing up.

Burke wiped his hands with a paper towel. "Odd that there's no front plate."

"What about the trunk?" Kevin asked. "Should we try to open it now or wait until you get the car downtown?"

"No, go ahead and see if you can get it open," Catherine said. "Who knows, there may be more remains in there."

Kevin borrowed some tools from the crane operator, and the trunk creaked open fairly easily, surprising everyone. The team peered in. They could see a spare tire, what looked to be a pair of suitcases, and something tube-shaped – maybe a rolled-up rug – all half-buried in silt.

"Better close it back up," directed Catherine. "We'll finish the job down at the lab."

It was after six o'clock and the sun floated over Dayton, shimmering like a mirage, as they wrapped things up. Two county flatbed trucks arrived, one hauling a large forklift; the car would go to a secure parking lot at the lab. The divers and the crane had left long ago, and now Catherine and her forensic team waved as they drove off.

Burke and Kevin were taking down the police tape when Lisa Fowler's car turned into the parking lot and pulled up next to Burke. Burke could feel the cool air coming from the car as she lowered the window.

"Hey, J.B., glad I caught you," she said. "I had to take Jason home – he was bored out of his mind. What can you tell me?"

"I'm afraid I can't give you much that you don't already know," said Burke. "There are indeed human remains in the car, and they'll go to the lab. The car is a black 1963 Chevy Impala, and we have no idea how long it's been down there. So far there's no hard evidence of foul play."

"No *hard* evidence?" Lisa asked.

"No evidence," Burke lied, correcting himself. He remembered the coroner muttering a quick "*hmmm*" when she'd pointed out some damage to the back of the skull.

"Okay, no evidence. Anyway, I got some photos," Lisa said. "I'm pretty sure I've got a scoop. No TV crews showed up the whole time I was here."

"Good for you, Lisa," said Burke, patting the roof of the car. "Just so you know, if we figure out whose remains are in the car, we'll have to try to notify the next of kin. Major Winston will probably want to set up a press conference after that."

"Thanks, J.B." Lisa smiled, looking Burke up and down. "Now go home and take a shower. You look like you've been playing in the mud all day."

7

Mary Lou Spaulding

Out in Kettering, at about the same time that Burke and Kevin were pulling away from the Eastwood Lake parking lot and heading back downtown, Mary Lou Spaulding was fixing herself a dinner of eggs and toast, broccoli, and sliced fresh tomato. The tomato came from a plant growing in a ceramic pot on the small terrace just outside the sliding patio door of her apartment. The door was closed today against the heat, and the air conditioner was on. She lived alone, and had for almost seventy of her eighty-seven years. In 1943, at the age of nineteen, Mary Lou had married a handsome young man, and one week later he left for boot camp. He died on a beach in Normandy. A widow at twenty, she never remarried.

Mary Lou's wedding had taken place at Holy Family Catholic Church on Dayton's east side, where she grew up. Her husband was buried somewhere in France, but there had been a brief memorial service at Holy Family. The day after the service, Mary Lou took a job at The National Cash Register Company, first building bomb sights, and later, carburetors for the new B-29 Superfortress bombers. She had always bragged that she helped build the carburetor for the *Bockscar*, the B-29 that dropped the *Fat Man* atomic bomb on Nagasaki, basically ending World War II. The *Bockscar* was now on permanent display at the Air Force Museum, and she had visited the plane many times.

Mary Lou stayed on at NCR, assembling cash registers for many years after the war. She lived with her parents and eventually bought a modest brick ranch house in one of the new eastern suburbs of Dayton. A parish had formed there, St. Nicholas Catholic Church, and she left NCR to become the housekeeper at the church rectory. She worked at the rectory for forty-five years, first when it was located in an old house across the street from the church, and then in the new facility built right next to the church. Mary Lou retired as housekeeper in 1999, sold her house eight years later, and moved to The Oakwood, a retirement community just south of Dayton in Kettering.

For several years after Mary Lou moved to Kettering, rather than joining a different parish, she made the drive back to St. Nick's every Sunday for Mass. Now, as she no longer drove, she would occasionally convince one of the staff at The Oakwood to take her there, but it had been months since the last time. She was beginning to feel some separation from her old parish, something she could never have imagined. She had cleaned and cooked and done laundry for many different men in her forty-five years at St. Nick's – pastors and assistant pastors – some who were transferred to other parishes, some who retired or died, and one who had simply disappeared, never to be seen or heard from again.

As she grew older, Mary Lou thought about these men more and more. Her fondest memories were of the handsome Father Ray, the assistant priest who mysteriously abandoned the parish one night without saying goodbye, not letting anyone know why he was leaving or where he was going. She'd been in love with Father Ray. It was an unrequited love that she had never revealed to anyone.

Tonight, after dinner, Mary Lou would do her few dishes and then maybe visit one of the other Oakwood residents. Most likely, she would settle down in front of the TV to watch the evening news, and then *Jeopardy*. She'd heard that watching *Jeopardy* and doing crossword puzzles could help keep her mind sharp. Her eyesight was still good enough for reading, and the apartment was full of books. She remained devoted to the *Dayton Daily News*, part of her morning ritual.

Mary Lou's evening would end as it had for almost fifty years. She would say a full rosary, keeping track as the beads slid quietly between her thumb and forefinger. Finally, she would offer a prayer to the souls of the three men who looked back at her from the framed photographs propped on a mantel over the gas fireplace. She dusted the glass and the frames every day, often changing the order of the pictures. Today, on the left, her husband smiled proudly, his Army hat tipped rakishly. In the middle, John F. Kennedy looked tan and dignified in an image that once hung in the homes of almost every Catholic family in St. Nick's parish. On the right, Father Ray struck a serious, even haughty pose, in a picture that had been taken in 1963 for the church directory. Mary Lou had never thought the picture was very good, but alas, it was the only one she had of him.

8

Always a Tune in His Head

Burke and Kevin checked in briefly at headquarters where they got an earful about their muddy appearance from Bones and Pete Skoff, the two detectives who were working the middle shift. Bones' real name was Ben Cooper and he was a year or two younger than Kevin. Apparently, when he was a little kid, Ben loved to watch TV shows about doctors and hospitals, and he'd always claimed that he wanted to be a doctor when he grew up. His dad started calling him Bones, which stuck, and everyone had been surprised when he became a cop instead.

Peter Skoff was in his early fifties and very laid back – at least for an *old* guy – according to the younger cops. All four of Pete's grandparents had emigrated from Croatia, and Pete could play the accordion and dance the polka. He was a scratch golfer, the current Dayton Senior Amateur Champion. After Marco Renzi had turned down Major Winston's offer to replace Burke as the top homicide cop, she'd offered the position to Pete, mostly out of respect for his seniority, and everyone knew he would turn it down; he'd rather be playing more golf than working longer hours. Burke teed it up with Pete whenever he got the chance, which was not very often, and playing more golf was one thing he was looking forward to when he retired.

Bones and Pete had the shift covered, so Burke and Kevin checked out and went their separate ways. When he got to his apartment, Burke turned up the air conditioner, opened a beer, took a shower, opened another beer, and ate a salad and scrambled eggs. The apartment was neat and spartan, the furniture modern. Burke didn't keep a computer in the apartment and no stereo. He had a flat screen TV, and his radio was also an alarm clock at the side of his bed. Burke was tired from the day and the heat, and he fell asleep on the couch after watching the first inning of a Cincinnati Reds game.

Had he not fallen asleep, Burke might have had one more beer or a glass of Jack Daniels on ice. Two or three drinks a night was his usual, and had been for most of his adult life. He often thought of alcohol as medicine, and it worked to help soften a long day.

Burke awoke during the top of the ninth inning, watched the Reds win, then turned off the TV and got into bed. Now that he was awake, he could hear the soft hum of the air conditioner moving cool air through the apartment. He thought about the day's events, about the beautiful '57 Chevy and the water-logged Impala, trying to imagine its former sleekness. He thought about the damaged skull.

Eventually he fell asleep and dreamed of the old neighborhood and the house he grew up in on Columbia Court. Most of the neighbors were Catholic, drawn there because of the closeness to St. Nick's. The families were usually large, and five to eight kids per family was fairly common. Burke's mother had once counted seventy-two children within the three blocks nearest their house.

A kid could always find a game going on somewhere, year-round. In the fall and winter, touch football, and even tackle football games, spread across the adjoining yards. One year some of the older boys erected actual goal posts in a small field at the edge of the plat. The two-by-four structure didn't last a week, done in by multiple impersonations of the Cleveland Brown's great fullback, Jimmy Brown, bulldozing his way into the end zone. Basketball was played year-round on asphalt driveways, with bent hoops and torn nets mounted on plywood backboards and bolted to the gable end of a garage.

Summer was the best. From sunup to sundown gangs of skinny, sun-bronzed kids roamed the neighborhood with abandon. Endless games of hardball, softball, whiffle ball or home-run-derby were played on a dead-end street, or on one of the circular court streets. A wire coat hanger was fashioned into a halo to scoop errant balls out of the storm sewer. Windows were broken by hard, line drive fouls. Games of tag or kick-the-can ran late into the long summer evenings. Sugar-rich Kool-Aid and popsicles, sometimes homemade from a recipe on a Jell-O box, fueled the games. Variety shows were organized by the mothers and played out in crowded, cool basements.

St. Nick's and the surrounding neighborhood were all built on what had once been corn and soybean fields. Over the years, beyond the plat, more farmland had been swallowed up by rapid development, to the point where Burke could now barely recognize most of the area to the east of University Park.

When he was a seventh grader at St. Nick's, Burke was persuaded by some of his friends to join the Boys' Choir. He had a nice voice and enjoyed singing in church, particularly the Latin hymns and Gregorian chant, and his favorite part of Christmas was singing carols. The assistant pastor, Father Nelson, directed the choir. The priest was tall and handsome – like a movie star, Burke thought – and had a beautiful, rich tenor voice. He was a very popular man, especially among the female members of the flock. He played the piano, and often led impromptu sing-a-longs at church events.

Burke sang all the time back then and always had a tune in his head. He loved Elvis Presley, Ray Charles, the Four Seasons and the Shirelles. But he quit the choir after only a few months, telling his parents that his voice was starting to change, and he wanted to try basketball instead.

At the start of eighth grade, his final year at St. Nick's, Burke announced to his parents that he wouldn't be going to the Catholic high school the following year. His father, not a very devout Catholic, didn't care where his son went to high school, but his mother thought she had somehow failed. A short while later, she was even more distressed when Burke informed his parents that he was no longer going to attend Mass with them on Sundays. Fortunately for Burke, his mother's distress was short-lived.

That spring, something happened that caused her to turn her back on St. Nick's as well. She had joined an unofficial group made up mostly of women from the St. Nicholas Altar Rosary Society, who decided to help promote the Civil Rights Act. The bill had already been passed by the House and was being discussed in the Senate at the time; open housing was part of the discussion. There were several black families in the parish now, and quite a few black Air Force families living in nearby base housing. The group wanted to open up the parish and reach out to black families interested in moving to the area. Burke's mother had been the one to approach the pastor, Father Krueger. She asked him to sign a petition that was being circulated throughout the country by groups like theirs in support of the legislation. When the priest refused to sign the petition, claiming that he preferred the status quo and didn't see the need for things to change, Burke's mother was horrified and disgusted. She and several other women in the group started getting anonymous phone calls accusing them of being "nigger-lovers" and "nigger-bitches." She quit St. Nick's and never went back.

The following fall Burke enrolled in the nearest public high school, Riverside, and that winter he joined the wrestling team, lettering as a freshman. He maintained a B average, made one or two Protestant friends, but kept mostly to himself. He slowly drifted apart from his Catholic friends, and often felt like an outcast in University Park. After graduating from Riverside, he got a job at a moving company and moved out of his parent's house. He rented a cheap studio apartment on Dayton's north side, and had rarely gone back to his old neighborhood in Riverside – almost never once his parents died. His only sibling, Mary, was two years older than Burke and now lived in Colorado. They spoke on the phone a couple of times a year but hadn't seen each other for a long time.

* * *

Burke's alarm sounded. He switched it off and rolled back into bed as the last image from the last dream of the night melted into the early morning light … *a gleaming black 1963 Chevrolet Impala with immaculate whitewall tires moved in slow-motion across the playground in front of St. Nick's school. A crowd of children parted like the Red Sea. They were smiling and waving to the handsome man behind the wheel.*

9

Dead or Dying

When Burke arrived at the squad room that morning, Kevin was filling in some of the other detectives on the events from the previous day. Tarisa and Marco had just arrived, and Jamal and Danny finished their late shift and were about to leave.

Danny Levine was the newest member of the squad. He was an actual Ivy-Leaguer, having graduated from Dartmouth, and Jamal often referred to him as "Ivy". He'd moved up to homicide after just two years in uniform. His plan was to go to law school eventually, but he wanted the street experience that, in his opinion, most criminal lawyers lacked.

Jamal Milton was the other African-American on the squad. A football star in high school, he'd been given a full ride by Ohio State, but blew out a knee in his freshman year. After that, he gave up football, but stayed in school and got a degree in criminology and criminal justice. He'd been in the department for ten years, the last five on Burke's homicide squad.

Burke greeted the detectives gruffly and went straight to his desk. Kevin followed, as did the rest of the squad, peppering Burke with questions. They were obviously intrigued by the remains found in the Impala. Tarisa was holding a copy of the *Dayton Daily News*, and the top headline read – **Human Remains Found in Eastwood Lake.** It was followed by Lisa Fowler's story and a photo of the forensics team working around the car.

"Cap," said Tarisa, "I'd like to help with this if you need anything checked out." The other detectives chorused her offer.

"Thanks, Tarisa," said Burke. "Everyone, thanks. Truth is, right now, there's not much of anything to check. I'll take the lead on this, once Catherine and her crew have something for us. So far there's no real evidence of foul play – it was probably an accident. And you all have better things to do than work on something that may be nothing, so I've got this for now. You've been razzin' my ass with that *short-timer* crap, so at least now I'll have something to do." They all laughed at that, even Burke.

After Danny and Jamal left, Tarisa and Marco asked a few more questions before settling in at their desks. Burke spent the next several hours working up a report on the discovery of the Impala, and dealing with the finance officer about paying for the crane and the divers. After that, he tried Googling different sites about vehicle identification numbers for a 1963 Impala. He found a lot of conflicting information about the location of the numbers, with some agreement on a VIN tag that could be found just below the upper hinge of the driver's door. Burke was hoping the damaged license plate would be able to tell him what he needed to know, even if the VIN wasn't found or couldn't be read. Just for kicks, he searched around to see if he had been correct about the middle taillight being the backup light, and discovered that he was right. He also found that lap belts were offered as an option in the 1963 Impalas.

Burke wrote himself a note to call Maggie. He was hoping he could take her out for dinner to make up for the last time he'd seen her. They'd argued again about his moodiness and his depression and his unwillingness to talk about it. It was a well-worn argument.

As much as he wanted to, Burke held off on calling the forensics lab. He knew Catherine would call him. At lunchtime Kevin, Tarisa, and Marco were busy searching through a stack of files, working on a west-side shooting from the night before. Burke went out alone to Lucky's, the little sandwich shop around the corner from police headquarters. He stopped and bought a copy of the morning paper from a rack on the sidewalk out front. Burke wasn't visible in the photo taken at the lake, but a small, stock headshot of him appeared alongside the story. He'd offered very little information to Lisa Fowler, and as usual, she got everything right. Looking at the picture of the Impala, his morning dream came back to him. Even now, he could easily picture the car in its new, pristine condition. The setting of the dream still puzzled him.

His cell phone rang as he was finishing his lunch.

"Pops, where are you?" Kevin asked.

"I'm around the corner having lunch. What's up?"

"The coroner just called. She said they've had a pretty good look at the remains and she wants you to come to the lab."

"What about the license plate? Did she mention that?"

"No mention of the plate," Kevin said.

"All right, I'll head over there."

The Dayton Police headquarters were located in the Safety Building, situated between the Dayton/Montgomery County Courts Building and The Miami Valley Regional Crime Lab. The lab was a state-of-the-art forensic science facility and served as a base for the Montgomery County Coroner. Burke walked to the lab, and the lobby guard directed him to the room where Catherine's staff had examined the remains. Catherine sat at a desk, writing. A beat up, rusty license plate lay on the desk.

"Hi, Catherine. How's it going?"

"Good, J.B. Just give me a second," she said, and nodded at the license plate.

Burke put on the reading glasses that hung around his neck and picked up the old license plate. Now that it had been straightened out, the embossed figures were easily readable. *1963-OHIO* was stamped at the bottom of the plate. The plate number in the middle was a small number 2, followed by a space and then four larger numbers – *3156*. Across the top of the plate appeared the word *DEALER*.

"Christ! It's a goddamn *dealer* plate," said Burke, tossing the plate back to the desk.

"I didn't think you'd be too happy about that," said Catherine. She finished what she was writing and stood up.

Burke shrugged. "Hell, if I'm *lucky*, all this will do is lead me to the dealer. And they probably swapped this plate around on a lot of different cars."

"Maybe if you can find the dealer, they'll still have sales records from 1963," said Catherine. "You could find out who all bought black Impalas."

"Fat chance," said Burke. "Shit."

"We worked on that plate because I knew you wanted it right away. We've hardly looked at the rest of the car. I put the whole crew on the remains this morning, but we'll work on the car this afternoon. Maybe we can find a VIN."

"Hell," said Burke disgustedly. "Could be the car was off the lot, just out for a test drive. If it hadn't been sold yet, it probably wasn't registered with the BMV. If that's the case, even a VIN won't help."

"Well, we'll look for it anyway," said Catherine. "You can take the plate."

"If you get the doors open, look on the driver's door hinge post, just under the upper hinge," Burke said.

"Will do. Let me show you what we found so far."

Catherine led Burke to another room. The bones had been cleaned up and were laid out on a paper-covered table. They formed a human shape, more or less a complete skeleton as far as Burke could tell. There were bits of human tissue still connected to some of the bones. The section of rib cage Burke had seen at the lake was there; the hip bones and the large arm and leg bones were all in good shape. The skull and jaw bone were posed at the top of the human shape. Other items, the metal ones quite rusty, were laid out at the end of the table. Among them were a watch with a metal strap, a belt buckle barely connected to what was left of a leather belt, a few buttons, a pair of degraded leather shoes, a few coins and keys, and a plastic comb.

"This stuff was in the mix," said Catherine. "No wallet, unfortunately, but we haven't really looked through all of the car and the other contents yet. A paper driver's license may not have survived anyway."

"Amazing," said Burke, shaking his head and looking at the artifacts. "Almost fifty years?"

"Yeah. Based mostly on the dealer plate, we figure the car was in the lake for forty-eight years," Catherine said. "If so, then the bones are in pretty good shape. The cold temperature at that eighty-foot depth and the pH level in the water probably helped. Most freshwater is usually slightly acidic, but the Eastwood Lake water we tested is barely acidic at all, almost neutral. We're not sure why. Could be all the moraine gravel may have something to do with it. Don't quote me on that – just a theory."

"Male or female?" Burke asked, pointing at the bones.

"Adult male," Catherine answered, "somewhere between thirty-five and forty-five years old."

"What the hell, Catherine. Do you think the poor guy just screwed up and drove into the damn lake?" Burke asked, shaking his head. "Is it a suicide maybe?"

"Well, I was wondering," said Catherine. "When we were at the lake yesterday, you said the spot had been your old swimming hole."

"Yeah, I did say that," Burke nodded.

"Could you have gotten a car back in there?"

"Well, I *guess* you could have," Burke surmised. "Yeah, I don't see why not. But you certainly wouldn't drive a car in there accidentally. Maybe suicide *is* a good bet?"

Catherine shrugged. "From the way the bones were situated on the seat and the floor of the car, and with the lap belt locked in position, we think the guy was strapped into the driver's seat when the car went in the water."

"Sounding more and more like suicide," Burke said.

"Could be I guess, but I doubt it, J.B. Let me show you something." Catherine pulled on a pair of latex gloves. "The only sign of trauma to the cervical vertebrate is a broken C-1. It's the bone connecting the spinal cord to the skull. There's no other sign of trauma to any of the other bones as far as we can tell. Just the skull."

She picked up the skull and turned it around. Burke saw instantly that the back part of the skull was caved in. He looked closely at the area and noticed a piece of skull bone missing. But before Burke could ask about it, Catherine picked up a small piece of bone from the table.

"This fits the hole," she said. "It's all here. No sign of a gunshot wound."

"But a pretty good blow, yes?"

"Yep, a good, sharp blow, resulting in a depressed skull fracture. The broken neck probably happened at the same time."

"Like with a hammer maybe?" Burke asked, miming a hammer blow.

"Like with a *sledge* hammer," Catherine said.

She set the skull back in its place on the table, pulled off the gloves and tossed them into a trash can. "Unfortunately, there's not much we can learn from what little tissue is left."

"So, no official cause of death?" Burke asked.

"Impossible to tell. Blunt force trauma? Broken neck? Drowning? Maybe all three. But try as we could, none of us came up with a reasonable explanation for the occipital head wound. I mean, how could an injury that severe occur to the back of the head, with the body strapped into the front seat of a car?"

"Christ! Do you think he was already dead when he went in the lake?" Burke wondered.

Catherine pondered the question. "Dead . . ." she shrugged, ". . . or dying."

10

The General

Retired USAF Brigadier General James McGowan was approaching the entrance to the Air Force Museum, but instead of turning right onto Springfield Street, he stayed on Harshman Road and turned into Eastwood Lake Metropark. He'd seen Lisa Fowler's story and the photo of the 1963 Impala in the morning paper and was curious about the spot where they'd found the car.

McGowan had retired from the Air Force two years earlier. He'd left Washington D.C. and his job at the Pentagon and moved back to Dayton where he'd spent several years as a young teenager. His father had been stationed there as a USAF officer and a pilot. He flew a B-52 Stratofortress for the Strategic Air Command wing based at Wright-Patt during the Cold War.

After high school, McGowan had taken R.O.T.C. classes, graduated from college in Texas, and followed his father into the Air Force. He was first stationed in Germany, but he ended up back in Dayton when he was transferred to Wright-Patt. In Dayton, he'd met and married his wife, Kathy. After that, and for the next twenty years, they moved around the world at the whim of the Air Force. They had lived on air bases all over the U.S. and in eight different countries before McGowan was finally installed at the Pentagon.

After her husband retired, Kathy wanted to move back to Dayton, so they bought a house in nearby Beavercreek, a few miles east of Riverside and the Air Force Museum. McGowan was now on the museum's board of directors and had been in charge of the museum's recent unsuccessful attempt to win one of the four retired space shuttles that NASA had donated to museums on the east and west coasts. Much to his chagrin, the entire middle of the country remained shuttleless.

As he'd read the story about the Impala in the morning paper, McGowan wondered if Police Captain John Burke, head of the Dayton homicide division, was the same John Burke he had gone to school with at St. Nick's and Riverside High, back when his father had been stationed at Wright-Patt. In the few years that he and Kathy had been back in Dayton, McGowan had seen the same stock photo of Burke several times in the news. There was certainly a resemblance, but he'd never been curious enough to look into it.

He parked in the lot above the lake, stepped over the guardrail and jogged down the incline and across the service road, where he spotted the tire tracks of the heavy crane. Walking slowly to the edge of the lake, he gazed across it. He looked to his left toward Dayton, and then to his right toward Harshman Road. Removing his sunglasses, he peered down into the water. The story in the morning's paper mentioned the Impala being found at a depth of about eighty feet. *No wonder we could never reach the bottom*, he thought. After a few minutes, he scrambled back up to the parking lot and turned around for a last look at the lake.

"Positively no," he said aloud, just to hear the words again.

11

Maggie

Through the August heat and humidity, Burke made the short walk from the lab back to police headquarters. When he got to the squad room Kevin was on the phone, and Tarisa and Marco were still sorting through a stack of files. Burke settled in at his desk and called the Ohio Bureau of Motor Vehicles. After explaining to two different operators who he was and what he wanted, he was finally connected to a BMV archivist named Nathan. Burke gave him the number on the dealer plate, and Nathan promised he would put someone on the case right away. It was possible they would come up with something by the end of the day, but maybe not until tomorrow. He would call as soon as they found something.

When Burke hung up, the other detectives gathered around his desk, curious about his visit to the lab. They were intrigued by his description of the damaged skull, and they passed around the dealer plate, agreeing that it would be "a real bitch" to trace.

Burke finished up some routine paperwork, checked the time, and then called Maggie. She usually took a class or two during the summer when she wasn't teaching, either at the University of Dayton or out at Wright State University, but she would be home by now.

"Hi Johnny," said Maggie. "I was hoping it was you."

"I was wondering if I could take you out to Jay's for dinner later," Burke asked. "And I'm sorry about last week. I know I'm an asshole, and I'm sorry."

"Yes, you are certainly an asshole sometimes, and yes, I'd love to go out to Jays," she said. "What time?"

Burke smiled. "I'll make a reservation. Can I pick you up at 6:30? That'll give me time to get cleaned up."

"I'll be ready," Maggie said.

Burke finished the day looking over reports. The previous night Bones and Pete had responded to a report of a young African-American male found dead in his car, shot once in the head. The car was found running with the air conditioner on, and the driver's window had been shattered. A passerby had spotted the body of the known drug dealer slumped over in the seat, and Tarisa and Marco had spent the day doing interviews and working up a suspect list.

Burke went through the reports, then sat pondering his short-timer status, coming to the conclusion that the squad was going to be just fine after he retired. *Hell,* he thought, *Kevin was pretty much running the show already.* He waited in the squad room until 5:30, hoping for a call from Nathan at the BMV, then headed for his apartment to get cleaned up for his date.

* * *

When they had first gotten to know each other, Maggie was drawn to what she regarded as Burke's *serious* side; he seemed more mature than most of the other young men she had dated. Burke's mother told Maggie that Burke had been quite different as a child, always singing and happy-go-lucky. She didn't know why he had changed.

Over the years, this serious side had overshadowed everything else about Burke. He'd always been shy and somewhat clumsy when it came to any kind of real intimacy, and Maggie's efforts to get Burke to open up, to shed some light on whatever demons were in his head, had failed. Eventually, after his second or third half-hearted attempt at therapy, Maggie had to ask Burke to move out, saying the drain and the strain were just too much. But she loved him, and she knew she always would.

Jay's Seafood Restaurant was crowded for a Tuesday evening, but Burke had made a reservation. The maître d' greeted them by name and led them to a corner table that had been held for them. As soon as they were seated, Burke stopped a passing waitress.

"Nancy, would you ask the bartender to please turn the music down?"

They ordered drinks and a dozen raw Blue Point oysters, and talked about what they'd been up to since they'd last seen each other. Burke felt relaxed, and Maggie even managed to get a smile out of him.

"Saw your picture in the paper this morning," she said, mimicking Burke's scowl. "They need a better shot of you."

Burke described the remains and the damaged skull. He told her about the dealer plate, and explained that the car might be difficult to trace.

"A lot of the car dealers have closed," Maggie said. "Some of the Chevy dealers."

Dayton was a factory town. It had been hit particularly hard by the near collapse of the auto industry and the sorry decline of manufacturing jobs in general. Much of the town's industrial make-up had been tied to Detroit over the years, and things had pretty much hit rock bottom. Huge plants like Delco Products, Delco Moraine, Frigidaire and Chrysler Airtemp had closed, or morphed into other, smaller companies that seemed to come and go. Other huge companies headquartered in Dayton, like McCall's Printing, the Mead Paper Company, and National Cash Register, first shrank, then took what was left of their dwindling empires and moved to other parts of the country.

Burke and Maggie split the oysters, ate their salads and fish, and kept the conversation light. It was the only way they could get through an evening without arguing. They talked about Kevin taking over the squad, and about Kevin and his wife Becky and their two little girls, Ashley and Megan. The girls called Burke *Grandpops*.

"Oh, it looks like *I* might be retiring, too," said Maggie, hoisting her wine glass. Because of state and federal cutbacks, the Dayton school board was working on a restructuring plan, and they were going to offer early retirement incentives to the older teachers, including Maggie.

"Good. You've done more than enough," Burke said. He offered a toast. "As Pete likes to say – *more time for golf.*"

They made a date to play golf the following Sunday, but didn't talk about living under the same roof again someday. They didn't talk about Burke's frustrating reticence, either. When Burke took Maggie back to her house – *their* house – Maggie asked Burke to come in. She fixed him a Jack Daniel's on-the-rocks, and they played Scrabble and watched a Red's game on TV, talking little. The Reds won it in the ninth, then Burke kissed Maggie on the cheek and drove home to his quiet, spartan apartment.

12

The VIN

Jamal and Danny were the only ones in the squad room when Burke arrived a little earlier than usual the next morning. They wanted to know what was happening with the *Impala Case,* as it was becoming known. Burke told them what he knew, about the dealer plates, his call to the BMV, and his hopes for the coroner finding the vehicle identification numbers. Jamal and Danny filled Burke in on the shooting of the drug dealer and what the squad had found out since – not much, as usual, and no witnesses. Nobody wanted to talk to them about it. The dead man was a gangbanger as well as a dealer, and the squad all figured there would soon be a payback shooting. "Just a matter of time, a matter of crime," Jamal rhymed.

Tarisa, Marco, and Kevin arrived, and everyone huddled to bring each other up to speed. Burke was happy with the way the squad was responding to Kevin's increasing responsibility; the transition would be seamless, he thought. Back at his desk Burke again resisted the urge to call Catherine at the lab – he knew she would call him. He told Kevin that Major Winston had set up a press conference for later in the day regarding the death of the drug dealer; they would be asking for the public's help. Kevin had taken the lead on the case, and would represent the squad at the press conference. "I'll be fine," he reassured his father. "I've watched you do this a thousand times."

Burke called Major Winston and filled her in on the forensics report from the *Impala Case.* He recommended that the suspicion of foul play be kept within the department for the time being, and told her that he hoped to have more information on the identity of the victim later that day, maybe the next.

Nathan, from the Ohio BMV, called at 9:00 a.m. sharp. He apologized to Burke for not getting back the afternoon before.

"The plate was in a batch of ten issued to Lang Chevrolet in Dayton, Ohio, on September 3, 1963," Nathan said. "They were shipped two days later on September 5th."

Burke leaned back in his chair. "I guess someone could have been using the plate, but not owned the car," he said.

"Well, yeah," responded Nathan. "It's possible that the dealership let someone test drive the car and keep it for a day or two. Some dealers still do that. Or the driver could have been an employee, or a relative of the dealer, a friend . . . who knows?"

"Shit," Burke muttered.

"But keep in mind, Captain, it's quite possible that the driver already bought the car, and just as a courtesy, the dealer let them drive on the dealer plate until the new plates came in the mail."

"Is that legal?" Burke asked.

"Not anymore. Actually, I'm not sure if it was ever legal, but from what I understand, it used to be done all the time back in the old days."

"So, the car may have been registered, or at least was in the process of being registered?"

"I suppose so," said Nathan. "Call me back if you can get the VIN. If it was entered in the system, I'm pretty sure I can find it for you."

Burke hung up. *What are the chances*, he thought? He could call the *Dayton Daily News,* to check their archives, maybe find a story about someone going missing in a brand-new black Impala back in 1963. Maybe there had been a missing person report filed with the DPD. Burke wasn't even sure they had records going back that far. Maybe Lang Chevrolet could help. *Maybe.*

Lang Chevrolet was one of the oldest Chevy dealers in the area. They had survived the cuts that General Motors made when things had gone to hell over the past few years. Burke called Lang's and spoke with a receptionist. She connected him with a vice president who told him that dealers were only required by law to maintain sales records for a period of seven years. There was no way he could trace a car that far back. Burke was not surprised.

"Just curious, Captain, but does this have something to do with the car that was found in the lake?" the VP asked.

"Possibly," said Burke. He asked the VP if he had ever heard any stories, maybe from one of the old-timers, about a new Impala disappearing back in 1963.

"There aren't any old-timers," the VP said, laughing.

Burke hung up and was about to call over to the DPD records division when Catherine DiMarco called.

"Good news, J.B." she said. "We got the doors open on the Impala and found the VIN. The tag was right where you said it would be."

"Is it readable?" asked Burke, grabbing a pencil from the *World's Best Grampa* mug on his desk.

"Absolutely," said Catherine. "It was pretty corroded, but we cleaned it up and applied a hydrochloric acid solution to it. I'm *amazed* at how readable it is."

"Catherine," Burke said, "I owe you one. How about I buy you lunch?"

"Thanks, J.B. Not today though. We're deep into this mess. The car has dried out a little, and we'll be going through the contents in the trunk. We're going to give the whole thing a good look."

Catherine read off the VIN, and Burke took down the long series of letters and numbers; hopefully they could be found in the BMV archive system. He immediately called Nathan at the BMV and passed the information on. Nathan said that if the paperwork for the sale of the car had ever been submitted, he was fairly certain they would be able to find it and match the car with an owner, probably by the end of the day. He promised to call Burke as soon as they got a match – *if* they got a match.

13

Raymond Nelson

Kevin's press conference went well that afternoon. Burke watched the proceedings from the back of a large meeting room that the DPD used for these events. He noticed Lisa Fowler, with her pen, pad, and recorder, right up front. She addressed Kevin as Detective Burke, and asked relevant questions about the shooting. When the conference ended, Burke saw her glancing around the room. She was probably looking for him, he thought, and he waved to her. She waved back, and headed his way.

"Hi, J.B.," she said. "That was different, having Kevin up there instead of you. Should I talk to him about the remains that were found in the lake?"

"No, I'll be handling that," Burke assured her. "In fact, I'm hoping to hear something later today. If we're lucky we might at least find out who owned the car. We can't assume that the bones belong to the owner, but we'll start from there."

"Will you set up a press meeting when you get that info?" she asked.

"I would think so," he said. "I imagine we'll be asking for the public's help with this, too. We're fairly certain that the car went in the lake back in 1963. Maybe someone will remember something about the car's owner – *if* we can find that out. Mum's the word for now though."

"You bet, J.B." Lisa promised. "I've gotta go write something on this shooting, but I'll see you soon, I hope."

Kevin and Major Claire Winston were discussing the shooting case when Burke returned to the squad room. Burke put in his two cents, and then settled at his desk. Claire finished with Kevin and pulled up a chair next to Burke.

"Kevin's doing a nice job in here. He's a real chip off the block," she said, punching Burke playfully on the arm.

Burke smiled. "Well, I hope that's a good thing," he said. "Thank God he's not a sour old curmudgeon like his old man."

"We're going to miss you anyway, J.B." she said with a laugh. "So, what's up with the Impala case?"

"Not much. The car probably went in the water sometime in 1963. The license was a dealer plate – not much help. But the lab found a VIN they could read, and I'm expecting a call sometime this afternoon from the BMV. Since it was a dealer plate, the car may or may not have been registered, but I've got my fingers crossed."

"What do you want to do if you get a name?" Claire asked.

"First we'll have to see if the name matches the remains, and right now I'm not sure how we'll do that," said Burke. "Catherine said most of the teeth were in pretty good shape, but I doubt anybody keeps dental records for fifty years."

"Probably not," Claire agreed.

"Would *Records* have missing persons files that far back?" Burke asked her.

"It's possible." She shrugged. "Everything that was on microfiche has been scanned into the system. Better keep those fingers crossed."

* * *

It was late in the afternoon when the office phone rang. "Homicide," Kevin answered, and then called across the room. "It's for you, Pops. The guy from the BMV."

Burke picked up. "Hi, Nathan. Any luck?"

"Hi, Captain Burke," Nathan said. "Yeah, I'm happy to say we have a name for you." Burke picked up a pencil.

"The car was registered on November 19, 1963, to a Raymond T. Nelson." He paused. "Umm…let's see, his date of birth was…September 12, 1925. The plates would have been shipped a day or two later."

Burke almost dropped the phone. The color drained from his face, and he leaned back hard in the chair as if he'd been slapped across the face.

"Hello?" said Nathan. "Are you there?"

"Yeah, I'm here. Sorry," Burke straightened up. "Nathan, is it *Father* Raymond Nelson?"

"Don't know," said Nathan. "You mean like a *priest*? That sort of designation wouldn't be on the registration."

"What about an address?" Burke asked.

"Umm, let's see," Nathan said. "5330 Belfair Avenue, Dayton 31, Ohio."

"Thanks, Nathan. Thanks a bunch." The color was returning to Burke's face. "Could you fax me a copy of the registration?"

"How about if I scan it and email it?"

"Either way," said Burke. "Thanks again." He gave Nathan the fax number and his email address. Kevin was standing at his side when Burke hung up.

"Jesus, Pops," he said. "What the hell was that all about? You looked like you were going to pass out."

Burke looked up at Kevin, but his eyes didn't focus. A chain of memories, like train cars zipping past, flashed through his head. "I think I know this guy, Kev, or *knew* him." He started to reach for the Dayton phone book he kept in a drawer, but stopped and turned to his computer, quickly Googling – *st. nicholas dayton ohio*. Burke knew that although Riverside was now incorporated, Dayton mailing addresses were still being used.

"5330 Belfair Avenue, just what I thought," he said. "I did know him."

"Who was he?" Kevin asked.

"He was a priest at my church . . . St. Nick's," Burke said. "An assistant pastor. He directed the Boys Choir. One day he just disappeared and nobody ever knew what happened to him."

"What do you mean *just disappeared?*" Kevin asked.

Burke snapped his fingers. "Just like that," he said. "Drove off one night in his brand-new Impala and never came back. I remember it was right around the same time as the Kennedy assassination."

"And you remember the car?"

"Yeah, it was a beauty. I can't believe I didn't put this together before." Burke put a hand to his head. "I even had a dream about the car the other night. But I haven't thought about Father Nelson in a long, long time."

"I've got to say, Pops, you seem a little freaked out," Kevin said.

"I guess I am a little," Burke admitted. "Do me a favor and keep this to yourself for now."

14

Riverside, Ohio: November, 1963

Heading for Dumbo's, Mike Donnelly walked through the starry November night. His eyes teared from the cold, and from the rage that he had barely been able to keep from his wife, Eileen. Dumbo's, his favorite local tavern, was squeezed between a grocery store and a drug store in a little shopping strip. The owner of the place was Bill Dombrowski, but everyone knew him as "Dumbo" and that's what he'd named his pub.

Mike stepped out of the cold and into the dimly lit tavern. He spotted his brother Jerry, who waved to him from the rear booth. Across from Jerry sat Frank McHale, Jerry's best friend. Frank's family was originally from Kentucky, and the three men had all grown up together on Dayton's east side.

Otherwise, the place was nearly empty. Martin Bigelow, the Riverside police chief, sat at a booth across from a pretty young woman. They were laughing, and Mike saw Bigelow reach under the table and grab the woman's knee.

Mike greeted Dumbo tersely, and ordered a draft. Dumbo was filling a glass gallon jug with "three-two" beer for a skinny teenager. The legal drinking age was eighteen, but only for beer that contained less than 3.2 percent alcohol. In most taverns you could bring in your own jug and get it filled with draft beer for about a dollar. The kid looked maybe sixteen, and seemed a little nervous, but Dumbo didn't ask to see any identification. Chief Bigelow looked up briefly from where he sat, then turned his attention back to the young woman. On a shelf behind the bar a black and white T.V. was tuned to *My Three Sons*, the volume turned off. A radio was playing "Dominique" by the Singing Nun.

"Dumbo, turn that shit off!" Chief Bigelow bellowed, and Dumbo switched stations.

Mike paid for his beer, then joined Jerry and Frank at the back booth. Frank gave his seat to Mike and slid in next to Jerry. Leaning forward across the table, and as quietly as he could while fighting back tears and a seething anger, Mike told them what Father Nelson had done to his son, Timmy.

"Jesus, Mike, you believe him?" Frank asked. Mike glared at his brother's friend through red-rimmed eyes.

"Goddamn right I believe him," he said, louder than he should have. His face was flushed and he looked ready to explode.

"It's okay, Mike," said Jerry, patting his brother's hand. "It's okay. If you believe Timmy, then I guess I believe him."

"Timmy made me promise not to tell Eileen, so don't tell her. Don't tell anybody," Mike said. He quickly drank off half his beer, and slammed the glass down on the table.

"Did you talk to Father Nelson about it?" asked Jerry. He peered over Mike's shoulder, toward the bar, to see if anyone was paying them any attention.

"You better believe I talked to him," growled Mike. "I waited for him after early Mass yesterday. The son of a bitch denied it. He said Timmy was probably having delusions, or fantasies or something. He said a bunch of bullshit, something about having gotten some psychological training in the seminary. He said it was very common for kids of a certain age to fantasize about this stuff. I almost punched him out right there."

"What're you gonna do?" Frank asked.

"Well, I told the bastard that I was going to talk to Father Krueger, and all he said was – 'That would be the proper thing to do' – just as cool as could be, like Father Krueger wouldn't have a problem with it."

"Did you talk to Krueger?" asked Jerry.

"Goddamn right! Krueger said he would '*intervene*'. Says he'll report it to the Archbishop and that I should keep the incident to myself – '*For the good of my son and my family*,*' snarled Mike loudly.

Jerry tried to calm his brother again with a little pat, but Mike went on.

"And when I told him it was more than just one goddamn incident, he said the Church was aware of Father Nelson's problem and that they would take care of it. He asked me to pray with him and I told him I didn't want to pray with him."

"You think he'll do anything about it?" Frank asked.

"I hope so. I guess so," said Mike, shrugging. "But I told him I was going to go to the Archbishop myself anyway. He said that was up to me and *begged* me not to tell anyone else. I told him I wouldn't, so don't you guys tell anyone else for now – okay?"

"What the hell can the Archbishop do about it?" asked Jerry.

"I don't know," said Mike. "But if they don't get Father Nelson the hell out of here, I swear to God I'll kill the son of a bitch myself. *I'll kill him.*"

15

Go on the Google

Burke slept poorly that night as more pieces of his childhood loomed up in confusing dreams. When the clock alarm finally went off, he woke up in a sweat. After a cool shower, he dressed, ate a banana and a piece of toast, and took a second cup of coffee with him when he left his apartment. He got to the squad room early and started to plan his investigation, making notes of what had been discovered so far, then laid out a procedure schedule for himself.

First, he would check with Records to see if they maintained missing person reports going back to 1963. If someone had reported Father Nelson's disappearance, maybe that person was still alive. Major Winston would have to be brought up to speed. Catherine DiMarco and her crew had had an entire day to look the car over – maybe there was some further evidence that would help to positively identify the remains as Father Nelson. If not, the priest's next of kin would have to be found, and possibly persuaded to provide a DNA sample in hopes of a match. He would call the current pastor at St. Nick's and see if anyone there could tell him anything at all. *Probably not*, Burke thought. But the Archbishop's office in Cincinnati may have some information on the missing priest, or any living members of his family.

Anyway, even with positive identification, Burke wouldn't be able to give the press anything until Father Nelson's next of kin – if anyone existed – could be informed. After that he would ask for the public's help with the investigation. Without giving anything away, the suspicion of foul play would have to be admitted. Better to do so up front than to have it leaked.

Kevin and the other detectives trickled into the squad room. Somebody started the coffee maker, and after Burke filled them in on the Impala case, they discussed the other ongoing investigations. Burke reassured them that he was content to work on *his* case without their help. He offered bits of advice on some of the other investigations, then retreated to his desk, followed by his son. He laid out his plan to Kevin and asked if he'd seen Major Winston yet that morning.

"Yeah, I saw her car in the lot," Kevin said. "Are you sure you don't want some help with this?"

"No, I'm fine," Burke said. "You have plenty on your plate. What time does Records open . . . eight or nine?"

"Nine," answered Kevin.

"Maybe I'll just go on the Google for now and see what I can find on my own," said Burke.

"*Go on the Google?*" Kevin grinned. "Geez, Pops. You sound like a *real* briar hopper."

Burke got a cup of coffee, then found Claire Winston in her office. He told her what he'd learned, and they agreed that the bones found in the car were more than likely the remains of Father Raymond Nelson, the car's owner. Since the coroner's report suggested a possible homicide, and even though it had happened almost fifty years earlier, Burke would have to follow standard procedure in the case.

"Let me see if I can find a family member before we go public with this," Burke said.

The Records Division was just opening when he got to the basement level of the building. A young clerk named Becky told him that if a missing persons report had been filed on Father Raymond Nelson, even back in 1963, they would most likely have it. Burke asked her to search three months out from November 1, 1963, even though he knew the car was registered around the middle of that month, and his best personal recollection was that Father Nelson disappeared right around the time of the Kennedy assassination.

"I'll get right on it," Becky said.

Back in the squad room, Burke found a website and phone number for St. Nicholas Catholic Church, and the pastor, Father Philip Metzger. He called the St. Nick's rectory number which was answered by a machine, and he decided not to leave a message.

He called the office of the Archbishop of Cincinnati and informed the man who answered that he was a police detective from Dayton, and that he was looking for information on a particular priest. He spoke with several different fathers-something-or-other, and was finally connected to a Monsignor Nicholas Stankowski, the Archbishop's archivist.

"Hello, Father," said Burke. "This is Captain John Burke from the Dayton Police Department."

"And what can I help you with, Captain Burke?"

"Well, Father, earlier this week we found a car at the bottom of a lake here in Dayton, and there are human remains in the car. We think the car has been in the lake since November of 1963, and we believe the remains may be those of a Catholic priest named Father Raymond Nelson.

"Holy shit!" the priest responded, then quickly added, "Please, excuse me."

"Yes, Father," said Burke, smiling. "That was my response, too."

"Was he one of our priests?" Father Stankowski asked. "A diocesan priest?"

"I believe he was," said Burke. "An assistant pastor at St. Nick's, in Dayton. St. Nicholas Catholic Church." He paused. "Do you know it?"

"Of course, I know it," responded the priest. "I believe Father Metzger is the current pastor."

Burke explained that the car had been registered to Father Nelson, and that he remembered the priest from his youth.

"Right now, I'm just trying to track down any living relatives," Burke explained. "Also, any other information that you might have in your records would be helpful, especially about his disappearance."

"I'll be glad to see what I can find," offered the priest. "Give me your number, Captain, and I'll call you back this afternoon."

Burke hung up, and the phone rang almost immediately. It was Catherine DiMarco calling from the coroner's lab.

"Good morning, J.B.," she said briskly. "We worked through the contents of the Impala yesterday, and I think you'll be interested in what we found."

"Should I come down?"

"Definitely. There's some stuff you'll want to see. We've developed what we're calling the *priest theory*," she said, laughing. "I would have called last night but we got out of here pretty late."

"I think I'm one step ahead of you on the priest bit," Burke told her. "I should have called *you* yesterday, but I'll be right down."

He made the short walk to the coroner's building and found Catherine writing at a desk. Several tables in the room were covered with material collected from the Impala. He told Catherine what he'd found out about the car being registered to Father Nelson, and she explained how they had come up with their priest theory.

"Almost all the clothing, or scraps of clothing, are black. One suitcase was jammed full. Black pants, black shirts, and a black suit coat. And the shirt collars are kind of odd. Short, like a priest's collar. The cloth scraps we found mixed in with the remains are also black, except for some smaller pieces which may have been his underwear or a handkerchief."

Burke looked at the material laid out on the tables. Some items were in better shape than others. He fingered the tattered suit coat.

"Anything synthetic seems to have survived in better shape, like the shirts, and one pair of pants," she went on. "Wool and cotton suffered the most. And everything was just jammed into the suitcase like it was packed in a hurry, not folded and stacked. Odd thing is – no extra underwear, no socks, no toothbrush or razor. None of those personal items you'd pack for a trip."

"You didn't find a white collar, did you?" Burke asked. "You know, like what a priest would wear?"

"I thought about that, too," said Catherine. "But no, none in the suitcase and none with the remains. I did some research and from what

I can tell, most collars were made of linen back in 1963, not synthetics. If it was there, it probably rotted away."

Burke examined the two suitcases that lay open on one of the tables. They had been cleaned up, and most of the trim and the hinges were rusty.

"Vinyl. Early Oleg Cassini we think . . . thanks to good ol' Google," she said with a laugh. "The suitcase did a nice job of helping to preserve this stuff. The contents of the other suitcase are a little more interesting. Follow me and I'll show you."

In another room, spread out on several more tables, were dozens of magazines, some in better shape than others. Catherine stood back and let Burke take it all in. For a full minute, he circled the tables in silence.

"Pornography," he muttered at last. "It's all pornography."

"Indeed," said Catherine. "Some of it's pretty raunchy, too."

Burke took a closer look. There were a few *Playboy* magazines and some other men's magazines. There were magazines in black-and-white with photos that looked as though they'd been shot at a nudist camp. There were also German and French magazines showing adult men with boys and girls, and boys with other boys and girls.

"The one suitcase was pretty much full of it," she said. "The stuff deeper into the suitcase was in pretty good shape."

Burke examined the magazines again briefly. "Anything else?" he asked, looking distraught.

"The glove box was empty, except for what was left of one of those manuals that come with a new car. We found those two beer bottles in the trunk, and the two beer mugs," she said, pointing. "From what we can tell from the color and shape of the bottles, it was probably Colt 45 Malt Liquor. Somebody Googled it. Apparently, it had just come on the market that spring."

"Colt 45. This stuff is pretty nasty," Burke said, picking up one of the bottles. "Strong, too."

"Besides the spare tire and some scraps of cloth, a towel maybe, this was the only other thing in the trunk," Catherine said, pointing to a remarkably well-preserved rug, maybe six feet by eight feet, laid out on the floor in one corner of the room. "Fake oriental. Some kind of blend, mostly synthetic."

"Odd," Burke mused, as he examined the rug. He made some notes in his notebook and took one last look at the magazines. Catherine led him back outside to the sidewalk.

"So, tell me, J.B." she said. "Who would want to kill a priest?"

Burke stood quietly, taking a long look up the street and then another long look in the other direction, almost as if he hadn't heard the question. He shrugged. "Hard to say. What will happen to the Impala now?"

"Well, unless you come up with a family member who wants it, I imagine it'll go to auction," Catherine told him. "Why? Are you interested, J.B.?"

"Nah," he said, smiling. "I'm holding out for a '57 Bel Air."

16

Nicholas Stankowski

That same afternoon, Monsignor Nicholas Stankowski stood in his bathroom and looked closely into a mirror, at the dark circles that had been forming under his eyes over the past few weeks.

"Good Lord," he said aloud.

His back, and sometimes his belly, had recently begun to ache, and it was affecting his sleep. He wasn't eating much, and often felt bloated and full of gas. He seemed to be losing weight. He'd been lucky all his life, he thought, never had any such problems, but maybe it was time for a checkup. He hadn't seen a doctor in a very long time.

Now sixty-three years old, Father Stankowski's official title was Moderator of the Curia – the Archbishop's right-hand man. He'd been the keeper of the Archbishop's records, the *archiepiscopi librarius*, for almost fifteen years, and lived in a small apartment in downtown Cincinnati, in a building on 8th Street owned by the Archdiocese of Cincinnati. The offices of the Archdiocese were next door, and the Archbishop himself had lived just up the street in a modest apartment above St. Louis Catholic Church. Recently, however, he'd moved to a $470,000 home purchased by the Archdiocese and located miles away from downtown in an upscale suburb. The move was not without controversy.

Personally, Father Stankowski did not approve of the purchase of the house. The timing was quite egregious, he thought, considering the state of the economy and the struggles and uncertainties that many members of the flock were dealing with. Born and raised in Cincinnati, he'd been devoted to the Catholic Church most of his life. Despite that devotion, he had often spoken his mind in opposition to what he considered irrelevant and outdated attitudes expressed by the Vatican. The Church's draconian past was especially abhorrent to him.

Unfortunately, this outspokenness had landed him in his current position in the Archbishop's office. As important as it was, it was a position he did not particularly relish. Once an up-and-coming diocesan priest, he had long ago been made a high-level monsignor. At quite a young age he'd been appointed pastor of St. Peter in Chains Cathedral, also located in downtown Cincinnati, not far from the St. Louis Catholic Church. But with age comes wisdom, Father Stankowski had always said. Some of his ideas about the direction in which he believed the Catholic Church should be headed on certain issues – homosexuality, for instance, and marriage for priests, women being ordained, birth control and abortion rights – were considered by his superiors as radical. He was eventually moved to the Archbishop's office, first as a vicar general, then chancellor of the Curia, and finally Moderator of the Curia. The Vatican wanted to keep an eye on him, keep him close, and each "promotion" was a means of doing just that.

Father Stankowski was thoroughly aware of the Vatican's intentions, but he didn't protest. Some of his friends thought he should, but he rationalized to them that there was a reason – God's reason – for the path of his career, and that someday God would reveal that plan.

He finished shaving and took a last look at himself in the mirror. Next week he would make an appointment with a doctor. The Catholic Church will survive without me for an hour or two, he thought.

17

Into the Arms of Our Lord

At lunchtime, over sandwiches at Lucky's, Burke told Kevin about the disturbing contents of the Impala trunk. Kevin was somewhat amused. "So, the priest was a perve," he said, grinning.

"Who knows," said Burke, unamused. "Pervert or not, he had a porn collection. And a lot of it was child porn."

"Have you talked to the priest out at St. Nick's?"

"Not yet," Burke replied. "I got an answering machine when I called. I thought I'd drive out there later – maybe take a look around the old neighborhood. It's been a long time."

After lunch, on his way back to the squad room, Burke stopped in at the *Records* division.

Becky looked up from the lunch spread out on her desk. "Hiya, Captain, I was going to call you right after I ate," she said. "No luck. I checked Missing Persons, everything from November 1963 to November 1964, but nothing showed up. Sorry."

Burke was a little surprised that a missing persons report had never been filed. It's possible, he thought, that a report could have been lost or misplaced sometime in the last forty-eight years. "Thanks, Becky. Sorry I disturbed your lunch."

"No prob."

Burke was back at his desk when his cell phone rang. "Hello, Captain. This is Father Stankowski calling from the Archdiocese Office. I have some information for you."

"Great. Thanks for calling back, Father." Burke took up a pad and pencil.

"My pleasure," said the priest. "So, according to our records, Father Raymond T. Nelson was ordained here in Cincinnati in May of 1951. It was a small class, probably because of the Korean War. Not only was there a draft, but I'm told a lot of young men left the program to volunteer."

"Do you have any personal records?" Burke asked. "Family members, that sort of thing?"

"Of course," said the priest. "Let's see. He was born in Richmond, Indiana, on September 12, 1925. His parents, Mr. and Mrs. Samuel Nelson, and his sister, Wilma, attended his ordination. According to our records, his mother's name was Maria, and Wilma was his only sibling. No other relatives are mentioned."

Burke quickly did the math. Father Nelson would have been thirty-eight years old in November of 1963, older than Burke remembered. But the priest had been handsome and trim, and may have appeared younger. Burke did a little more math. In 1963 Nelson would have already been a priest for some twelve years.

"Can you tell me where he was stationed before he was at St. Nick's?" Burke asked.

The priest did not immediately answer. "I'm sorry," he said at last. "That is just about all the information that I am at liberty to offer to you, Captain Burke. Church policy, I'm afraid. I *can* tell you that Father Nelson's file indicates that the archdiocese' last known contact with him was in November of 1963, and that he passed into the arms of Our Lord that same month."

Burke was stunned. *How had the Catholic Church known that Nelson was dead?*

"Wait a second, Father. No exact date of death?" Burke asked, quickly scratching a note. "Nothing more specific than that? Can you tell when that entry was made?"

Again, Father Stankowski did not immediately respond. The priest may have realized that he'd already revealed more than he intended.

"I'm afraid that's about all I can tell you," said the priest. "I hope it helps in your investigation."

Burke sighed and leaned back in his chair. "Yes, thank you, Father. You've been a great help. Thank you very much."

18

Suffer the Little Children

Burke hung up and closed his eyes, trying to wrap his head around what the priest had just told him. The Catholic Church listed Father Nelson as deceased, but the skeletal remains had just been found days ago. Burke realized that the entry of the priest's death in Father Stankowski's records could have been made anytime. *Who knows?* Maybe when Father Nelson failed to materialize, some scribe had just gone ahead and marked him off, using the last month that he'd been heard from. *That must be it.*

Burke got on his computer, and it didn't take long to find a phone number for the Wayne County courthouse in Richmond, Indiana. He dialed, and was eventually connected to a woman named Rosie. She was very chatty, and quite proud to tell Burke that all of the county census information, from as far back as when it was first collected, lived in her computer. Rosie quickly located the Nelson family.

From what she could tell based on the first appearance of Raymond's father, Samuel Nelson, in the 1910 census, he hadn't been born there, but came to the county from somewhere else. The 1920 census showed that he had married Maria (nee Esposito). The1930 entry revealed the birth of two children: Wilma M., born in 1923, and Raymond T., in 1925.

Rosie pointed out that Maria was the first Esposito in any record, so she, too, must have come from somewhere else. There were no other Nelsons from Samuel's line recorded after that, but Samuel, Maria, and Wilma appeared in all subsequent census records until their deaths –

Samuel's in 1967, Maria's in 1973 and Wilma's in 1999. There was no record of Wilma ever marrying or bearing children, and Raymond's last appearance was in the 1940 census. He'd most likely moved out of the county after that, Rosie surmised, and Burke realized that Nelson would have probably been in the seminary when the 1950 census was taken.

After writing everything down, Burke asked Rosie to fax him copies of the records. "You betcha!" she chirped. "This has been a load of fun, Captain!"

Burke realized that Wilma's death in 1999 was the end of the line for the Nelson family. As far as he was concerned, there were no relatives left to notify of the priest's death. Father Nelson could now, publicly, be associated with the remains found in the lake. Burke called his boss and told her the situation. They briefly discussed the possibility of exhuming one of the Nelson family members, in order to get a positive DNA match on the remains, but Major Winston decided such a measure was premature. "I'll set up a press conference for later this afternoon," she said. "How about four-thirty?"

With two hours to kill, Burke decided to drive out to St. Nick's and see if he could find Father Metzger, the pastor. He headed out Fifth Street, through the old Oregon district and into east Dayton, passing Holy Family Church, one of Dayton's older Catholic churches, where his parents had been married. Recently, Burke had heard that the Holy Family parish had forsaken modern times and reverted to using the old Latin Mass for some of their services. Women were once again coming to church wearing scarves on their heads, and the men were wearing coats and ties.

Burke angled off to the right when he reached Belfair Avenue, and a few miles later spotted St. Nick's. He slowed down as he drove past the school and then the church. The sign that he remembered still stood in a small lawn just to the left of the church. A large cross loomed over the sign that read simply – ***St. Nicholas Catholic Church*** – in large letters. Below that in smaller lettering, a Biblical quote read – *Suffer the little children to come unto me.* Another sign had been attached lower down, listing Father Metzger as the pastor, and the times for Mass.

As a child, Burke had never understood that particular New Testament quote, and he realized that it was still confusing to him. *Suffer? What the hell was that all about?* He made a mental note to research the quote. Just past the church, he turned into a small parking lot next to the rectory, which was exactly as he remembered it. He parked, then sat staring at the building for a full minute before getting out and climbing the few steps to the door. He rang the bell and stood quietly on the front stoop. A young priest, maybe thirty-five years old, answered the door.

"Father Metzger?" Burke asked.

"Yes, I'm Father Metzger. Can I help you?"

"Well, I hope so, Father, and I'm sorry to disturb you. I'm Captain John Burke from the Dayton Police Department." He showed the priest the badge hooked to his belt.

"Come in, come in, by all means," said the priest, shaking Burke's hand and laughing. "I hope I'm not in trouble."

Burke entered the rectory and it, too, looked the way he remembered it. To the right was a small waiting room, and beyond that a room that looked like an office. Another door led to the garage. The priest led him to the left, through a small coat room, and into a kitchen. They walked through the kitchen to a dining room and down two steps to a sunken living room. What had once been a wood-burning fireplace now contained a gas log insert. Father Metzger offered Burke a seat on a couch and asked if he would like something to drink. Burke said a glass of water would be fine. The room was air-conditioned and pleasantly dark. Burke peered down the hall that led off from the living room, back to where the bedrooms were located.

"So, Captain, what can I help you with?" said the priest, returning with two tall glasses of ice water.

"Well, Father, did you happen to hear about the car and the human remains that were discovered in Eastwood Lake? Earlier this week?"

"I did," said the priest, his eyebrows arching. "Grisly discovery! Have you identified the remains?"

"Not positively," said Burke. "I'm not sure if we'll ever be able to *positively* identify them. But there's pretty strong evidence suggesting that the car and the remains belonged to a Father Raymond Nelson. He was an assistant pastor here at St. Nick's a long time ago."

"Good Lord!" the priest exclaimed.

"Have you heard of him?" asked Burke.

"I *have* heard a few stories," said Father Metzger. "Some of the older parishioners mention him now and again. He's sort of legendary around here."

"Well, maybe you know the story then," said Burke, "about how he drove off in his car one night back in1963, and no one ever heard from him again."

"So I've heard."

Burke sipped the ice water. "Is there anyone in particular who might remember that far back?"

"Well, yes, as a matter of fact. Mary Lou Spaulding has some stories. She was the housekeeper at the rectory for many years, including when Father Nelson was here, I believe. She appears to have been very fond of him."

"Does she live nearby?" asked Burke. He had a dim recollection of the housekeeper.

"No, she's in a nice retirement community out in Kettering called The Oakwood. She used to come back here for Mass every Sunday. Now, not so often since she quit driving. Sometimes she'll get someone from The Oakwood to drive her over."

Burke took out a pad and wrote down the information.

"Do you keep any records here at St Nick's? Anything at all that might pertain to Father Nelson or his disappearance?"

"No, nothing like that. But I'm sure the archbishop's office could help you out. From what I hear, they keep pretty meticulous records."

"Yes, I already spoke with a Father Stankowski," Burke said. "He wasn't able to offer much info on the disappearance though."

"Ah, Monsignor Stankowski!" Father Metzger smiled. "One of the best. He should have been a cardinal by now."

"Is it possible that you have a photograph of Father Nelson?" Burke asked him.

"Hmm," the priest mused. "We do have a collection of old church directories. Let me see if I can find something."

He returned after a few minutes with a 1963 directory. He handed it to Burke, opened to a photo of Father Nelson. Burke stared at the photo for a long time without speaking.

"Captain Burke?"

"Oh, sorry." Burke said, looking up. "Can I keep this for now?"

"Absolutely," said the priest.

"There'll be an announcement to the press this afternoon," said Burke, handing the priest his card. "Thank you, Father. This is a big help."

He left the rectory and sat in his car for a long moment, staring at the building before finally driving away.

Burke cruised slowly through his old neighborhood – mostly modest, brick-faced or clapboard ranch houses and capes, built in the early to mid-1950s in the style of Long Island's Levittown – and pulled into the driveway of the house where he had grown up. The two silver maples in the front yard that Burke remembered had been replaced with tulip poplars. There were a few surviving maples in some of the other yards in the plat, and Burke thought back to the Halloween nights of his past. He remembered going door to door dressed as a hobo, his face blackened with burned cork. Gangs of kids, without their parents, stayed out in the dark for hours, with no fear of perverts or molesters or kidnappers. *How times have changed*, he thought.

Leaving the neighborhood, Burke turned left onto Belfair Avenue and headed back toward Dayton, again passing in front of St. Nick's. He read the Bible quote on the church sign again. *Damn*, Burke thought to himself, *I should have asked Father Metzger about that.*

19

A Murdered Priest

At four-thirty the press had gathered in the large conference room in the Safety Building. Burke and Major Claire Winston stood side by side at a podium marked with the seal of the State of Ohio and the seal of the City of Dayton. There were a few print journalists, Lisa Fowler among them, sitting in a row of chairs. Several photographers, and three or four local television cameras connected to their crews, stood at the ready.

"Good afternoon, everyone," Claire began. "I'm Major Claire Winston, Head of Special Investigations for the Dayton Police Department. Most of you know Captain John Burke, Supervisor of the Homicide Squad. As you are probably all aware, a 1963 Chevrolet Impala containing human remains was pulled from Eastwood Lake earlier in the week. Captain Burke's investigation has led to a likely identification of the remains, and, as no living relations could be verified or located, the department feels that this information can now be legally disseminated to the public. I'll let Captain Burke fill you in on the few details that we have." She stepped aside and motioned toward Burke.

"Thanks, Major Winston." Burke stepped up to the microphone. "We have reason to believe that the remains found in the car are those of one Raymond Nelson – *Father* Raymond Nelson – a Roman Catholic priest, who at the time of his disappearance in November of 1963 was the assistant pastor at St. Nicholas Catholic Church in Riverside." Burke held up an enlarged copy of the photo of the priest, taken from the old church directory. There was an audible buzz in the room, and Burke noticed Lisa Fowler, scribbling away.

"He was a white male, thirty-eight years old. The Impala was registered in his name. Some of the forensic evidence and the condition of the human remains suggest the possibility of foul play, and for the time being our investigation will be conducted as a homicide investigation. Now, does anyone have a question?"

Burke answered questions from some of the reporters who apparently hadn't been listening to the information he'd just offered. Lisa Fowler, on the other hand, asked several relevant questions. *Who would be running the investigation? Had a missing persons report ever been filed? Why exactly did they suspect foul play? Had the archdiocese been notified?* Burke declined to answer any questions regarding specific information about the condition of the remains, saying the full coroner's report had not been completed. He didn't mention the pornography.

"Thank you all," Burke said, wrapping things up. "Let me add, the DPD would like to ask that anyone with any knowledge of Father Nelson's disappearance, or any information that might help with this investigation, please call the Homicide Division at the Dayton Police Department. Thanks again."

He handed out copies of the photo of Father Nelson, and Lisa Fowler waited patiently until the camera crews and TV reporters finished up with Burke.

"Hi, J.B.," she said, shaking his hand. "Since you're taking the lead on this, I just wanted to let you know that I'll be *right* behind you. This is pretty fascinating stuff, don't you think? *A murdered priest?* Hell, depending on where this goes, I might even end up with a damn book."

"Don't get your hopes up too high, Lisa," said Burke, shaking his head. "And don't count on much help from the church."

He knew that trying to dissuade Lisa was a hopeless cause, and that she would, indeed, be right behind him.

"And, Lisa. You'll let me know if you get to something before I do?"

"You got it, J.B." she said with a wink.

Back at his desk in the squad room, Burke realized that he was exhausted. *What a week*, he thought to himself. He hadn't slept well, and the Impala case seemed to be leading him down a pot-holed road. Kevin and the other detectives were finishing up the week's last-minute paperwork and working out who would be on call over the weekend.

The squad room emptied and Burke sat alone. When he thought about his visit to the rectory, especially the dark hallway leading off from the living room, he suddenly felt more alone than he had felt in a long time.

Tomorrow was Saturday, and though he had the day off, he hoped to pay a visit to Mary Lou Spaulding. On Sunday he would relax and play a round of golf with Maggie.

20

Mike Donnelly

Sitting alone at a table, Mike Donnelly finished eating his dinner in the communal dining room at the Belmont Manor Home, a retirement center where he'd been living for the past five years. Clutching a walker, he returned to his small studio apartment down the hall. The television was already on when he unlocked the door; he rarely turned it off. Lowering himself slowly into a worn, plaid recliner, Mike cursed aloud his aching bones. The arms of the old recliner were darkened from years of contact with his oily, mottled skin, and the seat cradled his form exactly. The local news was just coming on.

Donnelly gasped – transfixed – when a photo of Father Raymond Nelson filled the screen. The lead story was about the identification of the human remains found earlier in the week. Mike watched the story intently on one station, then switched to another, then another, trying to catch just a second or two more of the image of Father Nelson. Finally, he turned off the television. The rest of the news didn't matter.

He'd read the story earlier in the week, in the *Dayton Daily News*, and seen the picture of the 1963 Impala pulled from Eastwood Lake. There was a skeleton in the car, and Mike wondered who it was. Now he knew. This was the watery end that Father Nelson had met almost fifty years ago. In all those years, not a day had passed when Mike hadn't thought about his poor son Timmy, and the horrible things that the priest had done to him. Timmy was long gone now, and Mike blamed his death on this evil man who'd been found at the bottom of the lake.

Forty-eight years ago, Mike had driven down to Cincinnati, and an old priest, the *vicar general* in the Archbishop's office, had assured him that the problem would be taken care of. He'd begged Mike to never speak to anyone of the things Timmy had told him. The priest did not deny there was a problem. The paperwork was already in place to deal with the situation, he assured him. Mike warned the vicar general that if the church was not willing to do something, he would deal with it in his own way. The aged priest assured him that wouldn't be necessary and asked Mike to pray with him. Mike had declined, and returned to Dayton.

And now he knew, for certain, after all these years. The church had kept its promise. Father Nelson had been buried in his own car at the bottom of the lake. Problem solved. No more perverted priest.

21

Mary Lou Spaulding

The hot weather broke overnight, and Mary Lou Spaulding arose to a beautiful Saturday morning. An old friend had taken her out to dinner the night before, and then she'd gone to bed early. Now, she put on some water for tea, turned off the air conditioning, opened some windows, and retrieved the *Dayton Daily News* from the box by her front door. Glancing at the front-page headline, she read – **Human Remains Identified as Priest**. Underneath was a photo of Father Ray, just like the one framed on her mantel. She gasped, suddenly light-headed, and quickly sat down, almost falling into one of the overstuffed chairs in her small living room.

Mary Lou had seen an article earlier in the week about the discovery of some remains, and had stared for a long time at the picture of the car that had been pulled from the lake. She knew it was the same kind of car Father Ray had driven off in, on a night long ago, never to return. *Could it really be him*, she'd thought? *It just couldn't be.*

But it *was* him. As she finished reading Lisa Fowler's story, a tear dropped from her cheek onto the newspaper. The tea kettle began to whistle, and she got up to turn off the burner. Sitting down at the kitchen table, she read the entire article. Father Ray was not just gone, he was dead, and *had* been dead for all these years. She leaned forward, laid her head on her crossed arms, and wept for a long time.

When Mary Lou finally sat up and wiped away the last of her tears, she returned to the living room. She rearranged the photos of the three men on the mantel, moving Father Ray to the middle. She gave all three frames a quick dusting, and returned to the kitchen to make a cup of tea. Tonight, she would say an extra prayer for Father Ray's soul.

22

Kenny Mason

Retired USAF Brigadier General James McGowan had also read the front-page article in the *Dayton Daily News*, tentatively identifying the human remains that were found earlier in the week at the bottom of Eastwood Lake. There was a photo of the priest, and the same, small stock photo of Captain John Burke that McGowan had seen before. Jim's wife, Kathy, had read the article earlier that morning.

"Jim, did you know this Father Raymond Nelson?" she'd asked. "Was he at St. Nicholas when you went to school there?"

"I knew him," McGowan had answered flatly. "He was the Boys' Choir director. I remember when he went missing. It was right around the time when Kennedy was assassinated."

Now that Kathy was off doing some shopping, McGowan read Lisa Fowler's article again. He put the paper down and found his wallet. It contained Kenny Mason's phone number, and McGowan wondered for a moment whether or not to call his old friend.

Kenny was the first friend Jim McGowan had made when he moved to Dayton, way back in the summer of 1963 when his father was transferred from a base in Texas to Wright-Patterson. The boys went to St. Nick's together for just one year, the eighth grade.

After St. Nick's, McGowan went on to the public high school in Riverside, and Kenny went to the new Catholic high school. They'd already begun to lose touch when McGowan's father was transferred to Vietnam in 1967, and Jim's mother decided to move back to her home state of Texas, taking Jim with her.

Just over two years ago, after retiring from the Air Force, McGowan had tracked Kenny down to his home in Ithaca, New York, and now they talked on the phone occasionally. Kenny still had family in the Dayton area, and he and McGowan had managed to get together a few times when Kenny came to town. McGowan dialed Kenny's number.

"Jim!" Kenny answered. "How the hell are you?"

"I'm fine. How the hell are *you?*" Jim asked.

"I'm good," said Kenny. They caught each other up, and then McGowan got to the point.

"Kenny, I have a bit of disturbing news here I thought you should know. And if you aren't sitting down, maybe you should."

"Go ahead, Jim."

"Well, it seems the Dayton police have found Father Nelson's car in the old gravel pit."

McGowan waited. "Kenny? You there?" he asked when his friend didn't answer.

"Yeah, I'm here," Kenny said. "Jesus Christ!"

23

Gone

Burke had enjoyed his first cup of coffee sitting in the morning sun on the small balcony of his apartment. The temperature had fallen, and after another restless night, the cooler weather seemed to cheer him up. He ate breakfast, paid some bills, and did a little grocery shopping at the nearby Kroger store. Around noon, he called Maggie to confirm their golf date for the next day, Sunday. At one o'clock Burke called the office at The Oakwood Retirement Community, got a number for Mary Lou Spaulding, and was transferred to the number.

"Hello," she said, picking up. "This is Mary Lou."

"Hi, Mrs. Spaulding. My name is John Burke, and I used to live in your neighborhood. I went to school at St. Nick's."

"Well, hello, John Burke," she said cheerily. "Were you the Burke family on Columbia Court?"

"That was us," Burke said. "Unfortunately, my parents are both dead now, and my sister lives out west."

"Oh, I'm sorry to hear about your parents. I'll pray for their souls."

"Thank you. The reason I'm calling is that I work for the Dayton Police Department now, and I was wondering if you've heard or read anything about Father Raymond Nelson."

"Yes, I have," Mary Lou answered. "I read about it in the morning paper. It breaks my heart."

"I'm so sorry, Mrs. Spaulding."

"Thank you, John, and please, call me Mary Lou."

"I was wondering, Mary Lou, if I could come and visit, to talk a little bit about Father Nelson."

"That would be fine," she responded enthusiastically. "Why don't you come for dinner? I could fix sandwiches for us, something simple. Or we could eat in the cafeteria if you like, but it's more private here."

"Well, if it's not too much trouble. That would be great. What time should I come?"

"How about six o'clock," she said. "I'm looking forward to it."

* * *

Burke drove to a sporting goods store and treated himself to a new lob wedge to add to his golf bag. On his way home he dropped in unexpectedly at Kevin and Becky's house out in Huber Heights. Burke's granddaughters squealed with delight when their Grandpops showed up. He and Kevin horsed around with the girls and watched a few innings of the Red's day-game on TV. When Burke got back to his apartment, he spent the rest of the afternoon practicing pitch shots with the new club on the long, open lawn behind the complex.

At five o'clock, showered and shaved, Burke left his apartment and drove through a nearby car wash. After that, he stopped at another Kroger store in Kettering and bought a small bouquet of white roses and a nice piece of aged Irish cheddar. When he arrived at the front office of The Oakwood, they gave him directions to Mary Lou's bungalow. She answered the door quickly when he rang.

"Hello, John Burke," she said, surprising him with an affectionate hug.

"Hi, Mrs. Spaulding – I mean, Mary Lou."

She stepped away, looking at Burke, and shook her head. "Please forgive me, but you don't look familiar to me after all these years."

"Well, I *was* just a boy when you saw me last, but I remember you. You look wonderful," he said, handing her the roses. "Here, these are for you, and I brought a little cheese. Hope you like cheddar." Mary Lou blushed.

"Oh, thank you, John. You know, I'm eighty-seven years old now," she said proudly.

As Burke followed her into the living room, his eyes were drawn immediately to the photograph of Father Nelson propped between two others – one of John Kennedy, and one of a smiling, handsome young man wearing an Army hat.

"That's my husband on the right," she said, noticing Burke's interest.

Over a dinner of ham sandwiches, homemade coleslaw, and iced tea, Burke and Mary Lou chatted about the old neighborhood, and she caught him up on a lot of his old acquaintances. She gave him what she called *the condensed version* of her life story, dwelling a bit on her involvement with the B-29 that bombed Nagasaki. She was delighted when she discovered their mutual interest in the Air Force Museum.

"Do you remember Jimmy McGowan?" she asked. "He was probably about your age. He became a general in the Air Force, and now he's retired. He's on the board at the museum. Anyway, he had a picture of me added to the *Bockscar* display. Actually, two pictures, one when I was young, and one taken recently."

Burke remembered Jim McGowan. He had lived in base housing and entered St Nick's as an eighth grader. Although they were in the same grade that year, they'd never hung out together. Burke remembered Jim as being older than his classmates, and already needed to shave. Both boys had gone to Riverside High, and Burke vaguely recalled that Jim had wrestled one year. McGowan was gone from Riverside by the time Burke graduated.

After dinner, Burke helped Mary Lou clean up, then they moved to the living room. He asked her about Father Nelson's disappearance.

"I remember it all like it was yesterday," she said, wistfully. "When I got to the rectory that morning, Father Ray – he let me call him that – he was already gone. The church was still locked and people were waiting to get in for the early mass. It was a Friday, the same day President Kennedy was killed," she said, pointing toward Kennedy's picture on the mantle. "My husband and John Kennedy were the very same age, you know."

She went on. "Father Krueger had spent that night at his mother's house in Piqua. When I called him there, he told me not to worry. He had me send everyone home and said he would be there in an hour. I checked the rectory garage, and it was empty. Father Ray's new Impala was gone – you know, the car in the paper. He *so* loved that car. His parents bought it for him. Anyway, I looked in his room, which was unlocked, and the closet was open and a lot of his clothes were missing off their hangers. His two brand new suitcases were gone – oh, he was so very proud of them – Oleg Cassini, top of the line. Very nice."

"Do you remember anything else unusual in the rectory, anything out of place, that sort of thing?" Burke asked.

"Just the rug. There was an oriental rug in front of the hearth that was gone. I remember thinking *that* was odd – why would he take *that*? It was nothing special – it wasn't even a *real* oriental rug. I picked it out myself at Rike's. You remember Rike's, I'm sure."

"I do. So, did anyone report him missing?" Burke asked.

"Not right away. When Father Krueger got back, he said we should wait, that perhaps there was a good explanation. Maybe Father Ray suddenly got called away for some reason. Maybe he went to Richmond to see his parents. Richmond, Indiana, that's where he was from. Anyway, Father Krueger didn't seem too alarmed or upset. I was *beside* myself." Mary Lou shivered.

"Then, that very afternoon, we started hearing about the assassination of the President. After that, everyone just seemed to forget about Father Nelson – even *me*, I'm ashamed to say. I cried for a solid week about Kennedy. I couldn't tear myself away from the TV. I saw Jack Ruby shoot Lee Harvey Oswald. *Right on live television!* Everyone in the parish was completely consumed by the assassination, and *nobody* was worried about Father Nelson."

Burke let her talk.

"By the middle of the next week I came to my senses and really started missing poor Father Ray. You know, to this day I can still recall his beautiful voice, almost like Andy Williams. Anyway, I discovered that someone – Father Krueger, I assumed – had cleaned out the rest of Father Ray's belongings from his room. It was empty. When I asked about it, Father Krueger said not to worry, that Father Ray was gone now and that a new assistant pastor would be sent by the Archbishop. I asked Father Krueger if he had called the police to report Father Ray missing and he said that wasn't necessary. I just cried and cried about Father Ray. I missed him terribly. He was always so kind to me, and he was so handsome. Handsome like my husband. Handsome like John Kennedy," she said, pointing again to the three photos on the mantel. "Father Krueger sent me home, and the next morning I screwed up my courage and called the police myself."

"Did the police come out?" asked Burke.

"Yes, Martin Bigelow came out and met me at my house," she said. "Do you remember Martin Bigelow from the Riverside Police Department?"

Burke *did* remember Bigelow *"the Gigolo."* He'd been the police chief in Riverside back when it was just a one-cop operation. Bigelow was divorced, and his reputation as a ladies' man was well known in Mad River Township. There were dozens of stories about Martin Bigelow and the lonely Air Force wives, stuck in base housing while their husbands were overseas. His police car was spotted regularly, day or night, parked in front of one of the hundreds of base housing units just across from Wright Field. The old, two-room schoolhouse that had been converted into the Riverside Police Station, was nearby.

"Do you know if he filed a missing persons report?" Burke asked, suddenly realizing that maybe one had never been filed with the DPD.

"I couldn't say what he did," said Mary Lou, "but he did take down some information. I told him that Father Ray had been alone in the rectory when I left for home that day, and that he had his regular Boys' Choir rehearsal scheduled for that evening. I think they were practicing for the upcoming Christmas show. Anyway, I suggested that he talk to the boys in the choir because they may have been the last ones to see Father Ray."

"Do you know if he did that?"

She shook her head. "No. Well, maybe. I don't know. He never came back to see me again after that," Mary Lou said. "But he did ask me out before he left."

"And did you go out with him?" Burke couldn't help but smile.

"Oh, gracious no," she said, blushing and waving a hand. "I was flattered, of course, but I never dated *anyone* after my husband was killed in France. Besides, Martin Bigelow was not a Catholic – and he had *quite* a reputation."

Burke asked Mary Lou if he could come back and see her sometime, that he might have more questions at some point.

"I'd like that," she said, getting up to see Burke out. "Oh, wait a minute. I have something here that may be of interest to you."

Mary Lou disappeared into her bedroom. When she returned, she handed Burke a stiff, yellowed, wax envelope, with an old-fashioned string closer holding it shut. As soon as Burke took hold of the envelope, he could tell what it was. He opened it and found two brand new, blue and white 1963 Ohio license plates nestled tightly together.

"It's the only thing I have of his," Mary Lou said. "They came in the mail the day after he disappeared, and I've kept them ever since. Maybe you should have them now."

Burke returned the plates to the envelope and handed it back to Mary Lou.

"You keep them," he said, spying a tear as it rolled down her cheek. He gave her a hug and held her for a moment.

"All the men I ever really loved," she cried into his shoulder. "Gone."

24

Hit Another One

Sunday was another beautiful day, the August heat having lifted the day before. Burke picked Maggie up at her house and tossed her golf clubs and pull-cart into the trunk of his car. He'd slept soundly for the first time in days and was feeling relaxed, and he always seemed to feel better when he was with Maggie. Even after living apart for all these years, she was still his rock.

"I hear you visited your girls yesterday," she said, once they were on the road.

"They're growing up too fast." Burke shrugged. "Seems like they were just babies last week. Hell, sometimes it seems like *Kevin* was just a little kid last week. Now look at him. Getting ready to take over for his old man."

Maggie reached over and put her hand on Burke's knee. "You're a good Grandpops, Johnny. You were a good dad, too, and I don't care *what* they say."

Burke laughed and patted Maggie's hand. "Thank you, dear. I needed that."

"Actually, I mean it, Johnny. Despite a lot of other things, you're *still* a great dad."

Burke told Maggie about his new golf club, and about his "date" with Mary Lou Spaulding. They rode in silence for a mile or two after that, not an uncomfortable silence, and then Burke was the first to speak.

"I've been thinking about seeing a shrink again," he said.

Maggie's eyebrows arched, and she stared at Burke. "Seriously?"

"Yeah. Something about this damned Impala case is bugging me. Everything about it."

"Like what exactly?" Maggie asked, still staring at Burke.

"Hell, I don't know, Maggie. Everything. I've been having weird dreams. And remembering things. Things I hadn't thought of in almost fifty years."

"Do you have someone in mind, Johnny?"

"No. Not yet anyway," he said, turning into the golf course parking lot. "But I'll look into it next week."

Burke had a city golf membership and knew almost everybody at Community; everyone there knew the head of homicide for the DPD. He and Maggie chatted with the starter, and teed off at ten o'clock. They walked, with pull carts. Burke didn't believe that riding in a motorized cart was the way to play golf. Golf was a game you *walked*, and he swore he would quit when he could no longer walk the course. On the other hand, he knew there were a lot of older golfers riding in carts, who had once made the same promise.

Starting with a par on the first hole and a birdie on the second – something he hadn't done in a long time – Burke was feeling good. They played the shorter inside course – Burke from the white tees and Maggie from the yellow. As was their habit, they kept the conversation light, mostly talking golf and grandkids. At the turn, they stopped for a hot dog, and Burke drank an iced tea. A beer at the turn wasn't always a good idea, and Burke didn't want to take a chance today. He'd shot a 41 on the front nine and was hoping to break 80, something he'd done only once before.

On the back nine, Maggie asked a few questions about the Impala case, but Burke was short with his answers and tried to concentrate on finishing with a good score. At the 18th hole they left their clubs at the bottom of a hill, and with only their drivers in hand, started the long climb up a set of stairs set into the hill, to the highly elevated tee box. The ladies' tee box was lower down at the bottom of the hill, but Maggie liked to drive this hole from the upper tee.

"Kevin said they found some child pornography in the Impala," Maggie said, following Burke up the steps. He stopped, and turned around to face Maggie.

"Kevin shouldn't have told you that." He knew instantly he'd said it too sharply.

"Oh, come on, Johnny. I'm his mother."

"It doesn't matter," Burke said. "That information's not public, and he should have known better. Please keep it to yourself."

"I promise," Maggie said, holding a finger to her lips. "Mums the word."

Burke needed a birdie to shoot a final score of 79. The hole was a short par 4, less than 300 yards, and Burke had driven the green more than once in the past. He teed up his ball, and halfway through the swing, he knew he had over-swung. He topped the ball, which dribbled on down the hill toward the ladies' tee box.

"Goddammit!" Burke wanted to slam the driver into the ground, but he refrained.

"Hit another one, Johnny," Maggie said, offering some consolation.

"No, I'll play that one," Burke grumbled, picking up his tee.

Maggie hit her own drive down the middle. They didn't talk after that, and going down the steps, Burke thought that if he could at least par the hole, he'd finish with an 80. But his concentration was gone. When he hit his second shot from the lower tee box, he over-swung again, hitting a huge slice. The ball went so far to the right that it cleared the neighboring fairway and headed for the parking lot where the grounds keepers and maintenance crew parked their cars. Burke cringed when he heard the ball smash into a car window, and he dropped his club. He turned to look at Maggie and watched as a smile slowly formed on her face. When she burst into laughter, Burke managed a smile, and the tension that had been building was suddenly gone.

Burke finished the hole with a triple bogie and a score of 83. He reported what had happened on the last hole to the guys at the pro shop, left his name and number for the owner of the car he had hit, and took Maggie home. Late that afternoon, Burke was in his apartment sipping a beer and watching the Reds on T.V. when his cell phone rang.

"Hey, Capitán!" said a friendly voice with a Spanish accent. "This is Carlos, from Community."

"Hey, Carlos," said Burke. "Please don't tell me it was your car I hit today."

"Sorry, boss," Carlos said, laughing. "Were you hitting a Pro V1 ball with three red dots?"

"Yeah, that's mine I'm afraid," Burke said.

"Good shot!" Carlos laughed again. "You took out my windshield. The ball was right there on the ground next to the car. Anyway, what you wanna do about it?"

Burke was about to say something about his car insurance, but stopped.

"Well, Carlos, next time I guess I'll have to loosen my grip a little," Burke said. "Maybe use a different set-up and try not to over-swing."

"Oh, that's a good one, boss," Carlos laughed. "But I'm just yanking your chain anyway. You don't have to do nothing. I got full glass coverage with no deductible. They came out already and gave me a new windshield. You the man, Capitán!"

25

White Cat in a Snowstorm

On Monday morning Burke and Kevin gathered the squad to review their ongoing cases. They discussed assignments for the week and established priorities for any reports or paperwork that had to be done. Again, Burke was pleased with Kevin's handling of the squad and their receptiveness to his role. With Kevin at the helm, Burke was free to concentrate on the Impala case.

The squad, especially Pete Skoff, the reigning city Amateur Senior Golf Champion, gave Burke a good ribbing after he related the story of his wild slice the day before. Pete was a great golfer, and famous in the DPD for the time he'd arrested two knife-wielding crackheads who tried to rob his foursome, right on the golf course. Pete had just hit his drive at the 16th hole on the outside course at Community when the punks popped out of the woods and told everyone to turn over their wallets and cell phones ". . . and no one gets hurt." Pretending to retrieve his wallet from a pocket in his golf bag, Pete had calmly pulled out a pistol and arrested the scoundrels.

Burke went to his desk, spent an hour with paperwork, and then called Scott Kaminsky, the police chief out in Riverside. They talked about the Impala case for a few minutes, and then Burke got to the point.

"I was wondering what the chances are that you might have any missing persons records going back to 1963," he asked.

"Well, believe it or not, the chances are actually pretty good," Kaminsky answered, to Burke's surprise. "Finding the one you want might be another story."

"Would you mind if I came over and had a look?"

"Not at all," said Kaminsky. "The deal is, the room containing all the old files is a mess. Everything in there's been moved three times over the last twenty-five years – every time we moved to a new building. There's stuff in there going back to the beginning of the department, before 1950. Nothing ever got transferred to microfiche, and now nothing's been scanned into the system. Lots of good intentions over the years, but not much got done. The good thing is, nothing got thrown out."

"Good," said Burke. "Can I come over this morning?"

"Sure," said Kaminsky. "I wish I could have someone look through the stuff for you, but we've had so many cutbacks, I can't spare anyone. Hell, I'll be the only one here before long, if this keeps up."

The Riverside Police station was located just off the highway, in the Riverside City Office building on Harshman Road, just north of the lake from where the Impala was found. Burke remembered when Martin Bigelow was the lone Riverside cop, working out of an old schoolhouse next to a little fleabag motel on Springfield Street. Over the years, the station had moved several times before landing at the Riverside City Building.

Scott Kaminsky greeted Burke at the front desk and led him back to a room containing the old files. "Bigelow the Gigolo had quite a reputation," he said. "But I've looked through some of his old reports and I think he was probably a pretty good cop. Couldn't type worth a shit, though."

The room was a total mess. Filing cabinets of every size and color lined all four walls of the windowless room, and three or four more rows filled the center of the room. Maybe half of the cabinets were labeled. Cardboard legal boxes were piled on top of most of the cabinets, and a cafeteria table and several folding chairs took up the only open space.

"I would start on that wall there if I were you, J.B.," Kaminsky said, pointing. "I think those are the oldest files. Would you like some coffee?"

Kaminsky brought him a cup, and wished Burke luck. Right off the bat, Burke found some files from the early 1960s, and his hopes grew. He soon realized, however, that they were mixed in with stuff from the 1970s and even the 1980s. After two hours of searching, he took a break and went to lunch with Kaminsky. They talked a little about the Impala case and about the city cutbacks, and Kaminsky told Burke a lot of the stories he'd heard about Martin Bigelow.

After lunch, Burke had been back in the file room for almost an hour when he opened a cabinet drawer near the floor and spotted an old paper file divider marked *MISSING PERSONS*. "Hallelujah!" he said out loud, and then, "well, maybe." There was a *1959* date on a report near the front.

"C'mon, c'mon," he muttered leafing through the rest of the papers. When he finally found one dated *1963*, he took the file to the table and sat down. Before long, he found what he was looking for and leaned back in the chair. "Bingo!"

Two thin pieces of typing paper, yellow with age, sandwiched a piece of carbon paper. Burke smiled. Martin Bigelow hadn't even bothered to separate the original from the carbon copy. A coffee ring stained the lower left side of the front page, and a handwritten note was scrawled across the bottom of the page. *Talk to housekeeper again.* Paper-clipped to the pages was a scrap of lined notepaper with three names printed in pencil. All three names looked as if they'd been written by different hands – *James McGowan, Steven Heckman,* and *Kenneth Mason.* Burke set Bigelow's scribbled notes aside, and read the typed report.

FATHER RAYMOND NELSON reported missing Nov. 28, 1963

Recieved a call Nov. 28 around 10:15 am from Mrs. Mary Lou Spaulding. She reprted that she is the houskeeper at St. Nicholas Catholic Church rectry located at 5330 Belfair Avenue Dayton 31 Ohio. She reported that Father Raymond Nelson, assist. paster at church has not been seen since the evning of Nov, 21. (six day ago) Reported Nelson is white male hieght about 6'2" weight about200 pounds. I went to her house and talked to her at around 11:00 am same day. She saw priest last before she went home the afternoon of Nov.21. He was to have choir practice thet evening. He was not in church as sceduled morning of Nov.22 for early mass. His car is gone from garage as well as clothes from a closet and suit cases. Black 1963 Chevr. Impala. Also one rug. Personal items of priest were still in rectry. She said choir boys may have seen priest after she did. Maybe no one else but not sure.

I then proceded to church and spoke with Father Kruger who had same information. He saw Father NElson last time also afternoon of Nov. 21 I asked him if I could talk to choir boys. He called Sister Roberta principal and she asembled choir boys in classroom at school. Choir boys pointed out three boys who saw priest last. All in grade 8. James McGowan, Kenneth Mason, Steven Heckman. These boys reported that they helped the priest move a piano in rectry after choir practice on evening of Nov.21and left around 8;30. This is last reported siting of priest. Last seen8:30pm Nov.21, 1963. Wearing black priest clthing. Current wearabouts unknown.

The report was signed, *Chief Martin Bigelow*. Back in his school days at St. Nick's, Burke had known all three of the boys mentioned in the report. Jim McGowan's name had already come up, when Burke visited Mary Lou Spaulding on Saturday, and apparently McGowan was currently living in the Dayton area; he would be easy to find. Burke knew that Steve Heckman was already dead, having jumped to his death from the top of Rike's parking garage in downtown Dayton a long time ago. Burke would have to try to track down Kenny Mason, if he was still alive. According to the note on the old report, Bigelow had wanted to talk to Mary Lou Spaulding again, and Burke guessed that he may have wanted to ask her about the piano that the boys mentioned moving – she hadn't mentioned it to Bigelow in the report, or to Burke, when he'd talked to her on Saturday. Burke thought about looking further for a follow-up report, but decided that had there been one, Bigelow would have put it in this same file.

Burke carefully peeled the carbon copy off, put the original report back into the folder, and returned the file to the drawer. He would ask Kaminsky if he could take the carbon copy, and was about to leave the room when he stopped.

"Shit," he muttered, rubbing his chin. Burke went back and sat at the table, read the report through again, and changed his mind. He found the file drawer again, removed all of the paperwork on Father Nelson, and put the folded bundle in his inside jacket pocket.

"I give up," he lied to Kaminsky, walking into the front office. "Talk about a needle in a goddamn haystack."

"Really?" said Kaminsky, looking doubtful. "Hell, I thought you'd find something. Shit."

"I found the right drawer, I think, but nothing on the priest."

"Oh, well, you're welcome to come back anytime and look some more."

"Thanks, Scott," Burke said, throwing him a quick salute. "I'll keep that in mind. And thanks again for lunch."

Outside, Burke was about to get into his car when another car pulled up next to his. It was Lisa Fowler.

"Fancy meeting you here," Burke said with a grin as she stepped out of her car.

"Hiya, J.B. Let me guess – you're looking for a missing persons report on Father Raymond Nelson."

"Now what in the world would make you think that, Lisa?" Burke asked, playing dumb.

"Well, a little bird named Mary Lou Spaulding thought such a thing just might exist," said Lisa, smiling. "She mentioned that she talked to you on Saturday. She thought you were *very* handsome by the way."

"How'd you find her?" asked Burke.

"Father Metzger, at St. Nick's. "He *also* mentioned he'd talked to you."

"Save yourself the trouble, Lisa," said Burke, nodding toward the building. "It's like looking for a white cat in a snowstorm with the mess they've got in there. I searched for over three hours and didn't come up with a damn thing."

"Kaminsky might not even let me look," Lisa said, shrugging. "We'll see."

"Well, if he does, good luck to you. Let me know if you find anything, all right?"

"Will do, J.B.," she said. "See you in the funnies."

26

Jim McGowan

Later that afternoon, back in the squad room, Burke Googled retired USAF Brigadier General James McGowan. He found quite a few entries, mostly regarding McGowan's Air Force career, including a full entry on Wikipedia. Burke read the Wikipedia page, then found several entries regarding McGowan's more recent connection to the Air Force Museum, some concerning his involvement in trying to procure one of the old space shuttles for the museum. Eventually, Burke found a phone number and a Beavercreek address through a White Pages search. The listing read simply, *McGowan, James & Kathleen*. Burke dialed the number.

"Hello," a woman answered. *Pleasant voice*, Burke thought. He told her who he was, and asked if he could speak to Jim McGowan

"Are you trying to raise money for something?" the woman asked.

"No," said Burke, smiling to himself. "This is actually regarding an investigation I'm conducting."

"Oh, sorry, we get a lot of calls," she explained. "Just a minute."

Burke waited for nearly a minute. He tried to picture Jim McGowan settled into his suburban home, far from the Pentagon world he had once been such a part of.

A man's voice came on the phone.

"Hello, this is Jim McGowan."

"Hi, Jim. This is John Burke. I don't know if you remember me, but we went to school together at St. Nick's – many years ago."

"I do remember you, John," McGowan said after a long pause. "And I've seen your picture in the paper a few times. I wondered if it was you."

"It's me," Burke said. "So, you probably know that I'm a homicide detective."

"Yes. I saw your picture just recently, in the story about Father Nelson."

"So, you remember him?"

"Sure, I remember him. I remember when he went missing."

"Well," Burke said, "that's what I'm calling about. You got a minute?"

"I'm retired, John. I've got all day."

"Good, good." Burke glanced at his notes. "So back in 1963, the housekeeper at St. Nick's rectory was Mary Lou Spaulding, and she was the one to report Father Nelson missing. Mrs. Spaulding told me you two know each other."

"We do," Jim said. "She's very involved at the Air Force museum. I'm on the board there now."

"Yeah, she told me all about it. It's a great museum, by the way. I get over there at least once a year myself," Burke said. "Oh, and I found some stuff online about you. Did you know you have your own Wikipedia page?"

"Yeah," McGowan sighed. "And I'm vain enough that I check it out once in a while. I'm always happy to see that most of what's on there is correct."

"Well, I was impressed," Burke said.

"Thanks, John."

"So, Jim, I found a missing persons report that the Riverside police chief – Martin Bigelow – filed back then in 1963. Do you remember him?"

"Bigelow the gigolo? Sure, I remember him. He took Sylvia out a few times when my dad wasn't around."

"Is that your sister?"

"No, no. Sorry. That's my mom. She always wanted me to call her Sylvia. Didn't like 'Mom' for some reason."

Burke thought about how different their mothers must have been.

"Anyway," he said, getting back to business, "the report mentions that you and Steve Heckman and Kenny Mason were possibly the last ones to see Father Nelson before he disappeared."

"Really?" said McGowan. "That's in the report?"

"Yes, it is," said Burke. "The report says that the three of you went to the rectory the evening before he disappeared, to help move a piano."

"Hmmm." There was a long pause. "I have a very vague memory of talking to Bigelow. I might have been in the rectory once, but I'm not sure why I was even there. We could have moved a piano, I guess."

"So, you remember being there with Steve and Kenny?"

"Well, sort of. I think maybe we *did* move a piano."

"Do you remember where you moved the piano to?" Burke asked.

"Not really. I can't really recall. Maybe from one side of the room to the other."

"And you all left the rectory together, after that?"

"I guess we did. Who knows? Hard to remember that far back. Most of my memories from that week involve the Kennedy assassination – my mom crying, the nuns crying, the T.V. on non-stop. Hell, you must remember, everybody was in shock. Nobody seemed to be too concerned at the time about Father Nelson disappearing. I guess he just sort of got lost in the shuffle."

"And when did Bigelow question you?"

"Hard to say. Maybe a week after Father Nelson left."

Burke thought that McGowan's memory was somewhat selective. He wondered why the general would have recalled that Father Nelson's disappearance had been *lost in the shuffle*, and why would he recall the correct time frame of Bigelow's questioning when he could barely recall being in the rectory and moving the piano?

"Did Bigelow talk to all three of you at the same time, or separately?"

"We were together, I'm pretty sure," said McGowan. *Selective memory.* Burke was taking notes and made no reply.

"Listen, John," said McGowan. "It said in the newspaper that there was a possibility of foul play. So, am I a suspect at this point? Is that what this is about? Are Kenny and Steve suspects?"

"No, no, no," Burke reassured him. "I'm just trying to figure out what happened, and you guys may have been the last ones to see Father Nelson alive. I'm just trying to cover all the bases."

"So, can I ask – do you *have* any suspects?"

"Not yet," Burke replied. "You know Steve is dead, right?"

"Yes," said McGowan. "Horrible. We were all out of touch for years and years, but after I retired, I was sort of curious about Kenny and Steve. I located Steve's wife in Florida – Maureen Heckman. She told me he committed suicide twenty years ago – jumped off the old Rike's parking garage. Maureen moved south after that."

Burke recalled Steve's suicide. No one had seen him jump, no note was found, and Burke had been part of the team that investigated the possibility of foul play. He'd interviewed Maureen, and remembered her breaking down and crying on his shoulder. In the end, Steve's death had been ruled a suicide.

"Any particular reason you wanted to get back in touch with Kenny and Steve?" asked Burke.

"Just old buds, I guess. Lots of time on my hands these days."

"So, did you manage to find Kenny?" Burke asked, as he jotted more notes.

"As a matter of fact, I *am* in touch with Kenny. He's living in Ithaca, New York. Builds houses. He still has family here and we get together sometimes when he's in town."

"Do you have a phone number for him?" Burke asked. "And one for Steve's wife in Florida?"

"Sure," McGowan said. "Hold on a minute and I'll find them."

Burke wondered if McGowan had bothered to contact any other kids from their class. He seemed to recall that he'd often seen the three boys together, back in the day.

McGowan gave him the phone numbers, and Burke asked him, offhandedly, if he was in touch with anyone else from their St. Nick's days.

"Not really," McGowan said. "Except for Mrs. Spaulding."

Burke thanked the general and asked if he could contact him again at some point. McGowan suggested that they stay in touch, maybe get together for lunch sometime. Burke hung up, but he knew he would be talking to McGowan again.

27

Riverside, Ohio: November 28, 1963

Riverside Police Chief Martin Bigelow entered the classroom where Sister Roberta, principal of St. Nicholas School, had gathered the members of the St. Nicholas Boys' Choir. Wearing his neatly pressed uniform and a short-brimmed police hat, he walked quickly to the front of the class. He wore a gun on one hip, and a baton hung from the other. The boys – fifth, sixth, seventh, and eighth graders – sat tensely at small wooden desks, staring straight ahead with their hands folded. They'd been pulled out of class for this unusual meeting, and the fact that it involved the school principal and the local police chief had them on their best behavior.

Sister Roberta had a brief, private conversation with Bigelow, then stepped in front of the choir, one hand fondling the beads of a large rosary that hung around her waist, the other hand clasping a contraption made of wooden parts and a strong rubber band. When she snapped the trigger on the contraption with her thumb, it made a sharp, loud click, gaining the attention of every boy in the room. Bigelow was impressed.

"Boys," said Sister Roberta, "Police Chief Bigelow is here and would like to have a word with you regarding the disappearance last week of Father Nelson. I expect you to give him your complete attention and cooperation. Chief Bigelow."

The nun stepped aside and Bigelow tipped his cap to her. He'd been trying to imagine what Sister Roberta would look like in a blouse and skirt. She was maybe forty-five years old, and her face was almost pretty. The bulky, black floor-length habit that she wore could not quite conceal the fact that she was heavy-breasted. He wondered what the color of her hair was, hidden behind the black-and-white veil that seemed to be pinching her face.

"Hello, boys," Bigelow began. "As you all must know by now, Father Raymond Nelson disappeared last week without any explanation. Also, his car is gone. According to Mrs. Spaulding, the housekeeper at the rectory, you choirboys were probably the last ones to see him. I understand there was a rehearsal on Thursday evening, and that the Father was nowhere to be found the next morning."

A low stir rippled through the room as the boys mumbled quietly to each other. With two quick snaps of the wooden contraption, Sister Roberta silenced the boys.

"I would like to know if any of you saw Father Nelson after that rehearsal," Bigelow continued. "Father Krueger said that Father Nelson would often let you boys into the gym to play basketball for an hour or so after you rehearsed. So, did some of you go to the gym, and did any of you see Father Nelson after that?"

Another buzz broke out and many of the boys seemed to be pointing at three of their choir mates in particular. Bigelow heard a mix of names in the hubbub – *Heckman, Jim, Mason, Kenny, McGowan, Steve*. Sister Roberta clicked the roomful of boys back into silence.

"Mr. Marcum," she said, addressing a boy in the front row. "Please stand up and tell Chief Bigelow what he wants to know."

Marcum stammered at first, but finally pointed at Jim McGowan and explained that he'd been picked that night to help Father Nelson carry the songbooks back to the rectory. "After a while Jim came to the gym and got Kenny Mason and Steve Heckman to help him and Father Nelson do something in the rectory."

He looked at Jim and continued. "Jim came back a little later and told us it was time to leave the gym. He said he'd turn out the lights and lock up for Father Nelson." As the boy spoke, some of the other boys nodded in agreement. When he finished and sat down, Chief Bigelow had another quiet conversation with Sr. Roberta.

"All right boys, thank you," she said. "Please return to your classes – except for Mr. McGowan, Mr. Heckman, and Mr. Mason. The three of you will stay here and speak further with Chief Bigelow. That's all. Now back to class, the rest of you."

Sister Roberta ushered the choir out of the room and left the three boys alone with the police chief. He asked them to move up to the front of the room, and they sat down side by side.

Bigelow noticed that Kenny and Steve were wide-eyed and looked very serious. Jim McGowan seemed relaxed and ready to talk. He looked vaguely familiar to the cop, and appeared to be a little older than the other boys, almost like he could have been their older brother, like Wally and the Beave on the *Leave it to Beaver* T.V. show.

"All right then," Bigelow said. "Tell me about that evening."

Jim jumped right in. "It was just like Marcum said. I helped carry the books for Father Nelson, then I hung out with him for a little while in the rectory. He wanted to move the piano and asked me to go to the gym and get two more boys to help. So, I came and got these guys and we helped move the piano. After that I locked up the gym and went home."

Kenny and Steve nodded, still wide-eyed and growing paler by the minute.

"You moved the piano?" Bigelow asked.

"Yes, sir. It was pretty heavy." Jim answered without hesitation. *Funny*, Bigelow thought. Mary Lou Spaulding hadn't said anything about the piano being moved.

"Did Father Nelson say anything about leaving town?" he asked.

"No, sir," said Jim. The other boys nodded.

"No one else was around?"

"No sir. Just us."

"Everything seemed normal?" Bigelow asked.

"Yes, sir," Jim said, smiling. "Perfectly normal."

"Humph," Bigelow grunted, looking quizzically at Jim. "Which one are you again?"

"McGowan, sir. James McGowan. You know my mom."

"*Sylvia McGowan?*" Bigelow grinned lecherously.

"Yes, sir."

"How old are you, McGowan?"

"Almost sixteen, sir."

"How come you're still in the eighth grade? Didya flunk or what?"

"No, sir. I was held back a few times 'cause of moving. This is my fourth school in five years." Bigelow knew this was the case with a lot of the Air Force kids.

"Humph," he muttered again. "All right then. Write your names down for me." Bigelow handed Jim a notebook.

28

Steve and Kenny

Burke hung up after talking to Jim McGowan, wondering if the retired general would contact Kenny Mason in Ithaca. He thought about calling Kenny immediately, but decided to wait. Instead, he dialed Steve Heckman's wife in Florida.

"Hello," Burke said. "Is this Maureen Heckman?"

"Yes, this is Maureen."

"Hi, Maureen. My name is John Burke and I'm calling from Dayton. I knew your husband, Steve. We went to grade school together at St. Nick's."

"Well, Steve passed away years ago – if you're looking for him."

"No, Maureen, I already knew that. And I'm sorry about his death. I remember when it happened. Must have been a little rough for you"

"So, you know how he died."

"I do. I was a cop back then – well, I'm still a cop – and I actually interviewed you during our investigation. You may not remember that."

"Jesus! John Burke! I remember you very well as a matter of fact," said Maureen. "I was blubbering away, and you were so sweet to me. And you knew Steve!"

"I'm surprised you remember that," Burke said. "That was quite a while ago. I hope things have worked out for you."

"Oh, I'm all right, I guess. Actually, Steve's death was a big relief in a lot of ways. Did you know Steve very well?"

"Just from St. Nick's. We were in the same class, but I went to Riverside after that. I do remember from the investigation that he was a heavy drinker. Maybe you told me that."

"Well, Steve had a lot of demons. Hell, I guess we all do. He wouldn't talk to me or anybody else about it. I tried to get him some professional help, but he thought shrinks were just a bunch of quacks."

Burke was quiet for a second. "Did he ever talk about his old school days?"

"Never. Mostly he just stayed drunk. He couldn't keep a regular job, so he just stayed home drinking while I supported us. Like I said, his death was a relief in a lot of ways."

"Well, the reason I ask, Maureen, is that I'm working on a disappearance case here in Dayton. We recently discovered the remains of a priest, in a car at the bottom of the lake here in town. He's been missing since 1963, and an old missing persons report mentions Steve as one of three boys who were possibly the last ones to see the priest alive. The priest was Father Raymond Nelson, and he was the assistant pastor at St. Nick's where Steve and I went to school together."

"I *saw* that story," Maureen said excitedly. "It was just a little article in our local paper here. I was surprised to see something about Dayton."

Burke realized that one of the national wire services must have picked up the story, probably from Lisa Fowler's article. There was, after all, a sensational aspect to the story. He wondered if Kenny Mason had maybe read about it, too, in Ithaca.

"So, Steve never talked about Father Nelson?" Burke asked. "Never talked about the disappearance of the priest?"

"Never," Maureen said. Burke scratched out a note on his pad.

"The other two boys mentioned in the old report are Jim McGowan and Kenneth Mason. Are you in touch with either of them?"

"I never knew Kenny Mason, but I think I heard Steve mention the name once or twice."

"What about Jim McGowan?"

"Jim called me a couple of years ago looking for Steve," she said. "He didn't know Steve was dead. Now he calls every once in a while, to see how I'm doing. Jim's very sweet – he always tells me to call him if I need anything. He retired from the Air Force, as a general I think."

Burke wondered about the strong connection that was growing ever more evident between McGowan and Kenny Mason and Steve Heckman.

"Well, thanks, Maureen. You've been a big help," said Burke. "Can I call you again if I need to?"

"Sure," said Maureen. "Anytime."

Burke hung up and made a few more notes. McGowan would now have had plenty of time to call Kenny Mason in Ithaca. Burke dialed the number Jim had supplied, and Kenny Mason answered.

"Kenny Mason?" Burke asked.

"Yes, this is Ken Mason."

"Ken, this is John Burke calling from Dayton, Ohio. We went to school together at St. Nick's. Do you remember me?"

"Sure, John, I remember you. It's been a long time," Kenny said. "How are you?"

"I'm good, thanks," Burke replied. "I got your number from Jim McGowan. Have you spoken to him recently?"

There was a short pause before Kenny answered.

"Not lately," he said. "We talk every once in a while. Sometimes we get together when I get back to Dayton."

"So how the hell did you end up in Ithaca, New York?" Burke asked.

"Oh, it's a long, long story, John. Mostly though, it's just that it's a nice place to live."

"Well, Kenny – sorry, *Ken*. Here's the deal. I'm a cop here in Dayton, a detective, and I'm working on a case that you may have heard about already. It actually got some national attention, I believe. Anyway, do you remember way back in 1963 when Father Nelson disappeared? He was the assistant pastor and the Boys' Choir director at St. Nick's. You must remember him?"

"Sure, I remember him," Kenny said. "I did see something in the news about it – about his car being found in the old gravel pit."

Burke tried to recall if Lisa Fowler's story had mentioned that Eastwood Lake had once been a gravel pit. Had the wire story mentioned it? But then Kenny could easily have known the gravel pit had become Eastwood Lake. Burke jotted a quick note.

"Yes. Anyway, I dug up an old missing persons report at the Riverside Police Station. It was written by Chief Martin Bigelow in 1963. He interviewed you and Jim McGowan and Steve Heckman. Bigelow thought you were the last ones to see Father Nelson before he disappeared."

"No kidding?" Kenny seemed surprised.

"Do you remember the interview?" Burke asked him.

"Boy, John. That was a long time ago. Tell me more."

"Well, the report says that the three of you were questioned at the school. You boys told Bigelow that you went to the rectory that evening to help move a piano. When I talked to Jim McGowan, he had trouble recalling the piano, but he said it was likely that you did."

"I have a dim recollection of being in a classroom with Bigelow," Kenny said. "As far as the night Father Nelson disappeared, we may have gone to the rectory to help. Moving a piano sorta rings a bell."

"Do you recall where you moved it to?" Burke asked.

"Not really." Kenny hesitated. "Maybe from one side of the room to the other."

Burke noted that McGowan had answered that same question the same way. Had McGowan called Kenny?

"And as far as you know, Father Nelson was fine when you saw him last, when you left the rectory that evening?" Burke asked.

"Well, John, like I said, I don't recall much about any of that, but I don't remember anything out of the ordinary."

"All right." Burke sighed. His instincts told him that there was something not quite right about Kenny's and Jim McGowan's stories.

"Thanks for your help, Kenny. Sorry, I mean Ken."

"That's okay, I don't mind," he said.

"I may want to talk to you again at some point."

"You know how to find me."

29

Lisa Fowler

Having rinsed the dinner dishes and loaded them into the dishwasher, Lisa Fowler sat down with her laptop at the kitchen table. She'd spent hours that afternoon at the Riverside police station, searching in vain for a fifty-year-old missing persons report. Tomorrow morning, she would go back and continue the search. Lisa sat staring at the blank screen. She was worried about her job.

Lately, the *news rumor mill* – as Lisa liked to call it – had been grinding out sketchy information about big changes coming down the pike. Someone had heard that Cox Enterprises was thinking of selling the *Dayton Daily News* to the Gannett Newspaper Group. The paper would shrink further, and its reputation would take another major hit. The staff would be streamlined, and Lisa knew that many of them would be out of a job.

At forty-five, she would almost certainly be put out to pasture. Gannett's staffs tended to be young, inexperienced, internet-savvy journalists who worked for peanuts. For now, Lisa took home a pretty good check at the end of each week, and between that and the child support she received from her ex-husband, she did all right. But what if it ended?

"Shit," she muttered, and closed her laptop.

Jason, her son, had retreated to his room after dinner – she could hear the sounds of a video game coming from his room. He would be a high school senior in the fall and was bored with summer. Lisa thought Jason spent too much time playing video games with his friends; she'd encouraged him to get a job for the summer, but nothing panned out. Her daughter, Jessica, was waitressing at a Mexican restaurant nearby and was out for the evening. Jessica had graduated from high school in June and would be starting at Wright State University in a few weeks. She'd been accepted at several other schools but the cost was too high, even with financial aid, and this way she could live at home and commute. Both kids were good students, and Lisa would be happy when they were back in school. She was proud that Jessica and Jason both enjoyed writing and had excelled in their English and creative writing classes.

Lisa owned her house in Kettering outright, as part of a divorce settlement. Her husband had decided he wanted a younger wife, and now he had one, and two more young children to boot. Jessica and Jason had little interest in their half-siblings.

Lisa had always been a serious newspaper junkie. She loved everything about newspapers. The smell of the paper, the feel of it in her hands, the newsroom, the headlines and the deadlines, the sound of the old presses, everything. She couldn't imagine doing anything else, and she couldn't imagine a life without a daily newspaper to hold in her hands.

As a youngster, she'd grown up with *two* papers, the *Journal-Herald* in the morning and the *Dayton Daily News* in the evening. Lisa's father wrote for both papers, until he was killed in the line of duty, struck by a police car while covering a fog-related, chain reaction pile-up. In 1986, the two dailies had merged. They had dropped the *Journal-Herald* name, and the one paper was now published only in the morning.

After high school, Lisa majored in journalism at Ohio University in Athens. She returned to Dayton, landed a job at the *Dayton Daily News*, and had worked there ever since. Over the years her beloved presses had been upgraded and eventually moved to a new facility outside of town. The offices, and the ancient, cigarette smoke-stained newsroom left downtown for a building near the university that had been abandoned by NCR. Home computers and the internet were changing the way the public got their news. The size, the content, and the readership of the paper had taken a major nosedive. And now Gannett might be taking over.

"Shit," she muttered again, and opened her laptop.

30

How to Kill a Man

The next morning Burke checked in a little late for work. It had been another long night of strange dreams, tossing and turning, and the sweats. Burke was grumpier than usual. When Kevin asked about the Father Nelson case, Burke was evasive. He hadn't told anyone about the missing persons file he'd discovered, and for now, that's the way it was going to be.

He'd missed the shift change, something he rarely did, and he forced himself to chat for a few minutes with Tarisa and Marco before settling in at his desk. He and Kevin spent most of the morning going through reports, and then Burke met briefly with Major Winston. She was also curious about the Father Nelson case, but Burke left her in the dark as well.

The missing persons report, and the conversations with Jim McGowan and Kenny Mason from the day before, ran over and over through Burke's mind. He called Mary Lou Spaulding and asked about the piano being moved on the night Father Nelson disappeared. She couldn't really recall, she said, and it seemed like something she would have noticed. Burke went online and looked up Lisa Fowler's original article. There was no mention of Eastwood Lake having once been a gravel pit. Kenny Mason would have known that anyway, Burke thought again. After all, Burke himself knew it was a gravel pit. Kenny had probably even gone swimming at "POSITIVELY NO."

Just before lunch, Kevin answered the squad room phone. "It's for you, Pop," he said, covering the mouthpiece with his hand. "Some old guy. Said he only wants to talk to Captain John Burke. Nobody else."

Burke picked up the phone. "Captain John Burke here."

"Burke? Captain John Burke?" The old man was almost shouting. Burke guessed he was probably wearing a hearing aid.

"Yes, this is Captain John Burke."

"Listen here, Burke. I saw you on TV. You said to call if anyone knew anything about Father Raymond Nelson."

"That's right, sir, I did. Thanks for calling."

"Well, listen here," said the old man, noisily clearing his throat. "I think I know who did it."

Burke had been trying to finish up a requisition form and had the phone wedged between his ear and shoulder. Now he sat up straight, dropped the pen he'd been holding, and took the phone in his hand. Kevin noticed the shift in his father's attention.

"Who is this please?" Burke asked the old man.

"Never mind who this is. I ain't gonna tell you that. But I think I know who put Father Nelson in the lake. Would you like to know who that is?"

Burke relaxed and sat back. He was starting to think maybe this was just some nut job with nothing better to do than bother the homicide squad.

"Yes, I'd be very interested to know who that might be," he said, with no particular enthusiasm.

"And just so you know, I'm calling from a public phone," said the man.

"Got it," said Burke, amused.

"Okay then. Listen to me. The guy's name is Mike Donnelly. He lived right near St. Nick's, in Riverside. And I heard him say he was gonna kill Father Nelson. Mike was a friend of mine, and I think he and his brother killed the priest."

Burke had a dim recollection of the Donnelly family. They lived just a few houses away from St. Nick's. The Donnelly kids were all younger than Burke, and he remembered that one of them had been killed, struck by a truck while crossing the street in front of St. Nick's.

"When did you hear this?" Burke asked, once again sitting up. "When did this conversation take place?"

"Listen, Burke, I can't recall the exact date, but it was sometime in November of 1963. The reason I remember is because it was around the same time President Kennedy got shot. My memory is clear on that."

"Where did this conversation take place?" Burke asked, the phone once again between his ear and his shoulder as he scribbled Mike Donnelly's name.

"It was in a bar called Dumbo's in the Belfair Shopping Plaza at the corner of Belfair and Seville, out in Riverside. That's where we liked to drink beer. I'm pretty sure it ain't there no more. Dumbo's, I mean. It's still a bar but I don't know the name of it."

Burke remembered Dumbo's. As a teenager, he'd purchased beer there more than once; Dumbo never carded anybody.

"I know the place," Burke said. "Tell me more."

"Well, Jerry called me, and I met him and his brother at Dumbo's. Mike told us Father Nelson had raped his kid, Timmy – *sodomized* him. And more than once! He said Timmy told him. I didn't believe it, of course. Back then I thought the little kid was making it up, but I'm not so sure anymore. Hell, just read the damn paper! Pervert priests everywhere. Ireland, Spain, Boston, Philadelphia – they're everywhere!"

"I know, I know," Burke said. "So, what did Mike say?"

"Well, he told us that if the Catholic Church didn't do something about it, he was going to kill the priest. That's just what he said. *I'll kill him.*"

"And you think he did?"

"Well, Father Nelson disappeared a few days later," the old man said. "Gone, vanished. Never seen again. Until now, that is. I think Mike Donnelly and his brother Jerry did it."

"And you say Mike was a friend of yours?" asked Burke.

"We grew up together," the man said. "Me and his brother were best buddies. About a year after Pearl Harbor, we all joined up. Mike went for the Army, but Jerry and I joined the Navy. We all made it

home in the end, thank God. But Mike, he killed him some Krauts –
killed 'em close up, too. He told me about it. He knew how to kill a
man. After we all got home, he went to college. He was plenty smart.
Got an engineering degree and a good job at the Delco. Me, I been in
the trades all my life, until I retired, that is."

"Did you ever talk to Mike about the priest vanishing?" Burke
asked him.

"Just once," said the old man. "After Father Nelson disappeared,
I figured Mike had something to do with it. Maybe Jerry, too. But
Mike told me the goddamn Church did it. The *Church*! Anyway,
nobody seemed to pay much attention to it. They were all wrapped up
with the Kennedy assassination. Then everybody just sort of forgot
about it. A new priest came in and that was that. But I don't think the
Church had nothin' to do with it. Hell, churches don't kill people.
That's the only time we talked about it. After that, I was kind of afraid
of Mike, knowing he could do something like that. I pretty much
stopped hangin' out with him."

"Do you know if he's still alive?" asked Burke. "Is he still in
Dayton?"

"As far as I know he is. I look at the obituaries every day, and I
ain't seen him in there yet. Somebody told me he was in the Belmont
Manor Home, out in Belmont."

"What about his brother?"

"Jerry's dead. Been dead for years." The old man cleared his throat
again.

"Is that it then?" asked Burke. "Anything else I should know?"

"Nope," said the man. "That's about it. Just thought you should
know is all. I ain't out to get Mike or nothin'. Hell, me and his brother
were best buddies. I just thought you should know."

"Okay then," said Burke. "Thanks for the call."

Burke hung up and Kevin looked at him with raised eyebrows,
having listened to only one end of the conversation.

"By God, I think I might have an actual suspect," Burke said,
thumping his desk.

31

Person of Interest

Burke and Kevin went to lunch around the corner at Lucky's. Kevin listened while Burke told him about the old stranger on the phone.

"Do you think this guy is for real?" Kevin asked.

"I think so," Burke said. "Everything he said made sense."

"So, if he's right, then the priest wasn't just a perve with a porn problem – he was a serious sexual predator," Kevin said. "A child molester. Hell, a goddamn *rapist.*"

Rap music was playing on Lucky's radio, and Burke found the music irritating. Lucky usually had an oldies station tuned in which Burke could tolerate it if wasn't too loud.

"Lucky," Burke called out in the direction of the kitchen. "Could you please turn that shit off!"

At the next table, two men in suits – lawyers, Burke guessed – nodded their approval. Lucky peeked out from the door leading to the kitchen to see who had called out.

"Sorry, Cap," he said, seeing Burke. "My new dishwasher likes it. I'll change it."

"I'll see if I can find Mike Donnelly this afternoon," Burke said, turning his attention back to Kevin. "What do you know about the Belmont Manor Home? Anything?"

"Not much," said Kevin. "Last time I drove by there I seem to recall it looked pretty run-down. From the outside anyway. I've seen articles in the paper – about staff violations, lack of qualified help, that sort of thing. It's probably pretty close to the bottom of the barrel for old fart housing around here."

Burke and Kevin finished lunch and were paying at the counter when in walked Lisa Fowler.

"Well! Lisa Fowler. Are you following me?" Burke asked with a pretend scowl.

"Absolutely," Lisa replied, laughing and shaking their hands. "Actually, I was up in the courthouse working on a story. I looked out a window and saw you guys walking this way. I thought I might catch you here."

"How'd you make out with Kaminsky in Riverside yesterday?" Burke asked.

"Not so good," Lisa said. "He didn't have a problem with letting me look through the old file room, but you were right about the mess in there. I looked through everything, six hours it took me. I had to go back this morning to finish up."

Burke couldn't help feeling a little guilty for taking Bigelow's original report. He hoped he could make it up to Lisa somehow, someday.

"How about you?" she asked Burke. "Anything turn up yet that you feel like sharing?"

"Not yet," Burke lied. "But I'm working on it. And you'll be the first to know, Lisa, I promise."

"Yeah, right," she said, rolling her eyes. "Do keep me in mind though, will you, J.B.?"

Lucky had tuned the radio back to an oldies station, and as Burke and Kevin were leaving, the Castaways were singing "...*liar, liar, your pants are on fire, your nose is longer than a telephone wire...*"

"What was all that about Kaminsky and the old files?" Kevin asked, out on the street.

"Just something I'm working on," said Burke with a shrug.

* * *

Back in the office, Burke phoned the Belmont Manor House. A friendly woman told him that they did indeed have a Mike Donnelly in residence, and that if Burke came to visit, he needed to stop at the front desk to check in. Mike Donnelly was pretty much always there, she said.

Burke drove southeast out of downtown Dayton and found the retirement home in a section of Belmont that had seen better days. Yards were brown from the summer heat, and several houses on the street looked empty. The Manor House needed paint, and the circular asphalt driveway was cracked and potholed. At the front desk a large black woman wearing a white nursing uniform signed him in and directed him to Mike Donnelly's apartment.

He found Donnelly's door and knocked. No answer. Burke could hear a TV, the volume turned up high. He knocked again, harder this time. There was a loud clatter on the other side of the door, and a lot of cursing.

"What? What the fuck! Who is it goddammit? Shit! Goddammit! COME IN!"

The door wasn't locked, so Burke opened it slowly, peering in. Donnelly was sitting in a ratty, plaid recliner. His sparse hair was one shade of gray, his skin another. His feet were tangled in a cheap, fold-out TV tray. A few dishes, a plastic cup, and some tableware were scattered across the worn, stained carpet.

"Goddammit, you startled me," Donnelly growled, looking up. "I was asleep. Who the hell are you?"

"I'm really sorry, Mr. Donnelly," Burke said, picking up some of the mess. "I didn't mean to scare you."

"You didn't scare me," Donnelly shot back. "You *startled* me, that's all. Who are you? And what do you want?"

"I'm Captain John Burke from the Dayton Police Department," he said, setting a dish on the nearby table and pointing to the badge on his belt. He put his hand out to shake, but Donnelly didn't take it.

"You *are* Mike Donnelly?" Burke asked, stooping to untangle the tray from around Donnelly's feet.

"Thanks," Donnelly said, calmer now. "Yes, I'm Mike Donnelly." He put his hand out to Burke. "I'm sorry, I was just taking a nap after lunch."

"I understand," said Burke. "Can I sit down?"

The old man motioned toward a kitchen chair. Burke pulled it up in front of Donnelly and sat down.

"Are you the Mike Donnelly who lived near St. Nick's, over in Riverside?"

"That's me. Why?"

"I'm investigating the disappearance of a priest that I think you knew, Father Raymond Nelson," Burke said. "He was the assistant pastor at St. Nick's back in 1963. He vanished one night and no one ever heard from him again."

Donnelly fixed Burke with a stare and didn't speak for a long moment.

"And now you found the sonofabitch at the bottom of Eastwood Lake," he finally said, a smile slowly forming on his gray, mottled face. The smile looked out of place, Burke thought, as if there hadn't been one there in a long time.

"Exactly. I'm assuming you saw it on the news," Burke said, nodding toward the TV where a soap opera was blaring.

"Where's the damn remote? Turn that shit off, will you?" the old man said, pointing at the set. "Yeah. I guess I saw *you* on TV, too." Burke found the remote on the floor and turned off the TV.

"I'll get right to the point, Mr. Donnelly" said Burke, sitting down again. "I got a call this morning from a man who claimed he was once your brother's best buddy. He wouldn't tell me his name, but he said he thinks you may have had something to do with Father Nelson's death."

"First of all, just call me Mike, okay?" Donnelly said, wriggling to get more comfortable in the recliner. "Second, it was Frank McHale you talked to, no doubt. And yes, he was my brother's best friend. Old friend of mine, too. I didn't know he was still alive."

"Apparently he is," said Burke. "He said you told him and your brother that Father Nelson had molested your son Timmy. He said that you threatened to kill the priest."

"*Molested!?* The sonofabitch raped Timmy!" shouted Donnelly. He was suddenly shaking with rage. "He fucked him! He ruined the boy, goddammit!"

The old man's graphic bluntness startled Burke, and he suddenly felt nauseous. He closed his eyes and took a few deep breaths.

"Ruined," the old man said again, still shaking. In an attempt to calm Donnelly down, Burke reached out and patted the old man's arm. Mike yanked his arm away. His face had gone from gray to red.

"My poor Timmy killed himself because of it!" he shouted. "My whole goddamn family was ruined by it! Everything was ruined!"

Tears welled up in the old man's eyes. He reached behind him, pulled a wrinkled handkerchief from his pocket and blew his nose loudly. "Sorry. I'm sorry. I can't help it. That sonofabitch priest deserved to die. I hope he suffered. I hope he suffered like nobody's ever suffered."

"So, you didn't kill him?" asked Burke.

"Hell no!" said Donnelly, quieter now. "I would have, though. After what he did, I could have killed him. The sonofabitch put his goddamn prick in poor Timmy's mouth. And he put his own mouth on poor Timmy's little pecker. He scared him to death and he raped him – three times. Three goddamn times he did it! First on an overnight choir trip to South Bend, and then one time in the rectory. And once right in the goddamn sacristy – right behind the goddamn altar!"

"Timmy told you all of this?" asked Burke.

"Goddamn right he told me," said Donnelly. "I had to beg him to tell me. Poor kid was about to shoot himself with my twelve gauge."

"Didn't you say he *did* kill himself," said Burke. "Is that how he did it?"

"Hell no, that's not how he did it," said the old man. "I got that shotgun out of the house the next morning, took it to work and sold it. Funny thing, too. After Kennedy got shot – it was right around that same time – Eileen, she's my wife, she told me she didn't want any guns in the house anymore. I think a lot of women felt that way. Anyway, I was able to tell her it was already gone."

"Did she know about what happened to Timmy?" Burke asked.

"No, Timmy made me promise not to tell her," said Donnelly. "I don't know why. He just didn't want her to know. He didn't think she would believe him. He knew she really liked Father Nelson. *All* the women liked the sonofabitch."

"So how *did* Timmy kill himself?"

Again, Donnelly fixed Burke with a stare and didn't speak for a moment. "He stepped in front of a truck," he said, tears welling up once more behind his glazed eyes. "It was two years later. He was thirteen years old."

The Donnelly child. Struck by a truck in front of the church. Burke remembered it clearly now. Suicide had never been mentioned.

"I remember when that happened," he told Donnelly. "I thought it was an accident."

"Now, why in the hell would you remember that?" Donnelly asked.

"I grew up in your neighborhood," Burke explained. "I was older than your kids though. Do you remember the Burke family? We lived on Columbia Court."

Donnelly thought for a second. "I remember," he said. "You have a sister."

"Yeah, Mary," Burke told him, standing up. "Do you mind if I get some water?"

"Help yourself. The glasses are in that first cupboard. Get me some, too." Burke got the water and sat down. Donnelly continued.

"Anyway, it wasn't an accident. That's just what everyone wanted to think. *Including* my wife. And that's what the police called it. But the truck driver told us he clearly saw Timmy standing on the side of the road. He swore Timmy was looking right at him. He thought Timmy was about to wave, and the next thing he knew Timmy was in his path and he had no time to stop. Eileen? She didn't believe it."

"Did Timmy leave a note or anything?" asked Burke.

"No note," said Donnelly. "But hell, I knew. Look where he died! *Right in front of the goddamn church*! That was all the note I needed. I knew why he did it."

"But Father Nelson – he was already gone," Burke said.

"Goddamn right he was gone – rotting at the bottom of the goddamn lake, I guess. But hell, the damage was done. Timmy was never the same and I didn't really know what to do about it. Eileen wouldn't let me take Timmy to a shrink – said she didn't believe in 'em. Said the Catholic Church didn't believe in 'em. Timmy made me promise not to tell her, so I never did. He made me swear, but I probably should have told anyway. She didn't know what the hell was wrong with him, and all I could do was try to love the boy and keep an eye on him. Hell, he didn't even want to talk to *me* about it after he told me the first time. I didn't really know what else to do."

Donnelly was crying now, and he blew his nose again. Burke patted the old man's knee, and this time he didn't pull away.

"After Timmy was killed, I finally told Eileen what Father Nelson had done to him. Timmy was right – she didn't believe me. She didn't want to hear about it. Thought I was nuts. That was pretty much the end of our marriage. I think she hated me after that. She took our two girls and moved back to her parents' house, pretty much turned the girls against me. I haven't seen any of them for years. We never did get a divorce. Hell, I'm not even sure if Eileen's still alive. They all moved away from Dayton years ago."

The old man wiped his eyes. Father Raymond Nelson had not only ruined Timmy, he had ruined this man's life as well, Burke thought.

"Your old friend said you thought the Catholic Church got rid of Father Nelson," said Burke. "What makes you think that?"

"They sure as shit did!" Donnelly said, getting excited. "It's not exactly the way I pictured it – drowning the sonofabitch in his own car – but they took care of it. I figured they'd just send him away, or kick the sonofabitch out of the church."

"But do you really think the Church would kill their own priest?" Burke asked.

"Who the hell else would do it?" said the old man with a shrug. "Father Nelson disappeared within a week of me talking to the archbishop. Well, not exactly the archbishop himself, but someone close to him, some high-up priest in the archbishop's Office. He told me they already knew about Father Nelson's problem and that they would take care of him quickly. He asked me not to talk about any of it to anyone. He said they would take care of it if I promised not to talk about it. I told him that if Father Nelson wasn't gone from St. Nick's within a week, I would take care of the sonofabitch myself. He promised me it would be done. Sure, they killed him. The Church can do whatever they want."

Jesus Christ! Burke thought. Could it be true! Did the Archbishop of Cincinnati actually have the power to have a problem priest eliminated? *Whacked?*

Burke's mind was reeling. He'd already decided that someone had indeed knocked Father Nelson on the back of the head – hard enough to break his goddamn neck – strapped him into his own car, and buried him in eighty feet of water. Gone without a trace. Could it really have been a professional job – ordered up by the Archbishop of Cincinnati?

No, Burke decided. *Impossible.* Things like that just didn't happen, no matter what the old man thought.

Burke thanked Mike Donnelly for being so forthcoming and apologized for dredging up a part of the old man's life that he probably had rather not thought about. Donnelly told him he was glad to have someone to talk to about Timmy, and he was happy to have helped.

"I'm afraid you're still a person of interest in this case," Burke said, grinning and shaking Donnelly's hand. "I'd appreciate a call if you have to leave town."

The old man laughed.

"Do I look like I'm going anywhere soon . . . *Captain John Burke?*" he said, reading the business card Burke handed him.

32
Toledo

That evening, Lisa Fowler jumped when her land line phone rang. It rarely rang anymore, with her and the kids all connected to the world through their cell phones. She looked at the answering machine and didn't recognize the number.

"Hello," she said, picking up.

"Hello," said a man's voice. "Is this Lisa Fowler?"

"Yes, this is Lisa."

"Are you the Lisa Fowler who writes for the *Dayton Daily News*?"

"That's me," she said, wondering what was coming next.

"I found this number on Google," the man said. "I'm really sorry to be bothering you, Miss Fowler, but I was wondering if I could talk to you about Father Raymond Nelson, the priest they found in Eastwood Lake."

"By all means." Lisa grabbed a pen and a pad of sticky notes. "It's not a bother at all. Who am I speaking to?"

"Well, I know you might think this is weird, but for the time being I'd prefer to remain anonymous, if that's okay?"

"Not a problem," said Lisa. "But you must realize that I have your number on my answering machine."

"That's okay, I thought of that," said the man. "This is a pay phone."

"Great," said Lisa, rolling her eyes. "So, what's up?"

"Well, like I said, this is kind of weird for me. In fact, I'm not really sure why I called you and not the police. I'm not so sure that what I'm going to tell you would help in their investigation anyway. But ever since I read your story and saw Father Nelson's picture in the paper, I wanted to talk to someone about it."

"I'm all ears," Lisa said.

"Okay. So, I hadn't thought about Father Nelson in like fifty years maybe. But when I saw his picture in the paper I almost passed out," said the man. "And then I threw up."

"Good lord!" said Lisa, dropping the pen.

"Yeah. Pretty gross. But I've never talked about this with anyone, not ever. I'm sorry to be dumping it on you."

"It's okay. Go ahead."

"Well, he was a horrible man, Father Nelson. Everyone thought he was so nice and all, but he wasn't. He did things to me that shouldn't have happened, but they did. He molested me many times when he was at my church. Not just molest, but he sodomized me. I didn't even know what sodomy was back then. I hadn't thought about any of it for years, until I saw his picture."

"Jesus!" said Lisa. "Excuse me, I'm sorry."

"That's okay," said the man.

"Did this happen at St. Nicholas Church, in Riverside?" she asked. "Is that where this happened to you?"

"No, no," said the man. "It was at the church where I grew up, in Toledo, at St. Joan of Arc. I didn't move to Dayton until after I got divorced, about fifteen years ago."

"So, this happened to you when? What years?" Lisa asked, picking up the pen.

"Oh, that would have been in '58 and '59, I guess," he said, and then he began to cry.

"Please sir, don't cry," said Lisa. "I'm so sorry about what happened to you. I'm so, so sorry."

"No, no," he said, sniffing. "I'm the one that should be sorry – for dumping this on you. I can't believe I told you. But I had to tell someone, and I thought maybe you could use the information. That's pretty much it. That's why I called."

"Well, I certainly appreciate you coming forth with this," Lisa said. "But don't you think maybe you should talk to someone else, like a psychiatrist or a counselor – maybe get into a group for abuse victims, something like that?"

"I will," said the man, "I will. I'm going to work on that."

"And please, please, sir..." implored Lisa, "...call me anytime. Maybe someday you'll want other people to know about this, and I'd be happy to help you. Maybe you could get other people to tell their own stories."

"Maybe someday," he said. "Maybe someday."

Lisa hung up and immediately started to dial the cell phone number she had for Captain John Burke. Realizing the time, she stopped, and instead sat down again with her laptop. She saved what she had been writing, and spent the next three hours Googling everything she could find on the sexual abuse scandal that had been rocking the Catholic Church for decades. Not a Catholic herself, she'd nevertheless followed the story over the years – from the U.S, to Spain and Ireland – to almost every country that had a Catholic population. The Boston diocese stood out, and most recently, the case involving dozens of priests in Philadelphia. She remembered crying when she'd watched a segment on *Frontline* back in April, about a priest and his friend who had abused nearly every single child in a small Native American village in northern Canada. The kids were now adults, and their stories were heartbreaking.

Lisa found an op-ed piece by Maureen Dowd that she remembered reading in the Sunday *New York Times* back in June, about the archbishop of Dublin and how he had been snubbed by the Vatican for reaching out to the victims of abuse in his diocese. And Jason Berry wrote a piece for *The Nation*, in April, on how the sex abuse scandal tainted the legacy of Pope John Paul II.

She revisited a series of articles written by one of her colleagues a few years earlier, about the long saga of a defrocked Dayton priest who had been part of a high-profile child sex abuse lawsuit that also involved the previous Archbishop of Cincinnati. A former seminarian had accused the two men of abusing him in the early 1970s. The seminarian had eventually recanted his accusation against the archbishop in 1992, but not against the priest. By then, the archbishop had been moved to the Archdiocese of Chicago and was eventually made a cardinal. The priest was forced by the archdiocese to give up his priestly duties in 1994, and in 2006 was defrocked by Pope Benedict XVI. The archbishop died a cardinal, in 1996, and years later it was discovered that while in Chicago he had hidden accusations against other priests. Lisa searched through several websites dealing with the phenomenon of repressed memories, and then closed her laptop.

"Damn," she thought. She knew she couldn't write an article based on an unsubstantiated accusation made by an anonymous caller. But tomorrow she would tell Burke about the call.

33

The Man on The Cross

Back in the squad room the next morning, Burke typed up the notes he'd made the evening before, after his visit with Mike Donnelly. He was searching through the Impala case file for a phone number for Father Nicholas Stankowski when his cell phone rang.

"Morning, J.B." It was Lisa Fowler. "Better hold on to your hat, partner!"

"Good morning, Lisa." Burke grinned, setting the folder aside. "What's up?"

"I got a pretty weird phone call last night, J.B.," Lisa said excitedly. She told Burke all about the anonymous caller from the night before.

"I've been researching online," she said. "There's a bunch of conflicting information on repressed memories. But if it's a real thing, I just wonder how many more victims are out there. And the Catholic Church doesn't do a damn thing. They just move the priest to a different parish. Boston, Philly, Chicago, L.A., Texas, Ireland, Spain – it's the same everywhere."

Lisa waited for a response from Burke, but none came.

"J.B.? You still there?" She thought maybe they'd been disconnected.

"Oh, sorry, Lisa. I was digesting what you said."

"You don't seem too surprised, J.B." said Lisa, slightly chagrined that the news of her anonymous caller had failed to elicit the response she'd hoped for from Burke. "What do you know that I don't?"

Burke didn't want to tell Lisa about Frank McHale, his *own* mystery caller, or his visit to Mike Donnelly the day before.

"Not much really," he said. "But I stumbled across a little something myself yesterday, sort of in the same ballpark."

"Stumbled my ass," Lisa said. "C'mon J. B., give me something. Anything! You know I can't do a story on this mystery caller."

"Listen, Lisa," said Burke. "You know that when I have something solid, I'll share it. Right now, I've got to play this pretty close. And I *really* do appreciate what you've told me. I'll make some notes and put it in the file. Sooner or later, we'll make a mountain out of all these damn molehills."

"I understand, J.B. I just hope the info helps."

"It's a tremendous help, Lisa. You have no idea."

After Lisa hung up, Burke thought about what she had told him. The only part that surprised him was the fact that Father Nelson had abused a child in another parish in another town. Burke found the number he'd been looking for and called the office of the Archbishop of Cincinnati. He was put on hold, and Monsignor Nicholas Stankowski eventually picked up.

"Hello, Captain Burke," said the priest. "What can I help you with today, my friend?" Burke was surprised at how weak the monsignor's voice sounded.

"Hello, Father. How are you?"

"I'm fine. And how are you?" The priest coughed. Burke sensed that maybe the priest wasn't so fine.

"Good, good," Burke said. "I was wondering if I could meet with you today. I could drive down to Cincinnati and meet you there at your office."

"Is this about the Father Nelson investigation?" asked Father Stankowski. "I'm fairly sure I already gave you all the information I can."

"Well, yes, it is about Father Nelson," said Burke. "But I'd like to meet with you if you're willing. I do have some other questions you might be able to help me with."

"I suppose I could do that," said the priest. "When would you like to come?"

"I could leave Dayton now and be in Cincinnati in an hour, maybe a little longer if the construction on I-75 holds me up," Burke said. "Will that work?"

"That's fine," said the priest. "Do you know where we are? On 8th street? Do you need directions?"

"I'll Google map it," said Burke. "What's the address?"

Burke told Kevin he was driving down to Cincinnati and would be back later that afternoon. Heading south out of Dayton on I-75, he passed the *Dayton Daily News* printing facility. That reminded him of Lisa Fowler and her anonymous caller, and then he thought about his visit with poor, broken Mike Donnelly. Burke was aware of the sex abuse scandals that had been rolling over the Catholic Church like waves, one after another, for the last twenty years, but he'd paid little attention. Now he seemed to be getting involved in something that he couldn't ignore. It was beginning to appear that Father Nelson was not only a criminal pedophile, but that the Archdiocese of Cincinnati knew about it and had done nothing other than to move him from one parish to the next, just as the Church had done all around the world.

How many times? How many parishes? How many children had Father Nelson molested? How many lives had been ruined? Burke was hoping he could get something more from Nicholas Stankowski, but his hopes were not high.

He got off the highway and drove into the center of Cincinnati. In a building housing the offices of the archdiocese, a friendly, forty-something priest led Burke to Father Stankowski's office. The room was lined with bookshelves, and dark curtains covered the windows, blocking the late morning sunlight. An oriental rug covered most of the floor and a large crucifix hung on the wall behind the priest's desk. Father Stankowski stood up and greeted Burke with a charming smile, and a very weak, two-handed hand shake. He was a small man, wearing a simple black cassock. His pallor was slightly jaundiced. *He doesn't look much better than the man on the cross,* Burke thought.

Father Stankowski had a brief coughing fit, and winced. He quickly sat down again at his desk and reached for a glass of water. He directed Burke to a leather chair across from him, and motioned toward the younger priest who stood nearby.

"This is Father Trevor Williams, my assistant," Stankowski said proudly, after wiping his mouth with a handkerchief. "He's just recently been appointed a vicar general."

Burke shook hands with Father Williams. The *vicar general* – whatever that meant – asked Burke if he would like some coffee. Burke accepted the offer and the younger priest left the room.

Burke leaned forward and asked, "Are you all right, Father?"

"I'll soon find out," said the priest, still smiling. "I'm going into the hospital tomorrow for a rather extensive series of tests. Hopefully they'll figure out what the problem is. I'm hoping it's nothing too serious."

"I hope so, too," Burke said. "It's good you're getting tested."

"Well, we are all tested, each and every day," said the priest, laughing. "Isn't that right?"

Father Williams brought in a tray with coffee, cream and sugar, and two tall glasses of ice water. Father Stankowski asked him to close the door as he left, and requested that he and Burke not be disturbed. "So, what can I possibly help you with, Captain?" he asked Burke.

"Well, Father, some things have come up regarding Father Nelson since the story broke. First of all – and for now, the press doesn't know about this – there was a collection of pornography found in the trunk of Father Nelson's car. A lot of it survived more or less intact, and some of it was child pornography."

The smile left Father Stankowski's face. Burke made a mental note of the reaction and gave the priest a moment to respond. When no response came, he continued.

"And yesterday I visited a man who claims his son was raped by Father Nelson almost fifty years ago, not long before he disappeared from St. Nick's," Burke said. "The man said his son was raped three times."

Father Stankowski clasped his hands as if in prayer and looked down at the desk, sighing loudly. Burke noticed his jaw clench and unclench several times.

"This morning, Lisa Fowler called me," Burke continued. "She's the reporter who broke the story for the *Dayton Daily News*. Last evening, she received an anonymous phone call from a man who told her that Father Nelson had raped him in Toledo. I guess Nelson was an assistant pastor at the St. Joan of Arc parish there in the late 1950s."

Father Stankowski raised his head slowly. His eyes were closed, and he finally spoke without opening them.

"Is she going to publish a story?" the priest asked. Burke was surprised by the question.

"She can't," said Burke. "She's a very good journalist, and she knows better than to write something based on innuendo."

"Does she know about the other accusation, from the old man you talked to?" asked the priest, again surprising Burke. He realized that Father Stankowski's first interest may not be in the victims, but with the reputation of the Catholic Church.

"I didn't share that," said Burke.

"And *will* you, at some point, share that information?" Father Stankowski asked.

"That depends on where my investigation goes," Burke replied. "Right now, the old man is a person of interest in the case, possibly a suspect."

The priest leaned back in his chair with another deep sigh. After a moment, he leaned forward, resting his arms on the desktop, and looked directly at Burke.

"Captain Burke," he said, "the Catholic Church is in crisis. As you are well aware – as is everyone else that reads a newspaper or watches the news on television – we have a rather large problem. We have a problem that is threatening to destroy our entire institution. The faithful are asking questions, and I am afraid the Holy See is not providing the proper answers. They are not providing a clear direction. They are not admitting to problems of the past, or at least not taking full and proper responsibility for these problems."

The priest stopped and drank some water. "Just yesterday, in fact, the archbishop flew to Rome for a meeting regarding this very problem. The Pope summoned all the American archbishops to this emergency synod, and they'll spend the next three weeks working toward an appropriate response to the crisis. Personally, I am not hopeful." Father Stankowski coughed. He closed his eyes and rubbed his forehead.

"Are you sure you're okay, Father?" Burke asked. "Should I get Father Williams?"

Stankowski raised his hand. "Let me finish," he went on. "Our last pope, John Paul, was a wonderful man and a gracious leader on many levels, but his record on dealing with the abuse of children by the clergy is abysmal. He couldn't, or *wouldn't* face the truth, and then just this May, he was beatified. The next step is canonization. Should the man be made a saint? I certainly don't think so. And I'm not alone."

"What about the current pope?" Burke asked.

"Benedict? As I said, I am not hopeful. What we need is a full disclosure of the past, and that is not happening. Last month, a new investigation in Ireland revealed that Church *and* civil laws regarding child protection have been completely ignored – repeatedly and for years, with the Vatican's knowledge. The archbishop of Dublin happens to share my disgust for what is going on. And how has *he* been rewarded for his valiant efforts at healing these wounds? He's been ostracized by the other Irish bishops and completely ignored by the Vatican. He should have been a cardinal by now, but I doubt that he ever will be."

"Apparently, some people think you should have been a cardinal yourself by now," Burke said.

The priest coughed again and reached for his water glass, waving dismissively.

"It seems to me that our canon law is being used to protect the integrity of the Church more than it is being used to protect the children," he said. "I am sickened by what has gone on."

"Is canon law preventing you from helping in my investigation?" Burke asked.

"Yes, it is, to a large degree," said Father Stankowski. "As moderator of the curia, and as a vicar general, I am charged with maintaining a certain level of protection for the affairs of the diocese."

"The *secrets* of the diocese," Burke corrected him.

"If you only knew," said the priest, sighing. "But for now, this diocese is totally committed to also following the civil laws and procedures regarding child sex abuse. We're doing criminal background checks, including fingerprinting, on any clergy or lay members having anything to do with the children in the schools and parishes and our other institutions. Anyone involved must attend an orientation session for what we call the Decree on Child Protection, before they're approved. Our website has links to both the Ohio and the National Sex Offender registry."

The priest put his hand over his heart. "We are trying here in Cincinnati, Captain Burke. Believe me, we are trying."

Burke finished the coffee. "And there's nothing else you can share with me about Father Nelson's past?" he asked, shaking his head. "You can't tell me if he was known to be a pedophile, or what parishes he served, or how many parishes? Nothing?"

"I'm truly sorry, Captain Burke," said the priest. "As I told you on the phone, I've given you all the information on Father Nelson that my position allows me to reveal."

Burke stood up, about to take his leave.

"Wait a minute, Captain," Stankowski said, holding up a finger. Burke noticed the hand was shaking slightly. The priest slowly pushed himself up from the desk and walked to a bookshelf, quickly finding what he wanted. He winced as he plopped back down in his chair. Opening the thick book, he scanned the index, then marked a page with a sticky note.

"Take this with you," he said, handing the book to Burke. "Our rules and regulations. The page I marked might help you understand my situation."

"Thanks, Father," Burke said, taking the book. "I'll get it back to you."

"Keep it. I got a million of 'em," the priest said, grinning. He coughed again.

"Father, I should let you go, but if you don't mind, there's one other thing I wanted to ask you about," Burke said, sitting back down.

"By all means."

"The old man I talked to. The man who said his son was raped by Father Nelson. He seems to be thoroughly convinced that the archbishop's office is responsible for the disappearance of Father Nelson. He claims he came down here in November of 1963 and talked with a representative of the archbishop. Said he was told they were aware of the problem and that they would take care of Father Nelson. He was asked never to speak of the problem to anyone."

"Captain Burke," said the priest, with an amused smile. "Do you really suppose the Church had something to do with this?"

"Not me, Father," Burke said. "But the old man seemed convinced."

"I'll just say this," Father Stankowski said, laughing weakly. "We may have our *secrets* as you call them, but I can honestly say, that as far as I know, we've never *disappeared* anyone."

They chatted briefly about the summer construction project on I-75, and about how the Cincinnati Reds seemed to be struggling since the All-Star break. Burke declined Father Stankowski's offer of lunch, and said goodbye to the priest, wishing him luck at the hospital the next day. As Burke was shaking the priest's hand, he remembered something else.

"Father," Burke said, "I'm really sorry for taking up so much of your time, but there's just one more thing."

"And what's that?" Father Stankowski asked.

"Well, on the sign in front of St. Nick's Church, there's a Bible quote. It's been there since I was a kid and I never really understood it. It says '*Suffer the little children to come unto me.*'"

"Ah! From the Gospels of Matthew, Mark, *and* Luke." The priest smiled. "The whole quote is something like, "*Suffer the little children to come unto me, and forbid them not, for theirs is the kingdom of heaven.*"

"But what does it really mean?" Burke asked.

"Well, *suffer* is the confusing word here, I'm guessing. It means *to allow* or to *endure*, perhaps *put up with*. I think what Christ was saying is that we should love and respect little children, accept them, welcome them and honor them, for they are the most blessed among us, innocent and unspoiled. I imagine that someone picked that particular quote when they named the parish in honor of St. Nicholas. Did you know that St. Nick is the patron saint of young children?"

"No. No, I didn't know that," Burke admitted, the irony slowly sinking in.

"And I was named for him – Nicholas," said Father Stankowski, smiling pensively. "I was always 'little Nicky Stankowski.'"

34

Knucklehead

Before leaving Cincinnati, Burke had lunch at a Skyline Chili parlor on the corner of 7ᵗʰ and Vine. Driving north on I-75 on his way back to Dayton, he wondered if he would ever see Father Nicholas Stankowski again. It was obvious that the priest was a very sick man. Burke liked him, and realized that the priest was sympathetic to the investigation, but shackled by his loyalty to the Catholic Church, an institution that he obviously cared a great deal for despite its shortcomings.

Kevin was alone in the squad room, a pile of paperwork in front of him, when Burke arrived. He was full of questions, and Burke could tell he was looking for any distraction from the mess on his desk. Burke filled him in on his visit to Mike Donnelly the day before, the call he'd had from Lisa Fowler that morning, and the meeting with Father Stankowski.

"Keep it to yourself for now, Kevin," Burke said. "And that includes your mother."

Kevin waived dismissively. "So, if you believe Mike Donnelly didn't kill Father Nelson, then that sort of leaves you without a suspect – except for the Catholic Church. Right?"

"And that's highly unlikely," Burke said. "Although . . . I'll bet that in the past the Catholic Church has actually done *worse* things than take out a problem priest. But maybe not in this day and age. It's an absurd notion on Donnelly's part."

"So, you've got nothing."

Burke shrugged. Kevin didn't know about the missing persons report that he'd found, or about Jim McGowan or Kenny Mason or Steve Heckman, and that's the way Burke was going to leave it for now.

"It's Ashley's birthday on Saturday," said Kevin, changing the subject. "She'll be ten. I don't suppose you remembered."

"You suppose correctly," said Burke, slapping his forehead. "Thanks for the heads up."

"We're having a party for some of her friends. You probably don't want to come to that."

"Correct again," said Burke with a wry grin.

"That's what I thought," said Kevin. "But we want you and Mom to come over on Sunday for a cook-out. Can you handle that?"

"I'd love to come," said Burke with a smile. "I'll call your mother and see if she wants me to pick her up."

Burke turned his computer on, and just as Lisa Fowler had done that morning, he searched for information on repressed memories. There seemed to be conflicting evidence as to the existence of such a phenomenon – sometimes called *psychogenic amnesia* – when traumatic or repressed memories are suddenly recovered years or decades after the events. It can happen spontaneously, triggered by a particular smell, taste or some other identifier related to the lost memory. Lisa Fowler's caller seems to have had his moment when he saw the picture of Father Nelson in the newspaper.

After Googling around for an hour, Burke turned off his computer, just as Tarisa and Renzi came in. Their shift was ending and Burke was surprised when he looked at the time. He and Kevin talked to them about another shooting, a drive-by, which occurred the night before on Keowee Street during Danny and Jamal's shift. A teen-aged, African-American male – the probable target – had been killed, and his little sister wounded, not seriously. Tarisa and Renzi had spent their entire shift unsuccessfully looking for witnesses. Pete and Bones came in, minutes apart, and joined the conversation. After everyone was brought up to speed, the group broke up. Burke chatted for a minute with Pete, about the upcoming city amateur golf tournament, and they made a tentative plan for a round of golf on Saturday. Burke walked over to Kevin's desk.

"Kevin," he said. "I need to talk to a shrink. Do you know any?"

"Duh!" Kevin said, looking up from his computer and laughing. "I've been telling you that for years."

"Not for me, you knucklehead," said Burke.

Everyone in the squad room heard the exchange, and suppressed snickering quickly turned into full-blown guffaws and high-fives.

"Yeah, yeah. Very goddamn funny," Burke said, patiently accepting the chorus of derision from his squad.

"Seriously, I need to talk to someone about this case," he said quietly to Kevin, when things finally settled down. "Someone who can tell me about repressed memories related to childhood sex abuse, and sex abuse in general, that kind of thing."

Kevin thought about it for a few seconds.

"How about that lady shrink who Claire brought in to do the seminar on child abuse last year? She seemed to know her shit pretty well. It was a good seminar."

"I wasn't there," Burke said. "I must've had something else on."

"Yeah . . . right," said Kevin.

"So, do you remember her name?" Burke asked, ignoring his son's barely veiled accusation.

"No, but I might have the program around here somewhere – I think I held on to it. Let me look."

Kevin opened a file drawer in his desk and bent to the task. Burke remembered the seminar; he had indeed skipped it.

"Here we go," said Kevin, handing the program to his father.

Burke glanced at the cover page, and then read it aloud:

"Dr. Cara Shannon, M. D. Psychiatrist / Researcher /Specializing in child sex abuse and treatment of child and adult sex abuse victims / Chair / Department of Psychiatry / Wright State University Boonshoft School of Medicine / Director / Child and Adolescent Psychiatry Program."

"Like I said," said Kevin. "I think she knows her shit."

"Thanks, Kevin," said Burke, slapping his son with the program. "She's just who I need. I'll go online and see if I can get a phone number for her."

Burke found a number for the psychiatry department on the Wright State website, and left a message on Dr. Shannon's voicemail. The phone rang minutes after he'd hung up, and Burke took the call.

"Hello," said a woman's pleasant voice. "This is Cara Shannon. I'm returning a call from Captain John Burke."

"This is Captain Burke. Thanks for getting back so quickly."

"Not a problem. Did we meet last year by any chance, Captain? I did a seminar there at the police station"

"I'm afraid I missed that," said Burke.

"Oh well, I imagine you're a busy man," Cara said. "So how can I help you?"

"Well, I'm working on a case and thought you might be able to help me out," Burke said. "My son Kevin is also on the homicide squad, and he *did* attend your presentation last year. That's how I heard about you. He said you seemed to know your . . . to be an expert on the subject of child sex abuse."

"Well, that *is* my field," said Cara.

"You'd have to keep anything we discuss about the case confidential," said Burke. "For now, anyway."

"Confidential is my middle name, Captain Burke."

"Good," said Burke. "I'd like to meet with you if that's okay. Would you be up for that?"

"Absolutely. Could you come to my office?" Cara asked. "Tomorrow morning at say, oh, ten o'clock?"

"I'll be there," said Burke. "Where can I find you?"

After he finished the call to Cara Shannon, Burke sat back in his desk chair with his fingers laced behind his head. Kevin was right about the investigation. He had nothing. Mike Donnelly had easily convinced him that he hadn't killed Father Nelson. The old man was broken and bitter, and rightfully so, thought Burke, but he didn't kill the priest. The archbishop's office had saved him the trouble as far as Donnelly was concerned, but Burke found that notion absurd. A pedophile priest would have been moved to another parish perhaps, but not whisked away in the night, knocked on the head, and dumped in the lake.

And what about McGowan and Kenny Mason, two of his old schoolmates and possibly the last ones to see the priest alive? Their stories were maybe a little too similar and not wholly convincing. Burke decided that he would have to talk to Jim McGowan again.

35

The Codex

That evening, Burke dined on a Marion's pizza that he picked up on the way home. He was feeling pretty satisfied with the day's work, despite the fact that he was not much closer to solving his case. He opened another beer and checked the sports section in the paper. The Reds were off for the night, and he was wondering what to do when he remembered the book Father Stankowski had given him. After taking out the garbage, he retrieved the book from his car, and settled on the couch.

The book title read, *Code of Canon Law* (Codex Iuris Canonici) *Latin-English Edition, New English Translation.* In the opening pages Burke found that the Codex had been promulgated by Pope John Paul II and copyrighted by the Vatican in 1983. Father Stankowski had spoken rather bitterly about this pope, Burke recalled. The pages of the book were set up so that the Church laws were written in English on the left side, Latin on the right. Burke turned to page 158, the one Father Stankowski had marked, and began to read . . .

Can. 486 §1. All documents which regard the diocese or parishes must be protected with the greatest care.

§2. In every curia there is to be erected in a safe place a diocesan archive, or record storage area, in which instruments and written documents which pertain to the spiritual and temporal affairs of the diocese are to be safeguarded after being properly filed and diligently secured.

§3. An inventory, or catalog, of the documents which are contained in the archive is to be kept with a brief synopsis of each written document.

Can. 487 §1. The archive must be locked and only the bishop and chancellor are to have its key. No one is permitted to enter except with the permission either of the bishop or of both the moderator of the curia and the chancellor.

§2. Interested parties have the right to obtain personally or through a proxy an authentic written copy or photocopy of documents which by their nature are public and which pertain to their personal status.

Can. 488 It is not permitted to remove documents from the archive except for a brief time only and with the consent either of the bishop or of both the moderator of the curia and the chancellor.

Burke could barely believe what he was reading. It would have been almost laughable, he thought, if it hadn't been so serious. The next few canons were frightening . . .

Can. 489 §1. In the diocesan curia there is also to be a secret archive, or at least in the common archive there is to be a safe or cabinet, completely closed and locked, which cannot be removed; in it documents to be kept secret are to be protected most securely.

§2. Each year documents of criminal cases in matters of morals, in which the accused parties have died or ten years have elapsed from the condemnatory sentence, are to be destroyed. A brief summary of what occurred along with the text of the definitive sentence is to be retained.

Can. 490 §1. Only the bishop is to have the key to the secret archive.

Burke was appalled. It was the most unbelievable thing he'd ever read. But he read on, repulsed and transfixed at the same time . . .

§2. When a see is vacant, the secret archive or safe is not to be opened except in a case of true necessity by the diocesan administrator himself.

§3. Documents are not to be removed from the secret archive or safe.

Can. 491 §1. A diocesan bishop is to take care that the acts and documents of the archives of cathedral, collegiate, parochial, and other churches in his territory are also diligently preserved and that inventories or catalogs are made in duplicate, one of which is to be preserved in the archive of the church and the other in the diocesan archive.

§2. A diocesan bishop is also to take care that there is an historical archive in the diocese and that documents having historical value are diligently protected and systematically ordered in it.

Burke stopped there, closed the book and sat up. He'd seen enough. Glancing at the cover, he opened the book again to page 158, as if to make sure he hadn't somehow dreamed what he'd just read. There it was, like something straight out of *The Da Vinci Code*. But this was not fiction. This was for real. This was the Catholic Church, and these were the rules Father Nicholas Stankowski was playing by.

Burke realized that he was shivering. With shock? Anger? The beer and pizza in his stomach suddenly felt as though he'd swallowed a chunk of cement.

36

Dr. Cara Shannon

Burke checked in early at the squad room the next morning. He'd been up since five o'clock, and his neck was still stiff, even though he had slouched under a steaming hot shower for almost twenty minutes. He still felt cold. But he wanted to make sure to talk with Jamal and Danny about the drive-by, and go over their reports before they went home at the end of their shift. Tarisa and Renzi arrived and joined in, comparing notes. Once again, the dead boy was a known drug dealer as well as a gang member. There were no witnesses and no suspects. The dead boy's sister would recover just fine; she said she hadn't seen the shooter or the car.

Burke went to his desk, and the squad huddled a little longer, talking quietly. Suddenly, Jamal burst out laughing and high-fived Marco Renzi. They were all looking in Burke's direction, and he guessed they'd been talking about what Kevin had said to Burke the day before, about the shrink.

"Yeah, yeah," he said, looking up. "Real funny."

Burke met with Major Claire Winston, and he told her about old Mike Donnelly, Lisa Fowler's anonymous caller, and his visit to Monsignor Nicholas Stankowski in Cincinnati. He was only a little surprised when Claire told him it wasn't the first time the archbishop's office had denied requests for information regarding a case. She recalled how, just the year before, the prosecuting attorney had been blocked by the Church in a case involving another priest who'd been accused of sexual abuse.

"He was spittin' nails," Claire said, referring to the prosecutor. Burke didn't mention anything to Claire about Jim McGowan and Kenny Mason.

Back in the squad room, Burke finished up some paperwork, and with time to kill before his meeting with Dr. Cara Shannon, he did some Googling, eventually coming across a site called *BishopAccountability.org*, an online archive on the sexual abuse crisis in the Catholic Church. Burke could click on any diocese in the country and see a list of every clergy member who had been publicly accused of sexual abuse. The site noted the nature of the accusations, the dates they were made, and included a brief synopsis of the outcomes, often with a photo of the accused attached. There were 29 cases listed for the Archdiocese of Cincinnati, a small number compared to some of the other, larger archdiocese – 238 cases in Boston – 117 cases in Philly – 258 in Los Angeles – 103 in Chicago. The Dayton priest Lisa Fowler had mentioned was on the list. Burke shuddered to think that these were only the *accused*. How many more could there be that no one knew about? Thinking back to his conversation the day before with Father Stankowski, Burke guessed there was probably not a link to *BishopAccountability.org* on the Archdiocese of Cincinnati website. No way.

At 9:40 Burke shut off his computer. It was a short drive across the Great Miami River to Dayton's west side. He'd been surprised when Dr. Cara Shannon explained that her office wasn't located on the main Wright State campus, but downtown in a complex called Elizabeth Place. The complex had once been a Catholic hospital – St. Elizabeth's. Burke and his sister had both been born there.

Burke parked and eventually found the psychiatry department in one of the old hospital wings. He located Dr. Shannon's office, and the door was open to the hallway. A matronly woman, around his age, sat at a desk facing the door. She looked up as Burke tapped softly on the door and entered the office. Another woman, much younger and very pretty, was looking through the top drawer of a file cabinet, one of several lining a wall. A few bookshelves and several straight-backed chairs lined the opposite wall.

"May I help you?" asked the woman at the desk.

"Yes," said Burke. "Are you Dr. Shannon?"

At this, the younger woman closed the file drawer and turned to face Burke, offering her hand. "Hi," she said. "I'm Cara Shannon. You must be Captain Burke. Let's go into my office," Cara said, leading him to an adjacent room. "Jackie, could you hold any calls or visitors for now? I'm not sure how long we'll be."

Burke found the large room organized and cluttered at the same time. Two walls were covered with floor-to-ceiling bookshelves, and more books were stacked on every surface that wasn't stacked with file folders. Several framed diplomas hung on one wall, and Burke looked closely at a photo of Cara wearing a dress and standing between Barack and Michelle Obama.

"That was at a fundraiser I helped organize a couple of years ago," Cara told him. "Have a seat, Captain." She pointed to a chair, then sat down behind her desk. "So how can I help?"

"Well, Dr. Shannon," Burke explained, "I'm investigating a case involving the remains of a Catholic priest we found in a car at the bottom of Eastwood Lake. You've probably heard about it."

"Yes, I have, certainly," she said. "And please, call me Cara."

Burke nodded. "Anyway, my investigation has turned up some alarming information about the priest, Father Raymond Nelson. First of all, a collection of pornography, some of it child porn, was found in the priest's car. Secondly, I discovered an old man here in Dayton who said the priest sexually abused his son – raped him – and another man who independently called a local reporter to say that he was also raped by Father Nelson. Years ago, up in Toledo."

"Ah, yes. Moved, but not *removed*, by the Catholic Church," said Cara. "Nothing new there. It seems to be the way they work. Have you talked to anyone in the Church about this priest?

"I've tried," said Burke. "They haven't been much help."

"Again, nothing new there either," Cara said, shaking her head. "It's horrible what's gone on. *Worse* than horrible! It's a tragedy, and it makes me sick."

"Are you a Catholic, Cara?" Burke asked her.

"Long ago and far away," she replied. "They'll never get me back. And if they don't get their shit together – excuse me – if they don't start putting a little effort into fixing this mess, there'll be a lot more like me. How about you?"

"Same for me," Burke said, nodding.

"So, how can I help, Captain?"

"I guess I just want to understand more about what makes a person do this – abuse children that is. I wanted to talk to an *expert*," said Burke, pantomiming air quotes. "Just to get a little better insight into this guy."

"And this will help in your investigation?" Cara asked, waving off Burke's flattery.

"Maybe, maybe not," admitted Burke. "So, what can you tell me?"

Cara rubbed her forehead. "Jeez. Where to start," she said, half to herself.

"What makes this guy tick, Cara? That's what I want to know."

She thought for a second. "Well, a sexual deviant, or sexually deviant behavior, is generally believed to be caused by early emotional, physical or sexual trauma, or a combination. The impact of the trauma can be devastating and can result in emotional immaturity. As the individual gets older, this arrested development can cause the molester to rely on children as sex objects – for the relief of sexual anxiety, for feelings of low self-esteem, things like that."

"So, the abuser was abused," said Burke.

"Almost always," said Cara, "and then *they* abuse. Once, twice, and then it becomes habitual, and it *does* seem to make them feel better when they do it, not worse. Freud believed that the abuser's ego is usually defective, as well as their moral conscience. According to him, the abuse can be a pleasant escape from reality."

"But if their reality was that they were abused, how can they be escaping it by abusing others?" asked Burke, leaning forward.

"Good point," said Cara. "Another theory is that the habitual sexual abuse is a repeated and unsuccessful attempt to overcome one's own early sexual trauma, through reenactment of the trauma. The molester identifies with his own abuser and tries to project, or displace the trauma onto his own victim. But the repeat behavior not only fails to resolve the feelings of conflict, it feeds the conflict by duplicating the circumstances. And then he'll abuse again and again."

"Does it ever stop?"

"Not usually," Cara said, shaking her head. "Each time seems to reinforce the problem. It's always one more time. And the negative reinforcement seems to be a big part of the problem. For instance, a child molester may be unable, or afraid, to relate to an adult female. Just being around them could make him anxious. He may molest a child as an escape from the stress caused by this internal conflict with women. He feels better after the act, not worse. Is he going to do it again the next time he feels that stress? Probably."

Burke thought about Father Nelson's relationship with Mary Lou Spaulding, and how many of the other women in St. Nick's parish had seemed to be smitten by the trim, handsome, priest.

"I just can't see how they don't understand that they're hurting the victims," said Burke. "Scaring the hell out of them, even scarring them for life."

"On the contrary," said Cara. "Many of them believe that if a child doesn't resist, he or she probably *wants* to have sex. And we hear that over and over from the abusers. Just a couple of weeks ago, an 87-year-old priest in the Bronx was accused of molesting a sixteen-year-old girl. Do you know what he said at his arraignment? *'She didn't mind getting a massage. She was wearing a short skirt.'*" Cara shook her head.

"But why do the victims want to keep it to themselves, like all these kids who don't rat out a priest until years and years later, when they've grown up?" asked Burke.

"Well, you already said it. They're scared to death. They don't think they'll be believed. The abuser is usually someone they know, someone with authority over them. They're afraid they'll get back at them if they tell. And, unfortunately, *that* behavior just encourages the abuser. They often think that if the child didn't tell someone about the abuse, then they must have enjoyed it. Then they'll go back to that victim."

"What about repressed memories, Cara?" Burke asked. "From what I've read, not all of you psychiatrists put a whole lot of stock in them."

"Well, I think those of us who don't are missing the boat," she said. "It's believed that abuse victims never really *forget* these memories. They can suppress them consciously because they just don't want to think about it, or they repress them subconsciously, where the memory actually becomes unavailable. The repression doesn't destroy the memory, and some external stimuli can restore it. I'm a firm believer in the phenomenon, and I've worked closely with several individuals who *have* managed to turn their lives around with a little help and treatment. I haven't done a lot of work with recovery through suggestion, but others have had great success. Unfortunately, I think some members of our profession have done a bit of fabricating and grandstanding, and it's damaged the credibility of a lot of good, legitimate work."

"I've read some stuff about lawyers and judges having a hard time with the idea of repressed memories," Burke said. "They don't think they're reliable."

"The courts are all over the map on it," said Cara. "Different states deal with it differently. Some favor the rights of the victims more than the accused, and vice versa. The laws and statutes are changing all the time. Here, the Ohio Supreme Court is still conflicted. We had a 1994 law regarding the statute of limitations on the use of recovered memories in abuse cases, but it was changed in 2006, and then again last year. I think it's being challenged again."

Burke hung his head. He thought about little Timmy Donnelly, and Lisa Fowler's mystery caller.

"What about rape?" he asked quietly, without looking up. "Sodomy."

"What about it?"

"Well, like how often is the abuser that violent?" asked Burke, still not looking up.

"Not that often. Maybe ten or fifteen percent of cases," said Cara. "And yes, sodomy would be included in that. Nonviolent abusers will often coax or pressure a kid into having some sort of sexual activity. They seem to know how to pick the vulnerable kids – kids that will trade sex for attention or acceptance – gifts even. Rapists are a different animal. They'll use intimidation, threat, brutal force. It's as much an act of aggression as it is sexual."

Burke was quiet for several moments.

"But how could a person do something like that to a child?" he finally said, looking up. "I just can't get my head around that. It makes me sick just thinking about it."

For the next three hours, skipping lunch, Cara and Burke poured over charts, graphs, statistics, and documentation from different books. She pulled piles of studies from the shelves. They dove deeper into repressed and recovered memory, the difference between the types of sexual molesters – fixated or regressed – and how abusers aren't a bunch of dirty old men in trench coats in the alley, but usually respectable, otherwise law-abiding citizens who often escape detection and blame for exactly that reason. They covered the difference between *pedophile* and *pederast*, *hebephilia* and *ephebophilia*. Cara explained that an abuser could target younger as well as older children based on his or her age as a victim, and the length and extent of his own abuse. She patiently explained, in laymen's terms, the assessment, diagnosis, and treatment for abusers. In the end, Cara picked out a small stack of books to lend to Burke, loading them into a cloth bag.

In the outer office, Burke shook Cara's hand and thanked her for her help. He was surprised when she handed him her card, and gave him a hug.

"I enjoyed this, Captain Burke," she said, smiling.

"Me, too," Burke said, blushing slightly. "Can I call you again if I need to?"

"By all means. Take care."

37

Bling

A very tall, muscular, black male nurse named Reggie pushed Monsignor Nicholas Stankowski's wheelchair down a hall in Cincinnati's Good Samaritan Hospital. They were headed to Radiology for a CT scan. Reggie had been assigned to guide the priest through the battery of tests that had been scheduled by Father Stankowski's primary care doctor.

"Make way, make way for the V.I.P.," Reggie sang out in a high, almost feminine voice that belied his burly physical appearance.

"You are my *V-I-P*," he had laughed, earlier that morning. "Very... Important... Priest!" Reggie and Father Stankowski had already been together now for a couple of hours. Two days earlier, when Stankowski had gone in for a checkup – his first in over five years – his doctor had been shocked by the priest's appearance and condition.

"This CT scan won't take very long," said Reggie. "Just a few minutes once they get started. Then you can go home. I'll get your discharge papers going as soon as we're done. You'll be out of here in . . . *no time.*" He snapped his fingers.

Father Stankowski had been in the hospital since mid-morning. Reggie had checked the priest into a private room as soon as he arrived and offered to put the priest's valuables into the hospital safe. When the priest started to undress, Reggie noticed a small, elaborate key hanging on a chain around his neck. While fastening the hospital gown that only partially covered Father Stankowski's jaundiced, bloated body, Reggie had asked the priest if he wanted to put the key in the safe with his other valuables.

"No, no," said the priest. "This key belongs to the archbishop. He's been called to Rome. I keep it for him whenever he travels out of the country."

When Reggie had Father Stankowski situated, he checked the priest's vital signs, managing to conceal his concern when he tested the pulse rate, but not when he measured the blood pressure.

"Oh, wow!" he said, under his breath. "That can't be right." He checked it again, with the same results. "Something definitely going on there, Father. Not to worry though, we'll figure it out."

The priest and the nurse had become fast friends, chatting away, mostly about subjects that interested Reggie – body building, food and wine, travel to South America, and Lady Gaga. Earlier, blood had been drawn from Father Stankowski's arm and sent off to the lab – *prioritized* – for testing. A chest X-ray and an ultrasound had been scheduled, but the doctors wanted to wait for the blood test results from the lab before moving ahead. After an hour's wait in the priest's private room, a doctor had called Reggie out into the hall. Father Stankowski could hear them talking quietly, but couldn't make out what was being said.

"Did they get the lab results?" he asked, when Reggie returned to the room.

"They certainly did. Something about an elevated level of CA 19-9, whatever that is," said Reggie, knowing of course, *exactly* what it was. "The good news is you get to skip the X-ray and the ultrasound. We'll get right to the CT scan. *Excuse* me . . . make that a CT scan with *contrast*."

Reggie gave the priest a Benadryl injection as well as some sort of steroid to avoid any allergic reaction to the contrast dye that would be injected into his arm for the CT scan. "Just sit tight now. I'll be back to get you."

Now, an hour later, they were on their way to Radiology.

"Okay, Father, this is it," said Reggie, turning the wheelchair into the scan room. "Oh good, it's not too cold in here today."

When Reggie came around to the front of the wheelchair, Father Stankowski noticed several gold chains hanging around the nurse's neck, one of which was attached to a large gold cross.

"Reggie, you've been holding out on me," said the smiling priest. "I hadn't noticed your lovely jewelry."

"Oh, you mean my *bling*!" Reggie said, looking down in surprise. He grabbed the necklaces. "Yikes! These are supposed to remain *under* my blouse at all times – hospital policy. I was just showing them off before I picked you up. Forgot to put them back."

He started to tuck the jewelry back under his blouse, but Father Stankowski reached up and stopped him, putting his small, pale hand over Reggie's massive mitt.

"No, wait," said the priest. "Let me see what you have there. Do I see a cross?"

"Why, yes, it is," said Reggie, spreading out the necklaces for the priest to see. "And here's the Star of David."

Reggie leaned down, and Father Stankowski reached out and hefted the cross and the star. They were both made of heavy gold, as were the chains.

"So, are you a religious man, Reggie?" he asked, releasing the necklaces.

"Oh, heavens no!" said Reggie, straightening up. "I'm a confirmed atheist! I just like all the symbols. I hope you're not offended, Father."

"Not at all, Reggie, not at all. But what was on the other necklace? It looked like a wedding band. Was it your father's?"

"I wish," said Reggie, sighing and pulling the ring out from his blouse. He showed it to the priest. "I never met my father. No, no – this is *my* wedding ring!"

"You're *married*?"

"Yes I am! I married my partner Phillip, just last month," said the nurse proudly. "We'd been planning a trip to New York City, like … *forever*. When we heard they were about to legalize same-sex marriage in New York, we decided to just go for it. We were there the day it went into law."

"Congratulations!" The priest smiled broadly and offered his hand.

"Why, thank you, Father," Reggie said, proudly.

He started to help Father Stankowski out of his gown, and there, around the priest's own neck, hung the elaborate key.

"Father! Your key!" said Reggie. "I'm afraid that has to come off. You can't wear that in the scanner."

The priest clutched the titanium key. "But it's very important that I keep it with me."

"Now, now," said Reggie, laughing. "We can't do the scan with *that* around your neck. It might explode or something! Here, let me have it. I promise I'll guard it with my life."

Father Stankowski let Reggie remove the key from around his neck.

"I'll tell you what," said the nurse, putting the key around his own neck, and dropping it under his blouse, "How about if I just keep it here with the rest of my bling, for safe keeping. You can have it back as soon as the scan is done."

Reggie got his patient situated on the movable scan table and covered the priest's legs with a heated towel.

"This won't take long, Father. Don't worry, you're in good hands," he said, nodding toward the nurse and the tech who would be performing the scan. "And this is the last time you'll get poked today! I'll be right outside, okay?"

The tech explained the process to the priest while the nurse inserted the IV and started the contrast dye into Father Stankowski's arm. The team left the room, and almost immediately the table began to move slowly into the scan gantry. A warm, slightly fuzzy feeling filled the priest's arm, spreading slowly to the rest of his body. He grinned broadly, about to laugh, but remembered that he'd been instructed to lie as still as possible.

What would my dear, dear archbishop say, he thought, *if he knew that right now, the key to the secret archive was hanging alongside the Star of David around the neck of a gay atheist who was married to another man?*

38

Confession

That evening, Father Phillip Metzger, pastor of St. Nicholas Catholic Church in Riverside, was hearing Friday confessions. He was tired, and trying his best to stay awake and pay attention to the confessors who came in one after another as he sat in the cool, dark confessional. *I shouldn't have had that second glass of wine with my dinner,* he thought. At one point, he'd peeked out through an opening in his door and was happy to see just a few more members of the flock waiting their turn. He recognized them all, mostly older parishioners who still took solace from the sacrament of penance.

Father Metzger absolved a woman of her sins and dismissed her, telling her to go in peace. *The last one,* he thought, and was about to leave the confessional when he heard the door on the other side open and close. The voice of a man he knew well – a devout, lifelong member of the parish – spoke to him.

"Bless me, Father, for I have sinned," the man began. "My last confession was one week ago."

The priest listened to the man's confession, almost the same confession as the week before, and the week before that. It was always the same. The man recited how many times he had used God's name in vain, how many times he'd had impure thoughts, and how often he raised his voice in anger, mostly toward his wife.

Father Metzger listened patiently, gave the man a short penance, and absolved him of his sins.

"Go in peace," said the priest, giving his blessing.

"Thank you, Father," said the man, and the priest began to close the small hatch through which they spoke. "Wait, Father, there's something else I wanted to talk to you about."

"By all means," said the priest, sliding the little door open again. "Go ahead."

"Well, Father," the man said quietly, "it's about Father Nelson, the priest they found in the lake."

"What about him?" Father Metzger asked. "Did you know him?"

"Yes, I did," said the man. "And I've tried my whole life to forget about him. But ever since they discovered him in the lake, it's all I've thought about."

"I don't understand," said the priest. "Do you miss him? Are you sad about him being gone?"

"No, no, nothing like that," the man said. "It's a terrible thing, Father. I've never told anyone, but I wanted to tell you. Father Nelson molested me when I was an altar boy – many years ago."

39

Birdie-Birdie

It was Saturday morning, the day after Burke's long session with Dr. Cara Shannon. After the best night of sleep he'd had in a long time, he played a round of golf with Pete Skoff and two retired ex-cops. Burke liked all three men, and the foursome seemed very relaxed and happy just to be on the golf course. The ex-cops usually played during the week when the course wasn't crowded, but they'd been eager to join Burke and Pete.

They played the longer, outside course at Community, and on a beautiful weekend day in August, the course was crowded. Play was slow, but no one in the foursome seemed to be in any hurry. Pete was surprised at how easygoing Burke seemed, and recalled that in the past, he would have been grumbling by now, bitching about having to wait on the group ahead of them.

But not today. Burke was smiling and chatty, and each time they waited to tee off, the men caught up on each other's families, talked about what was going on these days at the DPD, and laughed about the good and the bad aspects of retirement – mostly good. When the others expressed their curiosity about the Father Nelson case, Burke filled them in on as much as he felt he could share, which wasn't really much. The men joked and Burke laughed along. At Pete's urging, he told the story about shattering Carlos's windshield the last time he had played golf with Maggie. Somewhat amazed by his boss's cheerful mood, Pete would indeed have something to share with the rest of the squad on Monday.

Burke's demeanor also proved to be good for his golf game. While Pete shot the lowest score of the foursome, a two-under-par 69, Burke played the best round of his life, finishing birdie-birdie for a 78, easily beating the two ex-cops. What amazed Pete even more than Burke's score, however, was that his boss hung around for a few beers after the round, something he'd never done before.

Burke's sanguine mood lingered into Sunday morning. He woke up hungry, having slept well again – a deep, dreamless sleep. After a pot of coffee and a spinach and cream cheese omelet, he walked to a convenience store and bought a copy of the *New York Times.* He spent the morning reading the *Times* and cleaning his apartment, something he'd been putting off for too long. Late in the afternoon he drove to a nearby mall and found a toy store. After much back and forth, he bought a solar-powered grasshopper kit and had it gift-wrapped for Ashley. He also got a card game for Megan. At six o'clock he picked up Maggie, and they drove to Kevin and Becky's house for Ashley's birthday cookout.

It was just family, the way Burke liked it. He always made an effort to be on his best behavior when he was around Kevin's family, but today, for some reason, he didn't have to work at it. He felt relaxed. He played badminton with Maggie and the girls, helped Ashley put the grasshopper kit together, and played the new card game with Megan. At one point the squirt guns came out, and before it was over, Burke was pretty much soaked. Maggie, Kevin, and Becky watched happily, occasionally joining in the fun, and at dinner everyone agreed that the New York strip steaks were the best that Kevin had ever cooked.

During dinner Maggie informed everyone that she was retiring. As part of a restructuring process, the school board had offered incentives that she couldn't afford to pass up. She was finished teaching and wasn't sure what she was going to do – probably play more golf, and keep taking classes. Maybe she'd get another degree, *just for the hell of it*. They all toasted Maggie, and then Burke bragged about his golf score from the day before. No one talked about police work. After the girls went to bed Kevin and Burke sat in the dark smoking small cigars and sipping bourbon.

Kevin and Maggie had exchanged glances several times during the course of the evening as they watched Burke romping with the kids, laughing, and enjoying his steak. When it was time to go, Kevin hugged his mother goodbye, and whispered in her ear.

"Who's that guy you brought here tonight? I kind of like him."

"Me, too," Maggie whispered back. "Me, too.

40

Beautiful Ford

In the squad room on Monday morning, after yet another good night's sleep, Burke started his week as usual. He went through the reports that had been generated over what had been a fairly quiet weekend, and signed requisitions for supplies and equipment requested by his squad. Danny and Jamal had been on call, and they handled the weekend's lone incident on Sunday morning. A white, middle-aged man had driven a car over his white, middle-aged wife, killing her in their driveway. The man claimed it was an accident and wasn't being held at the moment, but the investigation would be ongoing.

Burke had a short meeting with Major Winston, filling her in on the driveway death and laying out the squad's schedule for the week. After turning in the requisitions, he went back to the squad room and checked his email, discovering his first Google *Alert* update of the day. He'd just found out about the alert system on Friday from Dr. Cara Shannon. That evening he'd set it up, typing in *catholic sex abuse scandal.* Email alerts had come on both Saturday and Sunday, highlighting three or four articles and several blog postings from around the world. The most troubling was an article in the *New York Times* that he'd read the day before, about a bishop in Kansas City who had waited five months before acknowledging to the police that he knew about a priest in his diocese who had been taking indecent photos of young girls. During those five months, the priest had continued attending children's birthday parties and spending weekends in the homes of parish families.

Burke waited until ten o'clock, put his computer to sleep, and called retired USAF Brigadier General James McGowan. The general picked up on the fourth ring.

"Morning, Jim. John Burke here. I was wondering if I could talk to you again about the Father Nelson case. Some new information has come up and I'd like to run some of it past you, if you don't mind."

McGowan didn't answer immediately, and Burke noted the hesitation.

"Sure, John," he said. "I think you pretty much have my story, but I'd be happy to talk to you."

"I'd like to sit down with you, face to face, if that's okay with you," Burke said.

"Um . . . sure. When did you have in mind?"

"Well, I'm free right now," said Burke. "I could drive out to your house if that's convenient."

"All right," said the general. "How about eleven o'clock? We could get lunch later, or maybe just have something here. Do you have my address?"

Burke took down McGowan's address, got directions, and hung up. He finished up some paperwork and told Kevin he'd be back sometime after lunch. Leaving Dayton, Burke could have taken Route 35, from downtown out to Beavercreek, but he decided to drive through the east end, past St. Nick's and his old neighborhood in Riverside. He drove by the church, and just beyond that, the Belfair shopping center where Dumbo's Tavern had been. There was still a bar there, and the whole area looked a little run-down.

Crossing into Beavercreek, Burke drove through several large, new housing developments, all located in what had been corn and soybean fields when he was growing up. He found Jim McGowan's red-brick-faced house in a neighborhood which had been built in an old woodlot filled with mature trees. The overhead doors on the attached three-bay garage were all open, and in it Burke saw a Subaru wagon, a newer Cadillac sedan, and a highly polished, light blue 1964 Ford Galaxie 500XL convertible with a white ragtop.

McGowan's wife Kathy answered the door. She was attractive, and Burke thought her smile seemed genuine. She shook his hand and invited him in just as McGowan came into the foyer. He was tan and fit, and he gripped Burke's hand firmly, patting him on the shoulder.

"I'm just off to the base to golf," Kathy said. "You boys have fun catching up." She gave McGowan a quick peck on the lips, and disappeared out the front door.

Burke and McGowan stood looking at each other for a moment, each trying to see through the middle-aged man to the teenage boy they'd last seen, probably forty-five years earlier. Neither man seemed self-conscious as they looked each other up and down.

"Beautiful Ford," said Burke at last, nodding in the direction of the garage.

"Thanks," said McGowan. "A friend found it for me in Texas last year. I always wanted one. Are you a Ford man?"

"Nah. I've always loved Chevys," said Burke. "But the '64 was my favorite Ford. Patty Crockett's dad had one, just like the one in your garage. Do you remember that?"

"I sure do. That's the very car I fell in love with," McGowan said, smiling. "Patty let me drive it once. Her old man would have killed me if he'd known. Let's go back to my study."

McGowan led Burke through a large, open living room filled with furnishings collected over the course of a life spent at Air Force bases all around the world. Burke recalled being intrigued by these trappings in the homes of his childhood friends whose fathers were in the Air Force. There was a hookah, several old leather Ottomans, oriental screens, exotic vases, a display of old Japanese swords, animal carvings, and several large, intricate tapestries.

"Wow!" Burke said, taking it all in. "Cool stuff."

McGowan's study at the back of the house of newer construction, probably a recent addition, and filled with Air Force memorabilia. There were dozens of black-and-white or color photographs of aircraft in flight, and many photos, some of them signed, of crews dressed in flight suits – including a much younger McGowan – posing in front of different aircraft. There were framed service medallions and insignias, commendations, group logos, awards, degrees, and several trophies topped with miniature aircraft. Model replicas of airplanes and jet aircraft lined the shelves and hung from the ceiling. There was a model cut-a-way of a jet engine, rows of baseball caps with different insignias, and floor-to-ceiling bookshelves packed full, including probably twenty feet of *National Geographic* magazines. A large, beautifully carved teak desk filled the center of the room. Burke noticed a putter leaning against the wall in one corner, and a half dozen golf balls on the carpet nearby.

He looked closely at a pair of cartoon-like caricatures, framed and hanging side by side, signed by Milton Caniff. Caniff had gone to high school in Dayton, and went on to create the old *Terry and the Pirates* comic strip. Later, he created *Steve Canyon*, a strip based on an Air Force pilot.

"That's me on the left and my dad on the right," said McGowan. "Milt and Dad were good buddies. He drew those for a lot of pilots."

The General sat down behind his desk while Burke moved slowly about the room, checking out each photograph, his reading glasses perched on the end of his nose.

"Good lord, Jim, did you fly all of these?"

"Sure did, but mostly the fighters. Not once in combat, though. I was in between wars – too late for Vietnam and too early for the first Gulf war. I was already on the ground in '91. I guess I should count myself lucky."

"So, how'd you miss Vietnam?" Burke asked him.

"Well, we moved back to Texas where I finished high school, and then I went to A&M on a ROTC scholarship. By the time I graduated and started pilot training, the war was pretty much over. How about you, did you go?"

"Nope," said Burke, shrugging. "I didn't want anything to do with Vietnam, but it was just dumb luck that kept me out of it. I was pretty much sick of school after I graduated from Riverside. I didn't want to go to college, so I had no deferment. Then somebody told me that they wouldn't draft cops, so I signed up for the Dayton Police Academy. My mom wasn't too thrilled with *that*. Anyway, it turned out they *were* taking cops after all. But then that first draft lottery came up and all bets were off. Mom was ready to move the whole damn family to Canada, but I drew a high number. Like I said, dumb luck."

"And you stayed in the police academy?" McGowan asked.

"Yeah," Burke shrugged again. "Funny thing that. Turns out I liked it."

Burke sat down in a wicker easy chair, and although they hadn't been close friends as boys, the two former schoolmates reminisced for nearly an hour, catching up with each other's lives and discovering that they had quite a bit in common. Like Burke and Maggie, McGowan and Kathy had only one child, a daughter now married and living in California. Kathy McGowan, like Maggie, had been a schoolteacher for many years. Both of McGowan's parents were dead. The general and his wife enjoyed golfing, and Jay's was one of their favorite downtown restaurants. Eventually, Burke got down to business.

"Jim," he said, his jaw clenching and unclenching several times, "some information has come up about Father Nelson and I wanted to ask you some questions,"

"Shoot."

"Well, first of all, from what I can tell, it looks like Father Nelson was a pretty serious pedophile. The worst kind – a rapist. And that's according to the father of a former St. Nick's choir boy, and another guy who said he was abused up in Toledo, before Father Nelson was moved to Dayton."

McGowan didn't respond. He stared off through a window as if he hadn't been listening. Burke waited.

"So why are you telling *me* all this?" McGowan asked finally, turning to look at Burke.

"Well, Jim, I think it has something to do with his death," Burke replied. "I'm just trying to figure it all out, and so far, I haven't come up with much except for this information about him being a pervert. I think the Church knows more about Nelson than they're willing to tell me, so I'm just trying to work up a profile. I hope you can help."

"Like how? How can *I* help?" McGowan said, almost bitterly. He leaned forward in his chair and locked eyes with Burke. "I already told you everything about that night that I can."

"That you *can* or that you *will?*"

"Jesus, John," said McGowan, sitting back in his chair. "I told you what happened. Everything I told you was the truth." Burke had heard thousands of lies over the years, and he knew he was hearing one now.

"Kenny told me the same story," said Burke. "You both recalled it almost exactly the same way, some of it word for word. I asked Mrs. Spaulding if she remembered the piano being moved in the rectory that night. She didn't. She said she probably would have noticed something like that."

"She's eighty something years old, for Christ's sake," said the general, leaning back and throwing his hands in the air. "And that was almost fifty years ago. Maybe we didn't move the damn piano. Hell, maybe we *did* move it, and then Father Nelson changed his mind and we moved it back."

"Maybe. But add it up, Jim," said Burke, and he counted it off with his fingers. "Nelson was a pervert. He was killed and dumped in the lake. You and Kenny and Steve were the last ones to see him alive that night, and all of your recollections differ from Mrs. Spaulding's. You can see where I'm coming from, right?"

"Okay, okay. Sure, I can see that," said McGowan, relaxing a little. "But . . ."

"Did Father Nelson molest you, Jim?" Burke asked, cutting him off.

McGowan gazed at Burke for several seconds, then dropped his head. After a moment he looked up. "No," he said firmly. 'No, he didn't. I wouldn't have put up with it."

"Do you know if he molested Kenny or Steve?" Burke was suddenly embarrassed to be asking these questions.

"Steve never mentioned it," said McGowan.

"What about Kenny?"

McGowan leaned back and sighed. He stared out the window.

"Maybe you should ask Kenny," he said, looking back at Burke.

"You're right," said Burke. "I should ask Kenny."

The two men sat silently. Finally, Burke stood and picked up the putter that was leaning against a wall. He made a few practice strokes.

"How about some lunch?" the general asked, standing up. "I could make us a couple of sandwiches."

"Thanks, Jim, but I'd better get back downtown." Burke put the putter back, and offered his hand to McGowan. "Maybe we should play a round of golf sometime. Do you ever play Community?"

"Mostly I play on the base. But yeah, I love Community. I have a city membership and play all those courses once in a while."

"Great. I'll give you a call sometime. And I hope you'll keep all this to yourself for now."

"You don't need to worry about that, believe me," McGowan assured him. He saw Burke to the front door and watched him take a quick peek at the beautiful Ford as he walked by the garage.

"John!" the general called out. "One question. Am I a suspect?"

"Let's just say you're a person of interest," Burke called back, waving.

41

Father Metzger

Again, Burke decided to avoid Route 35 and headed back into downtown Dayton the same way he had come out. Passing St. Nick's, he noticed the pastor, Father Metzger, standing with two other men in front of the large cross on the church's lawn. All of them were holding shovels. A wheelbarrow sat nearby, and black plastic pots full of mums were spread about. Burke was about to drive on past, but suddenly changed his mind, pulled over, and parked at the side of Belfair Avenue. He wasn't really sure why he stopped.

Father Metzger noticed Burke as he got out of his car, and they waved to each other across the road. As Burke waited for a truck and several cars to pass, he couldn't help thinking about young Timmy Donnelly, and how he had stepped in front of a truck close to this very spot, many years ago.

The priest shook Burke's hand and introduced him to the other men, volunteers from the parish. "We're trying to spruce things up for the opening of school," he said, pointing toward the mums. Without saying more, he led Burke out of earshot from the other men, to ask him how the Father Nelson investigation was going.

"Slowly," Burke replied. "I don't have much to go on, but there have been a few leads."

"Well, I'm kind of glad you happened by," said the priest. "Something has come up, and I've been struggling with whether or not I should tell you about it. But now you're here and I think it's a sign we should talk."

"God works in mysterious ways . . ." Burke said, smiling.

"Yes. Yes, he certainly does. Do you have time right now?"

Burke nodded, then followed the priest into the rectory, taking it all in as he had done before. They sat at a small table in the kitchen, and Father Metzger asked Burke if he'd had lunch.

"As a matter of fact, I haven't," Burke said, gratefully.

The priest made ham and Swiss cheese sandwiches, opened a bag of *Mike-sells* potato chips, and poured two tall glasses of iced-tea. They talked as they ate.

"Friday evening, I was hearing confessions," the priest told him. "A man that I know quite well came in, made his confession, and then wanted to talk about something else. He told me that Father Nelson had molested him when he was an altar boy."

"Jesus!" said Burke. "Sorry, Father."

"It's quite all right," said the priest, smiling. "I say it all the time myself. Anyway, he was the last one in the church, so I locked up and we came over here. He told me that Father Nelson had molested him several times – right here in the rectory."

"Did he mention if he'd been in the choir?" Burke asked.

"No, he didn't," the priest said. "If he sang then the way he sings now, I doubt it. The man can't carry a tune, I'm sorry to say."

"Did he mention that he was raped?" asked Burke. "Sodomized?"

"Good God, no!" Father Metzger leaned back in surprise. "*Molested.* That's the word he used. He said Father Nelson *molested* him."

"I'm sorry, Father, I wasn't trying to shock you," Burke said. "But my investigation has led to some pretty dark places. From what I can tell, Father Nelson was a serious sexual predator, even a violent one. There have been a couple of other allegations, and so far, all of the accusers have been boys, or they *were* boys when they were abused."

"Dear Lord," said the priest, wide-eyed.

"What else did he tell you?" asked Burke.

"Well, he said he was molested and that Father Nelson made him feel like it was all right, that it was a good thing. He said he just resigned himself to it, and he never told a soul. He pushed it out of his memory as he got older and tried not to think about it. He said all the news about abusive priests over the last few years kept bringing it back to him. And then when Father Nelson's remains were found, he said he couldn't *stop* thinking about it."

"Have you told the archbishop's office about this?" Burke asked.

"Well, no, not yet," said the priest. "But I will. Because of the circumstances, I've been struggling with what to do. You went to church, Captain Burke, so maybe you know about the *Seal of the Confessional.* As a confessor, I am absolutely forbidden to betray the penitent no matter what he's said, for any reason, not even to the archbishop's office."

"But you said he told you about it in the rectory," Burke reminded him.

"Actually, he told me in the confessional first," said the priest. "Granted, he was finished with his confession and was no longer confessing to anything. Instead, he was telling me about something that someone else did. But it *was* in the confessional and I wasn't sure whether I could talk about it. The fact that he chose to tell me about it in the confessional made me unsure of how much of his story he wanted me to share with anyone."

"But you told *me* about it," said Burke.

"I did," said Father Metzger. "Like you said, God works in mysterious ways. But I didn't tell you who it was."

"Did you ask him if you could talk to me, or the archbishop's office, about it?" Burke asked.

"No," said the priest. "I've been working my way through Church law and trying to figure out what to do. In criminal matters, more recent policy directs us to encourage the penitent to surrender to civil authorities. But then, he's not the criminal, he was the victim. I wasn't sure what to do. I did tell him he should contact you. I even gave him your card. He said he would think about it."

"I appreciate that, Father."

"I will, however, contact the archbishop's office and tell them what I've told you. I'll write to Monsignor Stankowski. If I've violated Church law, well, so be it. I'm willing to take the chance."

Burke finished the iced tea, and Father Metzger walked him to his car. They shook hands, said their goodbyes, and then the priest gave Burke a hug.

Why do people keep hugging me? Burke wondered.

42

Questions

The squad room was empty when Burke got back. He located Ithaca, New York, on Google maps, and figured he would have to fly into Rochester or Syracuse and then rent a car. When he called the airport, he was surprised to find that he could fly right into Ithaca. There was a flight the next morning that landed at 11:38, after a connection in Philadelphia.

He checked his email, and there, under Google Alerts, were another six or seven stories from around the world pertaining to the ongoing Catholic sex abuse scandal, including one about a town in the Netherlands. The discovery of old records showed that an unusually high number of mysterious deaths – 34 in all – had occurred in a Roman Catholic institution there for mentally disabled children between 1952 and 1954. Burke read several of the articles, then put his computer to sleep.

Unlocking the top drawer of his desk, he pulled out the Father Nelson file and found Kenny Mason's phone number. When Kenny answered, Burke could hear the sound of hammering in the background, and what may have been a nail gun blasting away.

"Hi, Kenny. This is John Burke, from Dayton."

"Hey, John," Kenny yelled. "Hang on a second, I can barely hear you."

While he waited for Kenny, he heard him holler to someone, something about 'the wrong goddamn trusses.' Burke pictured him walking away from a construction site, a tool belt strapped on, and a pencil behind his ear.

"That's better," Kenny said eventually. "How are you, John?"

"I'm good," Burke said. "You?"

"Not bad. What's up?"

"Well, some stuff has come up about the Father Nelson case. I was wondering if I could come out to Ithaca and talk to you about it."

"Sure, that's not a problem at all," said Kenny. "When would you like to come?"

Kenny hadn't hesitated, even for a moment, and Burke imagined that McGowan had already talked to him.

"Well, I know it's kind of short notice, but I could come tomorrow. I can get a flight that arrives there at 11:38 in the morning. There's a return flight later in the afternoon, so I wouldn't be staying overnight. Can you can get out of work?"

"I'm the boss, so that's no problem," said Kenny. "You want me to pick you up at the airport?"

"That'd be great," Burke said. "I'll see you then."

Burke called and booked the flight, then pulled up to his desk and spread out his notes. The first time Burke and Kenny talked, Kenny told Burke that he'd read about the discovery of Father Nelson's remains in the newspaper, and he'd mentioned the gravel pit. Burke had wondered about that because there had been no mention in the national press that Eastwood Lake had once been a gravel pit. Granted, Kenny could have known that the lake was the same body of water, but he'd left Dayton a long time before the gravel pit had been named Eastwood Lake.

Also, Jim and Kenny had used exactly the same words when describing how the piano was moved – *from one side of the room to the other.* Could be a coincidence, but probably not. In the old missing persons report that Bigelow the Gigolo had written, Mrs. Spaulding hadn't mentioned the piano being moved, and when Burke asked her about it, she had said it was something she likely would have noticed. When he told the general what Mrs. Spaulding said, McGowan had tried to skirt the issue, claiming it was a long time ago, casting doubt on the old woman's memory.

He was fairly certain that Kenny and Jim McGowan were staying in touch. Burke made a list of questions he wanted to ask Kenny Mason, then locked the file in his desk. Feeling an almost desperate need to talk to Maggie, he called to invite her out for dinner.

"Oh, Johnny." She sounded disappointed. "Not tonight. I'm just fixing a salmon casserole. But why don't you come *here* for dinner? There's plenty for both of us."

He accepted Maggie's offer, and as he was hanging up Kevin came into the squad room. Burke decided it was time to tell his son everything he'd been holding close to the vest. "Let's take a walk," Burke said.

They left the building and found a bench across the street, in a little park on the campus of Sinclair Community College. They sat almost nose to nose, Burke doing most of the talking, and before they knew it, an hour had gone by.

"Wow!" was all Kevin could say. "Nice work, Pop."

"Thank you, son," Burke said with a little mock bow. "And this is just between us for now, all right? I don't want anyone to know. Except your mom. I'm going there for dinner tonight."

Kevin grinned again.

"What?" said Burke, eyeing his son.

"Oh…nothin'."

Burke told Kevin about his plan to fly to Ithaca the next day, then headed home and showered. He picked up a bottle of white wine and arrived at Maggie's just as the casserole was coming out of the oven. While they ate, Burke walked Maggie through his entire investigation – every conversation, every note he'd made, every suspicion he had, and every dead-end he'd met.

"That's about the creepiest thing I've ever heard!" she exclaimed, when Burke told her about the Church's secret archive.

After dinner they set up the Scrabble board, and chatted away as they played. They finished the wine, and Maggie beat Burke 423 to 396.

Burke stood up. "I'd better go," he said, looking at his watch. "I need to be at the airport pretty early."

Maggie took Burke's hand, giving it a squeeze. "Thanks for coming tonight, Johnny. This was really, really nice." Burke could see that her eyes were a little misty. He put his arms around her and they hugged for a long moment.

"I love you, Maggie," he said.

"I love you, too. Have a safe trip tomorrow."

43

Show Some Class

It was still dark when Burke's alarm went off at 4:30. While making a pot of strong coffee, he tried to remember the last time he'd flown anywhere. It had been a while, and he was surprised that he couldn't even remember the last time he'd been away from Dayton. The thought depressed him a little.

The flights and the connection were worse than Burke had anticipated. A delay in Dayton and a late arrival had him running through the airport in Philadelphia. An hour later, as the cramped turboprop approached Ithaca, Burke could see the town nestled in the hills at the end of a long narrow lake – one of the Finger Lakes – surrounded by farmland and open countryside.

He tried to picture what an aged Kenny Mason would look like; Jim McGowan had certainly been recognizable. Kenny was waiting for him in the small terminal, and he and Burke recognized each another instantly. He was weathered and rugged looking, his face deeply lined, and wore a red ball cap with a stylized, white letter *C* on the front. What hair Burke could see under the cap was gray, and Kenny was wearing faded jeans and a white polo shirt. The two men shook hands and sized each other up, much the same way Burke and McGowan had done.

"Still a Redlegs fan, I see," said Burke, pointing to the cap.

"For life, I'm afraid," Kenny said, laughing. "And thanks for noticing. Everybody around here thinks it's a goddamn Cornell hat."

It was just about lunch time when they walked out to the parking lot and climbed into Kenny's Toyota pickup.

"I'll bet you're hungry," said Kenny. "What'd they feed you on the plane, a five-cent pack of peanuts?"

"You got it," said Burke.

"I'll take you to my favorite diner in my favorite neighborhood, Fall Creek. Maybe I can show you around town a little after lunch, some of our famous gorges. Have you ever been here?"

"Not even close," said Burke.

The airport was only a couple of miles out of town, and Burke took in the panoramic view as they drove down a long, sweeping hill into town. They skirted a wide lake dotted with small sailboats, stretching to the northern horizon.

"Cayuga Lake," Kenny said, pointing. As the highway descended, Burke looked north, and then scanned the hills and valleys to the south of the lake.

"Wow! Check it out," he said. "It's beautiful here, Kenny. Is that Cornell up there?"

"Nah, that's Ithaca College," Kenny said. "Cornell's up behind this hill on the left. You'll be able to see it when we get down into town."

The Lincoln Street Diner was tucked into an old residential neighborhood, next to a barber shop and a coin-op laundry. Otherwise, it was mostly single-family homes that looked like they could have been built anytime between 1900 and 1940. Chris, the owner of the diner, saw Kenny walk in ahead of Burke.

"*Loser!*" he shouted, pointing at Kenny from behind the long counter. The place was almost full, and everyone turned to see who'd come in. Besides some students, the mostly retired or blue-collar customers were regulars, and they all knew about the friendly feud the two had been carrying on for years. Chris was a big Phillies fan, and the Phillies had just beaten the Reds three games in a row. If they completed the four-game sweep in Cincinnati that night, it would be an historical first.

"Tonight, *asshole!*" Kenny shot back, laughing. They sat by a window at the only open table, and Kenny ordered a Tully burger.

"Why's it called a Tully burger?" asked Burke, as he perused the menu.

"Actually, I'm not really sure," said Kenny. "Probably something to do with the town of Tully, north of here. It's kind of a local specialty, but it's just a burger"

Burke ordered the daily special – a turkey dinner – and a glass of iced tea. Erin, their wisecracking waitress, assured him he'd made "an excellent choice." She knocked Kenny's cap off as she walked away. "Show some class, loser," she called back over her shoulder, grinning.

Over lunch Kenny and Burke talked mostly about the old days. Kenny told him that he had avoided Ohio for a long time, and only started going back the last five or six years, to visit his sister and a brother. He said he couldn't understand why his siblings – and a lot of their Catholic friends – had all become conservative Republicans.

"Yeah," Burke said, nodding. "What the hell is with that?" They both remembered a time when their parents, and most of the other Catholics they knew, were FDR and JFK Democrats who seemed interested in liberal social issues.

They laughed about the fact that John McCain had picked a venue in Dayton to announce the selection of Sarah Palin as his running mate. Getting back to baseball, they talked about the problems the Cincinnati Reds were having, and about the Dayton Dragons' amazing home game sellout record. At one point, Kenny took a call from one of his crew. Burke smiled when he noticed that Kenny's cell phone was even older than his own.

"Let's get out of here and go somewhere where we can really talk," Kenny said as they finished eating. He insisted on paying for lunch, and they stepped outside into the beautiful, late summer weather of upstate New York.

"Hell," Kenny said. "Let's just leave the truck here and walk up to the falls. It's just a couple of blocks. You feel like taking a little walk?"

Ithaca Falls was one of the largest and most spectacular waterfalls along Fall Creek. It dumped into Cayuga Lake from high above the town, where it bisected the Cornell campus, creating a cavernous, often treacherous gorge. A few road bridges crisscrossed the gorge, and Kenny explained that every so often a student leapt from one of the bridges, unable to handle the academic stress of attending the elite Ivy League school. The gorge had also swallowed "many a drunk, careless student."

Burke felt like a tourist, gawking away as Kenny led him to a small park at the bottom of the falls. They sat on a bench, and Kenny pointed up to the right. High on a hill, a tall, red brick smoke stack rose from the ground. *ITHACA GUNS* was spelled down the side of the chimney.

"That's all that's left of the old gun factory," Kenny said. "There's a plan to build some apartments up there, but the ground is still full of lead."

"I still see Ithaca Guns advertised in some of the supply books we get," said Burke.

"Yeah," said Kenny. "I think they moved out to Ohio somewhere."

Kenny pointed out that the water at this time of year was nothing compared to the spring, when a thunderous cascade would have made it impossible for them to talk where they were sitting. He leaned back against the bench.

"So, tell me, John. What have you found out about Father Nelson?"

Burke told Kenny pretty much the same thing he'd told the general – that he didn't have much information, and that McGowan's memory of that night long ago matched what Kenny had told him on the phone.

"You both said the same thing when I asked you about moving the piano," Burke said. "You both said 'from one side of the room to the other.'"

"Yeah. So?"

"You told me you hadn't spoken to Jim," said Burke. "I think maybe you had."

Kenny leaned back on the bench and rubbed his chin. Burke waited for a moment and then continued.

"I talked to Mrs. Spaulding, the housekeeper at the rectory back then. She said she didn't recall the piano being moved at all. Now, she may be an old lady, but I think she's still pretty sharp. She said she thinks she would have remembered that, and I believe her."

Kenny shifted his position on the bench, leaning forward and resting his forearms on his knees, his fingers interlocked, and looking down. Again, he said nothing.

"Another thing," Burke said, watching Kenny. "I'm pretty sure Father Nelson was a child molester. Abuser, pedophile, pervert — whatever you want to call it. Actually, he was even worse. He was a rapist."

Burke didn't expect Kenny to be surprised at this information, figuring McGowan had called him to let him know what Burke already knew. Kenny fidgeted, and continued looking at the ground. Burke thought maybe he was getting somewhere, that Kenny might not have the stomach for this.

"Did Father Nelson ever molest you, Kenny?" he asked.

Kenny leaned back and sighed. He stared at the falls for a moment, then turned his head and looked Burke in the eye. "Yeah. He did."

Burke looked away. *Maybe I don't have the stomach for this,* he thought.

Kenny took a deep breath, sighed again, took off his hat, and rubbed the back of his head. "He raped me twice. The second time, he promised he would never do it again. He never did."

"I'm sorry, Kenny," Burke said, shaking his head.

Kenny just shrugged. "Hell, it's really why I ended up here in Ithaca."

"What do you mean?" asked Burke.

"It's a long story, John. You sure you want to hear it?"

Burke checked his watch. "I've got about an hour and a half before you have to get me back to the airport. I'd love to hear it."

44

Satan's Choir

"After I graduated from high school, I couldn't wait to get the hell out of Dayton." Kenny gazed off toward the falls. "Twelve years of Catholic school, and I'd *had* it. Swore I'd never go back to school. Yes sir, I was a pretty fucked up kid."

"I didn't see you much after eighth grade," Burke remarked. "I don't know if you remember, but I went to Riverside."

"Nobody saw me much, really," said Kenny, shrugging. "When I was home, I pretty much stayed in my room and played the guitar. The only good thing about *that* is I got pretty damn good."

"Did you ever tell your parents what Father Nelson did to you?" Burke asked.

"Nobody," said Kenny, "I never told anybody. I wanted to quit the choir, but my folks wouldn't let me. I wanted to quit being an altar boy, but they wouldn't let me do that either. And they wouldn't let me go to Riverside. It was Catholic school all the way for me, baby."

"Did you think about it a lot?" asked Burke. "About Father Nelson?"

"It was *always* there. I got better at shutting it out as I got older, but it fucked me up pretty good." Kenny got up and walked a few feet to the bank of the creek.

"Do you know if Father Nelson ever molested Steve Heckman?" Burke asked.

"Steve never said, but I suspect he did. That night when we – well – no, he never said."

Damn! Burke had caught Kenny's hesitation. He let him go on.

"Steve and I were best friends once, but that just sort of petered out. We were both kind of loners in high school. Jim told me about Steve committing suicide. I guess he was kind of a drunk before that."

"So, what happened after high school?" Burke asked.

"I split," Kenny said. "I wanted to get as far from Dayton as I could get, so I ended up spending a year doing drugs and playing my guitar out in San Francisco. In August of '69 I hitched a ride to Woodstock. After that I landed in New York City."

"You were at Woodstock?"

"Yeah," said Kenny, laughing. "I *think*. I've been told I was there."

"Hell, I've never been to San Francisco *or* New York City," Burke said, remembering again how little of the world he had seen.

"Lived in the city for twenty years, man. Can you believe it?" said Kenny. "*Twenty fuckin' years*! And I did all right – played in some good rock and roll bands. Eventually, I was playing mostly jazz. I went on the road a few times, but mostly stayed on the East coast. Even did a little studio work for a while."

"Are you married?" asked Burke.

"Was," Kenny said. "Twice. Neither one worked out. No kids either. How about you?"

"Still married to my first wife – almost forty years. But we don't live under the same roof." Burke shrugged. "She's still my best friend, though."

"Wow! Good for you, man!" Kenny said, smiling. "Any kids?"

"One son. He's on the homicide squad with me."

For a few moments the two men sat staring at the water pouring over the falls, lost in their own thoughts.

"I was pretty fucked up most of those years in the city," said Kenny, breaking the silence. "I guess it was a good thing I didn't have any kids."

"Fucked up how?"

"Oh, drugs and alcohol. I was pretty much addicted to both – cocaine mostly. A little heroin for a while, but I couldn't play music when I was doing that shit. I snorted cocaine for years, but then when crack showed up – around '85 or '86 I guess it was – things really started going downhill. I got into it pretty heavy, and then I was *totally* fucked. Couldn't play, couldn't pay the rent, barely ate. I drank whatever I could get, and smoked crack, that was about it. Had to sell my guitars. Blew through all my money. I had this great little rent-controlled apartment and I couldn't keep up. They were trying to evict me."

"Jesus, Kenny," said Burke. "So, when did you turn it around?"

"Well, that's all part of how I got to Ithaca. It was weird. It was the middle of February, 1990, I think, and one day I picked up a *New York Times* that somebody left on a train. The first thing I read was a story about this priest that ran Covenant House – a big Catholic home in the city for runaway kids. Anyway, this priest was being accused of sex abuse by some former residents. It was a huge scandal. So, there in the paper it mentioned this group of shrinks in Ithaca, New York. They'd treated one of the guys that was abused and were somehow involved in the court case. And, BAM! Something just clicked. It was like a sign from God. Or the universe. Whatever. The next day I was on a bus to Ithaca, and I never looked back."

"And you found the shrinks?" asked Burke.

"Yeah, and they pretty much saved my life. They got me into rehab, they got me into AA, and they found me a job working for a contractor they knew. I started therapy, and they got me to open up about Father Nelson. It was the first time in my life I ever told anybody about it. I'm still in a support group they started for abuse victims. Actually, I help run the group now."

"Did the shrinks ever inform anybody about Father Nelson?" Burke asked.

"Nope. They left that totally up to me," said Kenny. "I chose not to do anything. I didn't want to go public with it and then have to deal with whatever happened. I figured he was dead, so what was the point."

"You figured he was dead?" asked Burke, pausing, "or you *knew* he was dead?"

Kenny turned and looked at Burke. After a moment, he smiled and shook his head. "I *figured* he was dead."

Burke let it go. They sat in silence, staring at the falls. Burke couldn't imagine the life Kenny had led.

"Do you still think about Father Nelson? What he did to you?" Burke asked.

"Sure, I do," said Kenny. "But it's okay now when I do." He leaned back on the bench and stretched his legs out in front of him. He was smiling, still staring at the falls. "Man, that son of a bitch had a beautiful voice, didn't he? Like Bing Crosby or Sinatra . . . Andy Williams . . . Perry Como . . . any of those guys."

"Yeah," said Burke, picking up a twig. "He could sing."

"Satan's choir," said Kenny, wistfully. "I remember that's what he used to call us when we fucked up, or if we got to horsing around during choir practice."

Neither man spoke after that. They just stared at the falls. Burke figured he wasn't going to get any more information out of Kenny regarding the disappearance of Father Nelson, but he took one last shot.

"So, Kenny, there's nothing else you want to tell me about that night?" he asked, tossing the twig toward the creek.

Kenny shifted on the bench, sitting up and taking a deep breath. He took his cap off, rubbed the back of his head, and put the cap back on.

"Tell me something, John," he said, looking at Burke. "Did you ever swear to something, or make a promise, like a vow, or an oath. Like a solemn oath?"

Burke thought for a second before he answered, wondering where Kenny was going with this.

"Well, sure I have," Burke said. "I pledged something when I graduated from the police academy. And I've given sworn testimony in court. My marriage vows – *that* was solemn."

"And did you keep your word?" Kenny asked. "Have you honored all of those promises?"

"Well, yeah," Burke said, thinking about it. "I guess I have. I've always tried to."

Kenny looked away, staring at the water. He leaned forward and rested his elbows on his knees. He flexed his hands and rubbed at the calluses. It was the first time Burke noticed that the tip of Kenny's right index finger was missing, down to the joint.

"I broke probably every goddam promise I ever made in my life," Kenny said. "All except for one."

He turned his head and looked at Burke, and Burke didn't know whether Kenny expected him to respond. He sensed it wasn't necessary, so he didn't. Kenny leaned back.

"I've got a pretty good life here, John," he said. "My conscience is clear. I've got my own contracting company. I've made some really good friends, and I have a girlfriend who puts up with my shit. I'm doing all right. Hell, I even bought a damn guitar and started playing again. I don't want anything to fuck this up."

Burke stood up slowly and looked down at Kenny. *Nor do I, my brother,* he thought. *Nor do I.*

"What happened to your finger?"

"Table saw," said Kenny, looking down at his hand. "I'm lucky it was my right hand. I can still hold a pick."

He played a little air guitar and laughed.

45

Capable of Murder

When it was time to go, Kenny insisted on accompanying Burke into the airport terminal. While Burke stood in line to check in, he watched Kenny inspecting one of the glass display cases spread throughout the building. Kenny was relaxed and smiling, hands in his pockets, leaning in to get a better look at whatever was in the display case. *He's comfortable in his own skin,* Burke thought. *He's had a rough ride and somehow managed to stay in the saddle.*

When it was time for Burke to go through the airport scanner, the two men shook hands, and Burke surprised himself by pulling Kenny in for a hug. He watched his old classmate walk away, and his gut told him that this man was not a murderer.

As the plane banked and headed south out of Ithaca, Burke looked to the west where he could clearly see three or four of the larger Finger Lakes stretching north. It was a quick flight to Philly, and then a long layover. He decided to make the most of it by killing time in an airport restaurant, eating crab cakes, drinking two pints of O'Reilly's stout, and watching the beginning of the Reds game against the Phillies.

The flight from Philadelphia landed on time in Dayton, and by 11:00 Burke was driving south on I-75 back into town. He turned on the car radio and learned that the Reds had just lost again, swept by the Phillies. *Poor Kenny,* Burke thought. *He'll never hear the end of that from the owner of the Lincoln Street Diner.*

Back in his apartment, Burke was exhausted from the long day. But more than that, he felt frustrated. He wasn't sure what to do next.

He didn't think Kenny – or Jim McGowan – would ever break whatever vow they had apparently made, but he was convinced that Father Nelson's death came down to his two old classmates.

There *was* a body, or what was left of it. There was no weapon. There were no witnesses – maybe Jim and Kenny, but they weren't talking. Was there a motive? Jim McGowan said he hadn't been molested by the priest. Kenny, on the other hand, had been raped.

Burke knew he didn't have enough to book the men on suspicion of homicide, and he didn't really think either man was a murderer. Although history had shown that someone as young as thirteen or fourteen was certainly capable of murder, Burke trusted his intuition. But whatever had happened to Father Nelson on that night back in November of 1963 still needed an explanation, and Burke wanted to know what it was.

Sipping the last of a glass of Jack Daniels, Burke decided that tomorrow he would talk to the county prosecutor. It might be his last chance.

46

The Prosecutor

On Wednesday morning, Burke arrived in the squad room just as the shift was changing. Tarisa, Renzi, Danny, Jamal, and Kevin were all there. Pete and Bones were off the clock. Despite the frustration Burke was feeling about the Father Nelson case, he'd had a good night's sleep and greeted the squad with a smile on his face. Burke's new demeanor over the past few days had been raising some eyebrows in the squad room.

Kevin and Burke looked over two days' worth of reports and paperwork. Burke checked in with Major Winston, turned in some supply requests and returned to his desk. He turned on his computer and read several Google Alerts that had come in regarding the Catholic sex abuse scandal. Day after day the stories poured in from around the world, and Burke could only shake his head and wonder if it would ever end.

He checked his watch and called Clifford Wolfe, the prosecuting attorney for Montgomery County. Wolfe was an old friend, about the same age as Burke, and they'd met years before when Wolfe was in private practice and defended a man Burke had busted. Their wives liked each other, and the two couples would play an occasional round of golf. At least once a summer they got together for a meal and a Dragons' game. Like Burke, Wolfe was a lifelong Democrat and had been raised Catholic. He'd gone to high school at Chaminade, once an all-boys Catholic school located in downtown Dayton.

"Morning, Cliff. John Burke here."

"J. B.!" said the prosecutor. "Your ears must be burning. We were just talking about you. Wondering how you were making out with the Father Nelson case. Major Winston's been keeping me up to date a little bit."

"Yeah, so you probably know it's a lot of dead ends so far," said Burke. "But I've got a few questions I want to run by you – *informally*, if you know what I mean. What are you doing for lunch?"

"No plan right now," Wolfe said. "I'm all yours."

"Great," said Burke. "How about we get a sandwich at Lucky's, say 12:30?"

"I'll see you there."

Back at his computer, Burke searched several Ohio criminal law sites. He knew there was no statute of limitation in Ohio for the prosecution of aggravated murder, but he couldn't remember the limitations for other types of homicide, like voluntary or involuntary manslaughter. He was curious about when the statute clock started for these types of crimes. Was it when the crime was committed, or when the crime was detected? He wondered whether a man could be prosecuted as an adult for a crime he committed as a boy. Burke found a few of the answers he was looking for, but some of the information was confusing, and none of it made him happy.

At 12:25, Burke headed to Lucky's. Wolfe had already walked there from the courthouse, and was sitting at the back table sipping coffee. The radio was set to the oldies station, and The Bobby Fuller Four's "I Fought the Law" was blaring through the restaurant. Burke smiled. He poked his head into the kitchen to say hello, and Lucky was surprised when Burke didn't ask him to turn down the volume; he turned it down anyway. The prosecutor stood up to greet Burke, and after they'd asked about each other's wives, they sat down and ordered Rueben sandwiches.

"So," began Burke, smiling, "I have some hypothetical questions for you about a hypothetical case."

"Hypothetical?" Wolfe's eyebrows arched.

"Yeah. And confidential."

"Hypothetical and confidential," the prosecutor said, rubbing his chin. "Got it."

"So, tell me this, Cliff. What would happen if two grown men — successful, law-abiding men, well thought of in their community — should come forth, *voluntarily*, and admit to a crime they had committed when they were teenagers?"

"Well, now that would depend on a lot of things, some of which I'm sure you are well aware of," said the prosecutor. "First of all, how serious a crime?"

"Murder, say," said Burke, "or aggravated murder. I do know there's no statute of limitation on either of those."

"You're right," Wolfe said. "And it's twenty years for manslaughter or voluntary manslaughter."

"You just answered my next question."

"So, are we talking about one of those, perhaps? If we are, then time would be on the side of these two men."

"I'm guessing that would more likely be the case," Burke said.

"Actually, let me think about this," said Wolfe. "If this hypothetical crime wasn't discovered until *now*, and if the corpus delecti wasn't discovered until *now*, almost fifty years later, the clock wouldn't start *ticking* until now. And there *is* corpus delecti in this hypothetical case, correct?"

"Let's just say there is," said Burke. "Let's say the hypothetical body belonged to a man who was now known to have been a serial rapist, an abuser of children. Let's say the homicide was more likely committed accidentally, or even on purpose to stop the rapist from raping again. Let's say one of these men had been raped by the . . . by the abuser."

"Well, an accident is one thing," said the prosecutor. "But killing a rapist to stop them from doing it again? It's still murder, J.B. If these kids had been abused repeatedly, I guess something like the *battered wife syndrome* could be a defense in court. It would create some sympathy, no doubt."

"And what if that *was* their story?" asked Burke.

"That would actually be up to you, J.B. You know, business as usual. You'd bring everything you had to me, and if I was a hard-ass, and I wanted to go after these guys, I'd have to decide if there was enough to take it to the grand jury."

"What if they didn't turn themselves in? What if I *brought* them in, on suspicion? What if they refused to talk?"

"Well, if I subpoenaed them to the grand jury and they wouldn't testify, I could ask a judge to hold them in contempt, and stick them in jail until they talked," said Wolfe. "For a while anyway. But a judge wouldn't put them in jail just for taking the fifth – only if they refused to testify about someone else's crime. It could get touchy. If I went ahead and charged them, and they pleaded not guilty, there would have to be a trial."

"What about trying them as juveniles?" Burke asked. "Why wouldn't they be tried as juveniles if they'd been teenagers when the crime was committed? Jesus, can you imagine sticking sixty-year-old men into a goddamn delinquent youth facility?"

"Good point," the prosecutor laughed. "But you're wrong about charging them as juveniles. That law changed a long time ago. Under the present statute, they would be tried as adults."

Burke had been hoping for a carrot. Something, *anything* that he could hold out in front of Jim McGowan and Kenny Mason, to soften them up so they would talk about what happened on that night long ago. Burke stared into the dregs of his coffee and sighed. The prosecutor could see that he hadn't been able to give Burke what he wanted.

"Listen, J. B.," he said. "We've known each other for a long time. You *know* I'm not a hard-ass. If these guys came forward, on their own, and told their story, I'd listen. If it turns out I believe this 'hypothetical' homicide was an accident, then there's no crime, no indictment. Or let's say what they did was even somewhat justified, and we all found the story to be believable. I would more than likely be very sympathetic. Throw in the fact that it happened when they were kids, and the fact that the 'hypothetical' victim was a known child abuser and a *rapist*. How likely is it I would prosecute that?" Burke looked up and smiled.

"Does this 'hypothetical' victim have any relatives?" Wolfe asked. Burke shrugged. "None that we can find."

"So, no one clamoring for justice. And, just for grins, let's say this 'hypothetical' victim was not only a known rapist, but ..." Wolfe leaned in and whispered, holding a finger to his lips, "...a *Catholic priest!* Hell, with what's going on in the Church these days, all the uproar around the world about the sex abuse – how could I even *think* about prosecuting these men? And don't forget, J.B., I get *voted* into this office. I got voted in the first time in 1996, and every four years since then I've been lucky enough to get re-elected. If I chose to prosecute these men, these nice teenage boys who'd put some awful pedophile out of commission, my ass would be on the street come next November. That's if I don't retire first." The prosecutor winked.

Burke was more than happy to pay for the lunches, and the two men parted company in front of the courthouse with a warm handshake.

"Hypothetical," said Wolf, with another wink. "*And* confidential."

"You are definitely the man, Clifford," Burke said.

47

Arnold's

Kevin was alone in the squad room when Burke returned from lunch. Several files were open on his desk, and he was typing on his computer keyboard. Burke certainly wasn't going to miss the paperwork part of the job when he retired in October, and he was glad that Kevin was handling most of it for him already. Kevin would be promoted to captain when he took over the squad room, and he would get a nice pay increase. Burke was proud of his son and knew he would do a great job running the squad.

Burke had no sooner settled in at his desk when the squad room phone rang. Kevin took the call. "It's for you, Pop," he said. "Father Stankowski from the archbishop's office."

Burke picked up. "Hello, Father," he said. "It's good to hear from you. How are you feeling?"

"Hello, Captain Burke," the priest said in a tired voice. "I'm not so well, actually. But I was wondering if we could get together again, today if at all possible. It's quite important that I see you very soon."

Burke wondered what was up, and looked at the clock. He'd been thinking about giving Jim McGowan a call and setting up another visit with him, but that could wait.

"Sure, Father," said Burke. "I could be at your office by three o'clock."

"Thank you, Captain. I would rather we didn't meet at my office, however. There's a bar just down the street. It's called Arnold's. It happens to be right next to the building that houses our archives – that's where I am right now. Do you know Arnold's?"

Burke *did* know the place. Arnold's Bar and Grill was the oldest bar in Cincinnati, and a bit of a destination. He and Maggie had gone there once or twice for dinner on their way to a Red's game. There'd been something in the news recently about a Hollywood film crew shooting scenes at the bar for a new TV show to be set in Cincinnati.

"I know it," said Burke. "I'll be there by three – if the highway construction isn't too bad."

"That's perfect. Lunch will be over by then, and there's a good chance the courtyard in back will be fairly empty. We can talk there," said the priest. "And one more thing, Captain Burke. You mentioned a reporter the last time you were here – the one who wrote about Father Nelson."

"Yes," Burke said, "Lisa Fowler."

"Can you tell me about her?" Father Stankowski asked. "Is she honest and trustworthy – intelligent – a decent human being?"

"From what I know of her, she's all of those things. She's also a very good journalist."

"And she writes for the *Dayton Daily News,* you said?"

"Yes, she's probably their top investigative reporter. She's been a staff writer there for a long time."

Father Stankowski began to cough, and Burke could picture him, holding the phone away from his mouth.

"Excuse me," the priest said finally. "Tell me, do you know if she's a Catholic?"

"I don't believe she is, Father," Burke said.

"Oh well, it doesn't matter, I was just curious. And it's Lisa Fowler. F-O-W-L-E-R. Is that correct?"

"That's it," said Burke.

"Okay," said the priest. "Thanks. I'll see you at three o'clock in Arnold's."

* * *

Right then, Lisa Fowler was at her desk in the newsroom, working on a story about the family of the brother and sister who had been shot on Keowee Street. The investigation was ongoing, but so far no one had been arrested. Her computer alerted her to a new email, and as she was saving her work she looked up and saw the managing editor, jacket and backpack in hand, rush out of his office and through the newsroom, headed for the stairway exit.

Lisa opened the new email. It had come from the managing editor who'd just hurried off.

"*Fuck!*" someone said loudly, from a desk across the room.

Lisa looked up to see who had spoken, and then looked back at the new email. It had been copied to the entire staff from the fleeing editor. *I regret to inform you . . .*

"Goddammit!" someone else called out.

Lisa read on. The *Dayton Daily News* was going to be sold to the Gannett Newspaper Group after the first of the year. The offices and staff would be relocated to a new, currently unknown location, and there would most certainly be a number of staff cuts. The managing editor was "extremely sorry" to be the bearer of this news, and he would let them know as soon as he was given more information regarding the sale.

Lisa closed her laptop and scowled at the exit where the editor had fled. "Chicken shit," she said. "Goddamn chicken shit." She put her head in her arms on top of the laptop, and started to cry.

48

A Greater Sin

Burke couldn't imagine what Father Stankowski wanted to talk to him about, but the priest's voice had sounded almost desperate. And what was all that about Lisa Fowler? Burke told Kevin he wasn't sure when he would be back, and hurried to his car. Once on the road, there were just a few short delays along I-75, and he drove as fast as he dared. When he got into downtown Cincy, Burke got lucky and found a parking spot right across the street from the bar. He walked into Arnold's at exactly three o'clock.

Burke waited inside the door for a moment until his eyes had adjusted to the darkness of the barroom. Two young waitresses stood at the near end of the bar, on the left, folding tableware into cloth napkins and chatting with the bartender. One of them asked Burke if he would be dining, and he told her he was meeting someone in the courtyard. He walked the length of the bar and turned left into a narrow dining area filled with high-backed wooden booths. The walls and the floor of the bar and the dining area were all red brick. Burke felt slightly claustrophobic in the darkness.

The courtyard, just off the far end of the dining room, was more to his liking – still a lot of brick, but open to the sky, and with a live tree growing in the middle, overhanging the wrought iron tables and chairs scattered around. There were windows high up on two of the brick walls, and a roofed-over stage in one corner built to resemble an old front porch. The sun was low enough in the sky that the high walls shaded the courtyard completely. No one was there.

Burke walked back to the bar and sat down on a stool to wait for Father Stankowski. He was debating whether or not to order a beer when someone tapped on his shoulder. Turning around, he was surprised to see Father Trevor Williams, Father Stankowski's young assistant. The priest greeted Burke and led him back to the courtyard. Burke wondered how he had missed the priest coming into the bar.

The older priest was sitting at a table under the tree, wearing black pants and shirt, a white collar and a black jacket. There was a cardboard file box tied up with twine sitting on a chair next to the priest. A walking cane was hooked over the back of the same chair. Father Stankowski greeted Burke warmly. The old priest did not look well. He was shrunken and his skin looked yellower than before.

His assistant disappeared hurriedly through a door in the brick wall on the right, and returned a minute later carrying another file box, also done up with twine. He set it down on the table next to the old priest. Father Stankowski said something in a language that Burke couldn't quite make out. Father Williams smiled, responded in what sounded like the same language, waved, and disappeared again.

"Was that *Latin*?" Burke asked.

"Yes, it was." Father Stankowski smiled. "When Trevor came on board, it was discovered that we'd both studied Latin in school, so we decided to try to keep our chops up. He's a bit better than I am. I'm actually quite rusty."

"So, what's this all about, Father?" Burke asked, quickly getting to the point, and motioning toward the boxes.

"Well, Captain," said the priest, "I've received some very unfortunate news regarding my health. You may recall from our last visit that I was about to go into the hospital for some testing. It took place last Friday, and that evening I was visited at my apartment by two doctors from the hospital – an oncologist and a cardiologist. They were quite candid and informed me that I was suffering from late-stage pancreatic cancer that has metastasized to my lungs and my liver. On top of that, the cardiologist said that my heart was a complete mess – major blockage everywhere – as bad as he had ever seen. He said it was a miracle I was still alive." Stankowski made the sign of the cross.

"Good Lord," Burke said, wincing. "I'm so sorry to hear this."

"It's not good," Father Stankowski said with a nod. "The oncologist said the cancer would probably kill me within a month, possibly sooner. The cardiologist said that my heart might get me first. However, he said there might be some steps he could take to reduce that chance."

"So, what are you going to do?" asked Burke.

"Nothing," said the priest. He smiled. "God and Mother Nature – I won't stand in the way of either one."

"I'm really sorry, Father," Burke said, shaking his head. "I don't know what to say."

"Say nothing," said the priest, suddenly straightening up in his chair. He patted the top of the file box closest to him. "Just thank me for what I am about to give you. Could you open this box for me, please?" Burke fumbled with the twine and removed the lid.

"After I received the diagnosis on Friday evening," Father Stankowski said, "I spent that night and most of Saturday morning in thought and prayer, seeking guidance, looking for an answer to one question and one question only. *What should I do with the time I have left?* I am aware that God chose a path for me long ago, and I have always believed that someday he would reveal to me the reason. My meeting you was part of the answer."

"I'm not sure I understand, Father," said Burke.

"Well, I now realize that the information I have failed to provide you with – concerning Father Nelson – is information that must be provided not only to you, and not only to all of the members of the Catholic Church, but to everyone – to the entire world. It sits there in the archives, rotting – festering away like the cancer in my own body. It's yellowed and stained and it's choking the life out of the Catholic Church."

The priest coughed several times into the crook of his arm, then went on.

"Short term, I think releasing this information may set the Church back a step. Long term, I think it can only help. Help to heal the wounds of the countless victims of sexual abuse not only here, but throughout the world."

Tears filled Father Stankowski's eyes but did not fall. Burke reached across the table and lightly patted one of the priest's thin hands.

"The book of John says it best, Captain. *And you shall know the truth, and the truth shall set you free.*"

He took his hand away from Burke's and wiped his nose with a handkerchief. "It also helps that my boss is still in Rome," he said, grinning. Burke laughed, and scooted his chair around the table to get closer.

"On Saturday afternoon, I had Trevor set me up with a copier in the archives. We . . . excuse me . . . *I* have been working on this ever since, trying to get it done before I take my last breath." He made the sign of the cross again, then pulled one of the files from the box and handed it to Burke.

"These are all copies that I made from the archives. As you can see, I've stamped every one with my personal seal. The originals remain in the archives. These folders here in the front hold documents concerning thirty or so clergy members from this diocese who have been publicly accused of sexual abuse – correspondence, police reports and court reports, records of civil sentencing, canonical sentencing and internal memos – even some mail correspondence."

Burke gazed at the box in disbelief.

"The thicker, more complete folders represent more recent cases. Most of the older files are smaller because much of the paperwork has been destroyed. Canon law stipulates that ten years after any Church punishment is handed down in a case, most of the documents pertaining to that case are to be destroyed, and only a summarized version of the information is kept. Same thing happens if the clergy member dies. Then most of his records are destroyed."

A waitress peeked in around the doorway from the dining room. A broad smile crossed her face when she saw the priest.

"Hi, Father Nick!' she said, waving. "Do you guys need anything?" The priest smiled and looked at Burke, who shook his head.

"No, we're fine, Peggy. Thanks."

Burke put on his reading glasses and quickly thumbed through the folder. It was probably twenty pages, all relating to just one case. He pulled out another folder and scanned a few pages randomly. There was a letter written on the archbishop's official stationery and signed by the archbishop concerning the reassignment of a priest to another parish, for "extraordinary reasons."

"Wow," Burke said, quietly.

"The rest of this box, and the other box, contain the files on 207 other cases that are *not* known to the general public, stretching back to around 1910. From what I've been told, a fire destroyed records previous to that. The bulk of these cases have occurred since around 1940. Unfortunately, I couldn't copy all the material in the files – it would have taken too long. I focused on what I thought were the most relevant documents. And again, many of these files are just case summaries. I've actually written quite a few of them myself. Father Nelson's file, by the way, is a mere summary. I believe you'll find it in the second box."

"*Two hundred and seven!*" gasped Burke, looking directly at Father Stankowski. The priest looked back at Burke, tears filling his eyes once more.

"I'm sorry," the priest said. He wiped his eyes, and the two men sat in silence until Burke spoke.

"Father, why are you giving this to *me?*" he asked.

"Because I firmly believe that is what God intended for me to do, Captain. This path I've taken – my journey – is clear as glass to me now. Maybe in the eyes of the Church I am sinning by giving you this material and by shirking my responsibility to the archbishop, but the archbishop is not my master."

He pointed toward the open sky above the tree. "*God* is my master, Captain Burke, and I will answer only to him. It would be a far greater sin if I died knowing what I know, not having tried to fix the damage that has been done."

If there is a God, Burke thought, *this is indeed a man of God.* "But, Father," he said with a shrug, turning his palms up. "What should I do with this stuff?"

"Well, not much really," said the priest, stopping to cough into his handkerchief. "I think I've figured out a way to keep you out of this, if that's what you want. All you have to do is deliver it."

"Deliver it to *who*?" Burke asked.

"To Miss Lisa Fowler," said the priest. "As a journalist, she may be very interested in the contents of these boxes. If she possesses the qualities that you have attested to, then I think she might be the perfect person to receive this . . . *stuff* . . . as you called it."

Father Stankowski reached into the breast pocket of his jacket and pulled out an envelope, and a sheet of paper which he handed to Burke. "Here's a copy of a letter I received this morning, just before I left my office," he said. "Please add it to the Father Nelson file if you would. I'd already tied up that box and didn't want to do it again."

Burke took the letter and gave it a quick glance. It bore a St. Nicholas Catholic Church letterhead and was signed by Father Phillip Metzger. It was a letter regarding the confessor who claimed to have been 'molested' by Father Nelson. Burke folded the letter and put it aside. "Will do," he said.

"And this one is from me," said the priest, glancing down at the envelope. "It's written on Archdiocese stationary and stamped with my seal. Basically, it states that being of *extremely* sound mind, and *eminently* clear of conscience, I am knowingly and purposefully breaking an oath of secrecy by giving the contents of these files, almost 1700 pages, regarding charges of sex abuse against members of the clergy in this diocese, to one Lisa Fowler, an employee of the *Dayton Daily News*. The letter also states that these pages were copied from the secret archives and personally stamped, and that I have done this without the knowledge of any other individual. The responsibility for this action is mine and mine alone."

Father Stankowski smiled, pretending to wipe his hands. "How's that, Captain?"

"Nicely done," said Burke, with a small bow toward the priest. He took the envelope and placed the two letters in the box, put the lid on, and retied the twine.

"And Father Williams doesn't know what's in the boxes?"

"I'll pretend I didn't hear that question, Captain Burke. But I will say that young Trevor and I are of like mind on most subjects," said the priest, smiling. "He'll be dealing with the fallout from this, but he's a big boy. He's also very smart, *and*, he had a very good teacher."

"What will you do now, Father?" asked Burke.

"Well, I reckon I'll just ride off into the sunset," Father Stankowski said with a grin, slouching back in his chair and talking like a cowboy. Burke realized that the priest was simply trying to lighten the moment.

"Actually, Captain Burke, when I head outta this here saloon, Trevor is driving me straight to a hospice facility. I reckon this is just about my last rodeo."

Suddenly, the priest grabbed the arms of the chair and sat up straight.

"Good Lord, Captain Burke! I almost forgot something. It's quite important. I meant to ask you not to turn these boxes over to Lisa Fowler until I'm gone." He crossed himself yet again. "Trevor will call and let you know. I gave him your card. Will you promise me that?"

"Absolutely," said Burke, nodding.

"I guess that's it then." Father Stankowski reached into his pants pocket and pulled out a cell phone. "I'll call Trevor now and let him know I'm ready to go,"

"I'll stay until he gets here," Burke offered.

"No, no, Captain. You should take the boxes and skedaddle on outta here," the priest said. "I'd like to just sit here by myself for a minute, maybe sip an ice-cold beer while I wait."

Burke half squatted and hugged the seated priest awkwardly. He thanked him, and told him he would never forget him. Father Stankowski dismissed the praise with a wave of his hand, and Burke stood up. He stacked one box on top of the other, said goodbye one more time, and headed out the way he'd come in.

"Captain Burke?" the priest called after him. Burke stopped and looked back. "Would you kindly ask one o' them purdy little waitresses to come in here?"

"You got it, pardner," Burke said, playing along. He supported the boxes with one hand, saluted the priest, and left him alone in the courtyard.

49

Make it Go Away

Leaving Arnold's, Burke carried the file boxes to his car. It was after four o'clock by the time he got back to Dayton, and Kevin, Marco, and Tarisa were in the squad room. Burke really wanted to talk to someone about his trip to Arnold's, but wasn't sure who that should be. He decided it would be better if he didn't share the information with anyone, not even Kevin. Not for now, anyway. He started to dial Maggie's number and stopped. *No, not even Maggie,* he decided.

Burke told Kevin he had some errands to run, left the squad room and drove straight to his apartment. He carried the file boxes in, opened a beer, and settled in on the couch. He cut the twine on the second box and started flipping through the files. Back at Arnold's, when he'd looked briefly at the material in the first box, he hadn't noticed how the files were arranged. Now he discovered they were in alphabetical order by last name, and he quickly found the file for Father Raymond T. Nelson. Burke could hardly believe what he was holding in his hands.

There were four pages in the file. They contained only a "mere summary" of the material that had once been included, and as Father Stankowski had explained, this paring down of the file would have been done years ago. There, at the top of the first page, was the information that Burke had already been given regarding Father Nelson's 1951 ordination, the date of the Church's last known contact with Father Nelson, and the vague, curiously worded entry regarding his death – *passed into the arms of Our Lord in November of 1963*. Again,

Burke realized that the time of death could have been entered anytime – when someone in the archbishop's office had decided that Father Nelson must be dead.

After that, the entries began. Father Nelson's first posting as an assistant pastor was at St. Patrick's parish in Hillsboro, Ohio, in July of 1951. The church pastor's name was noted. Also listed were the extracurricular activities in the parish in which Father Nelson had been involved – choir director, children's choir director, Holy Name Society director, and festival committee. After that there were four dated entries. Two were marked *Molest* (1) and two were marked *Molest* (2). Next to the first three of those entries was typed the word *Pastor*, and next to the last was typed the word *Parent*. At the end of each entry, in upper case, appeared *MOLLI. SUCC.*

In September of 1953, Nelson had been transferred to a parish in Barnesville, Ohio, where once again, choir director and children's choir director were listed among his activities. There were two *Molest* (1) listings and one *Molest* (2) spread over a period of two and a half years, all preceded by the word *pastor*, and *MOLLI. SUCC.*

Nelson moved next to Bellefontaine, Ohio, in March of 1956. Again, there were similar notations, but it was at this parish that the first *Molest* (3) appeared, followed by the word *alcohol*. Shortly after the date of this entry, Nelson was transferred again, this time to St. Joan of Arc parish in Toledo, and after that to St. Nick's in 1960, when Burke was ten years old. The St. Nick's entry listed two Molest (1)'s, four (Molest) (2)'s, and two Molest (3)'s.

Burke had to stop for a moment when he realized his hands were shaking. He took several deep breaths, a sip of beer, and continued to read.

In every parish, Father Nelson had directed a children's or a boys' choir. In every parish after 1956, *alcohol* appeared over and over. Molest (1), (2) or (3) also appeared again and again, in every parish, with more and more (2)'s and (3)'s as time went on. Burke noticed that sometime around 1955, the *MOLLI. SUCC.* designation had changed to *AMELIO. SUCC.*

He read a few more of the older summaries. They were similar to the Father Nelson file, but Burke was confused by the odd numbering and notations. *Was it abbreviated Latin?* The numbers never rose above three, never a four or a five, and Burke reasoned that the numbers following the word *molest* had nothing to do with the number of times the offense occurred, as he had first thought. Instead, he figured it must be some sort of rating system based on the severity of the incident. Maybe the *pastor* or *parent* notation referred to whoever brought the incident to the attention of the archbishop's office in the first place. The final Molest (3) notation in the St. Nick's entry was followed by the word *parent*. Burke thought of Mike Donnelly and little Timmy.

He ordered a pizza and opened another beer. *MOLLI. SUCC.* and *AMELIO. SUCC.* really had him stumped, and Burke wondered again if they were some sort of arcane Latin references. He wished he'd spent a little more time looking at the files and asking questions at Arnold's. He thought about trying to reach Father Stankowski, but quickly decided against it. The poor man deserved to be left alone.

The pizza arrived and Burke opened another beer. He took out some of the more current case files and found page after page of internal Church correspondence related to the transferring of abusive clergy members. The rating system had disappeared, and in these later files the details of the accusations were spelled out graphically. Throughout the letters and the memos, Burke was shocked by what seemed to be a lack of remorse on the part of the Church. The general attitude in almost everything he read was clear – *how do we make it go away? How do we shut them up?* In one random letter, the word *amelioration* came up several times, and something suddenly clicked for Burke.

"Jesus!" he said out loud. "That's it!" *Amelio* was short for *amelioration!* Could *molli* mean *mollified,* or *mollification?* They were almost interchangeable. Burke couldn't believe he hadn't figured it out sooner. But what about *succ?* Maybe it stood for success, or succeeded or successful, as in *mollification successful.* He took a sip of beer. Either way, he thought, it all came down to the same thing. *How do we make it go away?*

Stopping occasionally for a bite of pizza, Burke perused the files. He realized that the abusive clergy members were being passed back and forth among the six dioceses in Ohio, traded around like major league baseball players. Offenders – including some nuns – were almost always sent to another diocese, and occasionally there was an out-of-state swap. The church implored and cajoled, and money was paid. *Lots* of money.

On a positive note, Burke noted that the Church *had* attempted to remove many abusers from positions that put them in contact with children, especially in the more recent cases. He was curious, and looked to see if there was a file for the former archbishop, the one who had become a cardinal. Sure enough, there was.

Around ten o'clock, halfway through his fifth beer, Burke went to sleep on the couch. He awoke a while later, put the leftover pizza in the refrigerator, and crawled into bed with a whopping headache. Tomorrow was Friday, and he would call Jim McGowan.

50

Just a Goddamn Kid

After a troubled, fitful night of sleep, it was cold pizza and a pot of hot coffee that got Burke going the next morning. He looked through a few more of the files while he ate the pizza, and then showered. Once he was dressed, he reread the letter written by Father Stankowski – *his confession.* Smiling, Burke put the letter on top in one of the boxes. He taped the lids on with packing tape, carried the boxes down to his car, and locked them in the trunk.

Burke got to the squad room a little late. Kevin, Pete, and Bones were there, making follow-up calls and dealing with the death of a young woman who had fallen, jumped, or been pushed from a seventh story window of her apartment. Danny and Jamal had responded to the scene, and had called Kevin in the middle of the night. Kevin had been up since three o'clock and had sent Danny and Jamal home at the end of their shift. Apparently, the body at the scene had been in pretty rough shape, and Kevin was in a dismal mood. Burke knew his son was dead tired, and he was proud of the way Kevin was keeping it together.

Burke spent an hour working through the routine paperwork that Kevin asked him to help with. He talked to Tarisa and Marco when they came in, about the reports that Danny and Jamal had written, and made some suggestions regarding follow-up. A person of interest – the boyfriend – was called in for further questioning, and Burke sat in on the interview. At eleven o'clock he sent Kevin home to get some sleep, and then called and made a dinner date with Maggie.

When he got off the phone, Burke took the Impala case file from the locked drawer and spread everything he had across the top of the desk. He made some additional notes about the conversations he'd had with Kenny Mason in Ithaca, and with Clifford Wolfe, the county prosecutor. Based on those conversations and his meeting with Father Stankowski the day before, Burke planned his next meeting with Jim McGowan. When he called him, the general agreed, somewhat reluctantly, to meet with Burke at his house in Beavercreek at two o'clock.

Burke got a sandwich at Lucky's for lunch, and with time to kill before his meeting with McGowan, decided to drive out to Eastwood Lake. Just that morning, he'd wanted to kick himself when he realized he had neglected to ask either Jim or Kenny about the old swimming hole. At the very beginning of the investigation, the connection between "POSITIVELY NO" and the discovery of the Impala had seemed merely coincidental – just a serendipitous jog of an old, pleasant memory. Maybe now it deserved a second look.

He drove to the lake and parked in the lot, just above the spot where Father Nelson's Impala had been craned out. Walking down the slope to the edge of the lake, he looked around. The area was very different now than it had been nearly fifty years ago, and he tried to remember the lay of the land back then – the privacy from passing cars, the chained-off access lane into the area, the trees and the scrub. *How in the hell had it happened?* Burke shook his head. *Did three young boys actually pull this off?* The conundrum was driving him nuts. He had to know, and he decided he would ask Jim straight out.

At two o'clock, when Burke pulled into McGowan's driveway, all three garage doors were again open; the Subaru was gone. *Good*, he thought, *Kathy's not around*. Jim met him at the door and led him back to the study. He sat down behind his desk, and Burke took the easy chair across from him.

"I talked to Kenny," Burke began. "I flew out to Ithaca earlier this week and we spent a few hours together."

"Kenny called me," said McGowan. Burke was only a little surprised that McGowan admitted talking to Kenny.

"We had a nice talk," said Burke. "He's had a rough time. Seems like he's pretty much got it back on track now."

"He's doing all right," McGowan said. "Did you meet his girlfriend?"

"No, she was working."

"She's a real sweetheart," said the General.

"Look, Jim," said Burke, getting to the point. "Kenny told me he was raped by Father Nelson. Twice. He said it fucked him up for a long time. I asked if Steve Heckman had been raped and he said he didn't know, but he thinks he probably was. He said they never talked about it, but I think it happened to Steve, too."

McGowan gazed out the window, not speaking.

"Out in the trunk of my car is a file on Father Nelson that I got yesterday from a priest in the archbishop's office in Cincinnati," Burke continued. "Hard evidence from the Church that Father Nelson was a known abuser. He raped boys, Jim. Maybe a lot of boys. He raped Kenny, and he may have raped Steve, and I think all of this has something to do with why the sonofabitch was killed."

McGowan continued staring out the window, almost as if he wasn't listening to a word Burke was saying.

Burke tried a new tack. "Do you remember the swimming hole out at the gravel pit, across from the base? We called it "POSITIVELY NO" because part of the sign was missing. Do you remember that? I'm pretty sure I saw you there once or twice."

No response.

"Goddammit, Jim," Burke said. "Talk to me! I know you're not telling me the truth. I knew it the first time we talked. You think you're the first person who ever lied to me?"

McGowan's jaw clenched. He stood up and walked to the window, cranked it open, and sat back down in the chair. He looked at Burke.

"I told you everything that I'm going to tell you," he said flatly.

Burke fixed the General with a hard stare. "Did you make a goddamn vow, too?" he asked. "Like Kenny?"

McGowan half grinned. "Kenny told me he sort of mentioned that to you."

Burke's eyebrows arched. "Do you think this is *funny*, Jim?"

"No, I don't think it's funny at all," the general snapped, looking fiercely at Burke. "But you're wasting your time, John. Forget it."

They stared at each other, McGowan swiveling from side to side in his chair, hoping that Burke would just throw up his hands in frustration and leave.

But now it was Burke's turn to lie.

"Look, Jim, nobody knows about you and Kenny and Steve. I'm the only one. I have the only copy of Bigelow's missing persons report. It's the only thing connecting you guys to Father Nelson, and nobody has seen it. Nobody."

McGowan sighed and shook his head. The swiveling began to irritate Burke.

"I talked to the county prosecutor," Burke went on. "He's a close friend of mine. He's a good man and he's fair. I explained the whole situation to him. I laid it out, everything but your names. He knows all about Father Nelson's past, and about the abuse. He knows it's been almost fifty years and that you were just kids when it happened. He knows that people are getting fed up with the Catholic Church. He knows that nobody gives a rat's ass about Father Nelson, and that nobody's going to be screaming for your neck."

Burke detected what he thought was a glimmer of interest in McGowan's eyes. He'd stopped swiveling, and folded his hands in his lap.

"He more or less guaranteed me he would never prosecute," Burke continued. "He said he'd probably be voted out of office if he went after you guys, even if it turned out to be murder or aggravated murder. If it *was* murder, then we all know the sonofabitch had it coming, and I'd bet my life that you guys only did what you had to do."

McGowan let Burke finish. He sighed, got up and walked to the same window he'd just opened, cranked it closed and sat down again.

"Listen, John," he said. "I can't tell you anything more. But I really, *truly* appreciate your coming to bat for us. Please understand that. I mean it with all my heart."

Burke sat back in the chair. *I can't believe it*, he thought. *I can't believe this fucking guy won't talk to me!*

"Okay, Jim, now listen to me," he said quietly. "This case has gotten very personal for me – something I've never, *ever*, let happen before. I feel like I'm drowning – like I'm going to die if I don't find out what the hell happened to that sonofabitch. If you tell me now, I promise you it will never leave this room. It'll be between you and me, Jim. Just you and me. I'll end the investigation and I'll destroy Bigelow's report. I'll *shred* the goddamn thing. Please, Jim, I'm *begging* you."

Burke was close to tears. McGowan spun around in the chair, turning his back to Burke, and neither man spoke for almost a full minute. Over his shoulder, the general could hear Burke get up from the chair and walk to the corner of the room.

Burke picked up the putter that leaned against a wall, and softly tapped a golf ball across the carpet. Then another. Then one more.

"I'm sorry, John, I really am." McGowan said. "But I made a vow."

And Burke finally broke.

"*GODDAMMIT!*" He raised the putter and smashed it down with all of his might, snapping it in half over the back of the chair he'd been sitting in. McGowan spun back around to face him. "*That goddamn sonofabitch raped me, Jim*," screamed Burke. "*Me, goddammit! He fucked me! He stuck his goddamn cock in my goddamn ass and he fucked me!*"

The General had faced plenty of angry men over the course of his military career, but this anger topped anything he had ever seen. Burke's face was crimson, his eyes bulged, and spit flew from his mouth. He dropped the destroyed putter and leaned across the desk, gulping for air and half choking. He was pounding his fist, and tears of rage welled up in his eyes.

". . . he . . . he . . . he . . ." Burke spluttered, trying to catch his breath.

And then he stopped.

He stopped just as quickly as he had exploded. Slowly, he straightened up, wiping his mouth with the back of his arm. He pressed the palms of his hands into his eyes, then collapsed back into the chair.

When McGowan recovered from the shock of Burke's explosion, he pulled several tissues from a box on a shelf behind him. He leaned across the desk and gave them to Burke. Burke blew his nose loudly and wiped his eyes again. The general sat back, letting out a long, deep sigh.

Burke's breathing slowed. He stared at the floor in front of him. For half a minute neither man spoke.

"Jesus, Jim," Burke said softly, breaking the silence. "I'm sorry."

"It's okay," said McGowan. "I'm sorry, too. I didn't know."

When Burke looked up, tears were falling from his eyes. "*Nobody* knows," he said. "I never told anyone. Not my parents. Not even Maggie."

Jim moved the tissue box to the desk, and Burke wiped his eyes and blew his nose one more time. McGowan got up and left the room. A minute later he came back and handed Burke a glass of water. Burke drank it quickly, wiped his mouth, and set the glass down.

"I wanted to kill him," Burke said, looking down, his voice hoarse now. "I was twelve years old. Twelve fucking years old, and I wanted to kill the man. I thought something was wrong with me because it was all I could think about. I thought about how I would do it. I *dreamed* about doing it. I knew that if he ever touched me again, I would kill him. But the sonofabitch never did, thank God. He avoided me, almost like he knew. I was glad when he disappeared. I *hoped* he was dead."

"I'm sorry, John," McGowan said. "I don't know what else to say. It's terrible."

"I was just a goddamn kid," Burke said. "All I wanted to do was sing in that choir." He wiped his eyes again. The two men sat quietly, and McGowan waited for Burke to continue.

"I don't know which haunted me more – getting raped, or wanting to kill Father Nelson." Burke looked up at McGowan. "Did you ever want to kill someone, Jim? I mean, have you ever hated a man so much that you could have killed him?"

McGowan sighed and closed his eyes. "No," he said. After several seconds his eyes opened and he looked back at Burke. "But I killed Father Nelson."

Burke stared at McGowan.

"You deserve to know," said the general.

51

Riverside, Ohio: November 21, 1963

Father Nelson had his eye on the McGowan boy. He seemed older, and more physically mature than the other eighth graders. There was certainly more definition in his arm muscles. He was almost a man, Father Nelson thought, but still a boy.

"All right," he said loudly, as the choir came to the end of *Adeste Fidelis.* "That's enough for tonight."

The choir was rehearsing in the church for the annual Christmas school concert. They would also be singing for the midnight Mass at St. Nick's, and as part of a combined choir in an upcoming performance downtown at Memorial Hall.

"Please pass the song books to the front," the priest said. "Mr. McGowan, would you please stay and help carry the books back to the rectory? And I'll open the gym for an hour if anyone wants to shoot some baskets."

This was something Father Nelson did every week. The boys looked forward to it and considered it a privilege. Most of them stayed after – shooting baskets, shouting, horsing around, and roaming the dark halls of the school with no adults about to rein them in.

Jim McGowan loaded the books into the boxes as they were passed up, and Kenny Mason handed him a stack. Steve Heckman was at Kenny's side, as usual. The boys were best friends and had befriended Jim when he moved to St. Nick's parish from Texas, earlier that year.

"See you in the gym," Kenny said, handing the books to Jim.

"Dipshit," Steve added, out of the side of his mouth.

Jim raised a book like he was going to hit Steve, and the two friends ducked away, laughing.

After turning off the church lights and locking the door behind him, Father Nelson told Jim he would meet him at the front door of the rectory, after he opened the gym and turned on the lights for the other boys.

It was a cold night and already dark. Jim waited for the priest on the stoop at the front of the rectory, right next door to the church. There were no lights on inside, and he thought that the pastor, Father Krueger, must not be home. Jim knew that Mrs. Spaulding, the housekeeper, had her own house nearby. He'd never set foot inside the rectory, and he was curious about what it would be like.

Father Nelson joined him on the stoop and unlocked the rectory door. The priest explained that Father Krueger spent every Thursday night at his elderly mother's house in Piqua. He turned on some lights and told Jim to put the books down on a bench in the entryway, then locked the door.

"Jim," said the priest, "there's something else I'd like you to help me with if you would. Follow me."

He led the way into the kitchen, turning lights on as he went, and on into a dining room. Jim could see into the sunken living room, two steps down from the dining room. There was a fire burning in the fireplace, casting a warm glow.

"Take your coat off and have a seat," said the priest. He went back into the kitchen, removing his own jacket as he went. Jim looked around and thought the place looked like any other nice house. There were Venetian blinds on the windows as well as curtains. The dining room furniture was kind of modern looking, and he could make out a couch and several overstuffed armchairs in the living room. A baby grand piano took up one corner of the room. All of the blinds were closed.

Father Nelson took a quart bottle of Colt 45 malt liquor out of the refrigerator. He'd purchased two of them earlier that day and stashed them there after Father Krueger left for his mother's home in Piqua. Jim could hear some clattering coming from the kitchen, and soon Father Nelson came back carrying two large, glass mugs full of beer. Jim was surprised at first, but then thought it was really cool that Father Nelson hadn't even asked if he wanted one. Jim's mom let him have sips of her beer all the time, and he even snuck a few out of the house every once in a while.

"I hope you like beer," said the priest.

"I love beer," said Jim.

"Well, drink up, there's more where that came from," Father Nelson said, smiling. He handed the beer to Jim and they clinked their glasses together. Jim knew that Father Nelson liked to drink. Everybody knew it. Jim had seen him pretty drunk once, at a Friday Night Fish Fry. His mom had sent him on his bike to the school cafeteria to pick up fish sandwiches for their dinner. A strictly men-only-event, with carry-out sandwiches available to everyone else, the Fish Fry was sponsored by St. Nick's Holy Name Society every other month. The men drank beer, ate fish, smoked cigars, and played poker.

"Cheers," said the priest, and he motioned toward the dining room table. "Have a seat."

Jim took a big swig of beer and pulled out a chair. The priest set his beer on the table and went down the steps into the living room, disappearing in the dark hall at the other end of the room. He returned shortly and sat down in the chair next to Jim, tossing a small stack of magazines on the table top. Jim could see immediately that they were dirty magazines, and his eyes widened.

"I need your help with this, Jim," Father Nelson told him. "The archbishop has asked several of us, those of us who have had some training in psychology, to help with a study they're conducting on the dangers of pornography. You know what pornography is, right?"

"Yeah," Jim said. "Dirty magazines."

"Exactly," said the priest. "And dirty movies, too."

"Right," said Jim, nodding, trying not to show his shock at what he was seeing.

"Anyway, I want you to look through these, "the priest said. "I want to know how you feel about what you see. You know, how you react to the pictures, which ones you like or don't like, that kind of thing. So, go ahead and have a look. Take your time. And don't worry, it's not a sin to look at this material. You're doing it for me, for the study."

Jim felt funny about what the priest was having him look at. He wasn't worried about it being a sin. He didn't think that at all. He'd seen his father's *Playboy* magazines plenty of times. He even had a couple of them squirreled away in his room at home, and used them when he jerked off. The only other time he'd heard a priest talk about sex was maybe a month before, when Father Krueger held a special assembly in the cafeteria for the seventh and eighth grade boys. It was supposed to be about *sex education,* but it had all been a load of crap. Father Krueger kept referring to jerking off as *boxing Oscar,* and said it was a mortal sin.

Father Nelson got up from the table and stepped back down into the living room. Jim took another big drink of beer and started leafing through the magazines as he had been asked to do. There was a *Playboy* or two, but most of the others weren't even in color. They were extremely graphic, by far the dirtiest magazines he'd ever seen. Men fucking women and young girls, and men sucking and fucking other men and young boys, and boys sucking and fucking other boys. There was very little print matter in the magazines, unlike *Playboy*, and no cartoons. The printing that *was* there – and on the covers – was mostly in a foreign language. French and German, Jim thought. He could feel the erection rising in his pants.

"Drink your beer, so we can have another one," called Father Nelson from the living room. Jim finished his beer, and he could hear the priest poking the fire in the fireplace. Father Nelson tossed another log on the fire. He came back to the dining room, picked up Jim's glass and went into the kitchen.

Jim was already feeling light-headed from the beer when the priest returned and set another full mug on the table in front of him.

"Are you enjoying some of these?" the priest asked, standing behind Jim and looking over his shoulder.

"Yeah," Jim said, truthfully. "Some. Some are pretty sick, I think."

"Are they giving you a hard on?" asked the priest, nonchalantly. He patted Jim's upper arms and gave them a squeeze. Jim froze. The hands moved up and began to squeeze and massage his shoulders. The priest leaned forward, and his hands moved down to Jim's chest and squeezed his teats. Jim could feel Father Nelson's stomach rubbing against the back of his head as the priest leaned even farther forward, reaching down and squeezing his stomach. He put a hand on Jim's crotch.

"*What are you doing?*" Jim cried, jumping to his feet and knocking Father Nelson's hands away, all in one quick, violent motion. He turned around and watched as the priest lost his balance, tripped backward over the top step of the sunken living room, and went completely off his feet. As he came down, the back of his head struck the corner of the raised concrete hearth with a sickening sound, and his head bounced forward with an audible crack. He landed on his left side, and his head was twisted oddly, back and to the right.

"Jesus!" Jim cried, and rushed to the fallen priest. The priest was out cold, completely motionless, and his eyes were wide open. Blood began pouring from a cut at the back of the priest's head.

"Jesus!" Jim said again, in a panic now. He ran down the dark hall, grabbed a towel from the bathroom, and ran back to the living room. By the time he got there, he could see the bleeding had slowed somewhat. He shoved the towel under Father Nelson's head, pressing the towel tight against the wound. After a few seconds, he lifted the towel and looked at the wound. The bleeding had slowed even more and soon stopped completely. Father Nelson's eyes were still open wide, staring up at Jim, and he didn't seem to be breathing.

"Jesus fuck," said Jim. He jumped up, ran back to the bathroom, and puked into the toilet. He waited a moment, and then puked some more. Running back through the living room, Jim didn't look at the priest. He took the steps in one stride, ran through the dining room and out to the front door. His hands were shaking as he fumbled with the lock. Once he got it open and made sure it wouldn't lock behind him, he ran past the church to one of the doors that led from the schoolyard to the gym. As usual, the boys had propped the door open with a shoe to keep it from closing and locking if someone went outside to pee. Jim took a deep breath and tried to compose himself. He opened the door and stepped into the gym.

"Steve! Kenny!" he yelled, trying to get their attention. His two friends stopped what they were doing and ran to the door, as did several other curious boys.

"What's up, doc?" Kenny said, shifting a basketball from one hand to the other. One of the other boys grabbed the ball out of his hands.

"Dumbass!" Kenny yelled as the boy ran off with the ball.

"Father Nelson said to get two guys to help move some stuff in the rectory," Jim said, trying hard to act normal. "You and Steve should come with me."

"Do we have to?" Steve whined.

"Yeah, dipshit, you have to," said Jim, scowling at his friend.

"I'll go," said one of the other boys.

"Yeah, right, asshole," Jim said, again with a scowl. "C'mon, let's go. Just Kenny and Steve."

"Your breath stinks," Kenny said, as they went out the door. "Like beer."

"Fuck you," said Jim. "C'mon."

Jim ran ahead, and his friends followed him back to the rectory. When they got inside the front door, Jim stopped and turned around.

"I think Father Nelson croaked," he said. "I think I killed him. He's in the living room, so don't crap your pants when you see him."

The boys could tell Jim was serious, and their eyes widened. Following him through the kitchen, they saw the large Colt 45 bottles on a counter. One was empty and the other was opened, but mostly full.

"Were you *drinking* that stuff?" Steve asked. Jim didn't bother answering.

The boys had all seen dead bodies before, at Catholic funeral homes, but mostly older relatives – great aunts and uncles, and grandparents. When they saw Father Nelson, crumpled on the floor with his head at an odd angle and his eyes open, they both stopped dead in their tracks.

"Jesus!" said Steve.

"Holy fuck!" Kenny said. "What the fuck happened? Where's Father Krueger?"

"He tried to feel me up!" Jim said, pointing toward the priest. "He tried to grab my pecker!"

Steve and Kenny exchanged a quick glance.

"He's some kind of pervert queer or something!" said Jim, sitting down and pointing to the dirty magazines. "Look at this shit he was showing me!"

His friends glanced at the table, then quickly away.

"So, you *killed* him?" Steve asked in a shrill voice.

"No, you dumbass. I didn't kill him. Not on purpose! I just shoved him away, and he tripped. His head hit the cement."

"Where's Father Krueger?" Kenny asked again.

"He's gone for the night," Jim said. "Spending the night at his mom's house."

Kenny crept down into the living room and got on his knees next to the priest. They'd learned how to check for a pulse in health class, and he did so now. After a few seconds he dropped the limp arm and leaned forward, his ear close to the priest's mouth, listening.

"He's dead all right," he told the others. "Nothing."

Steve knelt down beside Kenny and put the back of his hand against the priest's forehead. "He's already cooling off," he said, his voice trembling. "Holy crap! Look how white he is!"

"Eww!" Kenny exclaimed, wrinkling his nose. "I think he pissed himself. Can you smell it?"

All three boys looked down at the priest's crotch. It was hard to see in the faint light, but the priest's pants were indeed wet. Jim joined his friends around the priest.

"Close his eyes, Kenny," he said. "It's giving me the creeps."

"*You* close his eyes!" Kenny retorted. "Why is his head all crooked and shit?"

"How the fuck do I know!" said Jim, trying to close the priest's eyes. They wouldn't stay closed, and after several tries, Jim dashed down the hall to the bathroom. He came back with another towel and draped it over Father Nelson's head. The boys seemed to relax a little.

"Did he ever do anything like that to you?" Jim asked Kenny. "Any of that queer shit?"

Kenny looked away and didn't answer.

"Jesus, Kenny! He did, didn't he?" Jim said in amazement. He looked at Steve who also looked away.

"You too?" Jim asked. "You fuckers! Why didn't you ever tell me?"

Kenny and Steve were both looking down, not making eye contact with Jim. Steve started to cry.

"I can't talk about it," Kenny mumbled.

Jim looked from one boy to the other, and shook his head. "What the fuck are we supposed to do now?"

"Whattaya mean *we*?" Steve said, crying even harder and looking back at Jim. "We didn't do anything."

"I know you didn't do anything, you dipshit. But you're *here*, aren't you?"

"Yeah, well I . . . I . . . I wish I wasn't!" Steve stuttered. "Wha . . . wha . . . what'd you have to come and get *us* for?"

"Yeah," said Kenny.

"Because you're my friends!" Jim said. "What else was I supposed to do?"

"Why didn't you call the cops?" Kenny asked. "Or an ambulance?"

"Because I came and got you guys!" said Jim. "I just got scared, I guess. The cops'll think I killed him."

"Not if you just tell them what happened," Steve said, wiping his nose on his sleeve.

"Yeah right, like the cops are going to believe that a *priest* grabbed my dick!"

"Just show them the dirty magazines," Kenny said.

"N . . . n . . . n . . . no! Don't do that!" Steve said. "They'll just ask us a m . . . m . . . million questions."

Jim and Kenny looked directly at each other. They knew they had to come up with a plan – and fast. Steve was still crying.

"What if we just leave," Kenny suggested, his eyes wide. "Let's just lock the door behind us and leave. The cops'll think he tripped and fell on his own."

"We'd have to get rid of the magazines," Jim said. "And the towels – we'd have to get rid of them, too."

"B . . . but everybody knows we're here," said Steve. "All the guys in the gym know we're here. They'd . . . t . . . t . . . tell on us for sure."

"Fuck!" Jim plopped down to the couch. Steve and Kenny followed suit, wide-eyed and scared. Nobody spoke, and Jim's knee was bouncing nervously.

Suddenly, he jumped up. "Where's the garage?"

"I think there's a door in front," said Kenny. "In the hall by the kitchen."

Jim jumped the two steps and ran toward the front of the rectory. Kenny and Steve didn't move. A minute later, Jim came back and faced his friends.

"Let's get rid of him," he said.

Steve and Kenny stared at him in disbelief.

"We could do it," he went on, before they could protest. "We could put him in his car and drive it out to the gravel pit and shove it in. Right there where we swim, at "POSITIVELY NO." It's so deep nobody'll ever find him."

"You're kidding, right?" said Kenny.

"No," Jim insisted. "I'm not kidding. We can do this. He'll just disappear with his car and nobody'll ever know what happened. We can put the magazines in the car, and nobody'll ever see them. The towels and the beer, too. Tomorrow, everyone will think he just drove away."

"But everyone in the gym will know we were here," Steve countered.

"So what? If anybody asks, we say we helped him move some stuff, and then we went home. As long as we never talk, nobody will ever know. Maybe they won't even ask."

"Move what stuff?" Steve asked. "What if they do ask?"

"Fuck, I don't know!" Jim said, looking around the room. "The piano! We helped move the piano!"

The boys sat quietly, thinking. Kenny stood up and went down the hall to the bathroom. He came back to the living room, zipping his fly. He looked at Steve, then turned to Jim.

"Can you drive, Jim?"

"Oh, shit," said Steve, and he started to cry again.

"Hell yeah, I can drive!" said Jim. "I got my temps in Texas when I was fourteen. Sylvia let me drive all the time down there."

Kenny turned to Steve. "Shut the fuck up! Stop crying! Jim's right. As long as we don't tell anybody, it'll work. C'mon, Steve, we can do this. Don't pussy out on us."

"Okay, okay," Steve said quietly, throwing up his hands. "Stop yelling." He wiped his nose and stood. "And I ain't a pussy."

"Good. Let's shake on it," Kenny said, sticking out his hand.

Jim and Steve took hold of Kenny's hand and they all shook on it. Jim smiled and gave Steve a friendly punch on the arm.

"We'll need his car keys," Kenny said.

"I think he tossed them on the bench by the front door," said Jim.

"Wait!" Steve stopped them. "How long is this going to take? My parents are going to wonder where I am. It's already pretty late and I usually get home about now."

"Shit," Jim said. "What about you, Kenny?"

"I'm okay, I think," said Kenny. "My parents went over to see my new baby cousin. They said they'd probably play some cards. I'm pretty sure I'm okay. What about *your* mom?"

"Sylvia won't even notice," said Jim, shaking his head. "She doesn't care too much if I come home late. I'll make something up. Can't you do that, Steve? Call and make something up?"

"Like what?" Steve said with a shrug.

"Shit, I don't know. Tell them Father Nelson is giving us extra singing lessons or something."

"Okay," said Steve. "That's pretty good."

Jim and Steve headed for the kitchen and found the wall phone. Jim saw the Colt 45 bottles, and called back to the living room. "Kenny, we should get rid of these beer bottles, too. I'll go kick everybody out of the gym and lock up."

When he ran to the gym, the shoe was gone from the door, replaced by a folding chair; only a dozen boys were still in the gym.

"Everybody out!" he yelled. "Father Nelson said it's time to lock up!"

Jim got the gym cleared, threatening one boy with "serious physical harm" if he didn't get his ass moving, and turned out the lights. He made sure the door locked behind him, and ran back to the rectory. Steve met him at the door.

"I called my mom," he said. "It's okay."

"Good," said Jim, again giving him a little punch. "Where's Kenny?"

"He's in Father Nelson's bedroom. I just dumped all the beer — from the glasses, too. We figured we should get rid of it all."

"Good idea. We'll put everything in the trunk." The two boys went back to the dining room, and Jim saw that the magazines were gone from the table.

"Make sure everything seems nice and tidy, okay, Steve?"

He found Kenny in the bedroom, packing the magazines into a suitcase. "This was open on the bed. It was full of this stuff," said Kenny, holding up a magazine. "The other one in the closet feels like it's empty. Maybe we should put some of his clothes in it so it looks like he packed up and left."

"Brilliant," said Jim. He opened the other suitcase, grabbed some shirts, pants, and a jacket from hangers in the closet, and stuffed them in. They made sure the room was tidy, turned out the light, and carried the suitcases to the garage. Steve was already there. He'd found Father Nelson's key ring on the bench and had opened the trunk of the brand-new Impala. The garage lights were on.

"You dumbass," Jim said, quickly turning them off. "There's windows."

"Sorry," Steve said. "I'm an idiot."

The trunk light was bright enough for them to see what they were doing. It was a huge trunk, and they shoved in the suitcases, the beer bottles, and the mugs.

"Okay," said Jim. "Let's go get him."

The boys went back into the living room and huddled around the dead body. Kenny lifted the towel from the priest's face. His eyes were still open.

"Holy fuck," said Jim. "That's creepy." He wrapped both towels around the priest's head as tightly as he could.

"Looks like there's a little blood on the rug right there," Kenny pointed out.

"Shit," muttered Jim.

"Probably some pee, too," Steve added. The rug was one of several oriental rugs that were spread around the living room, covering a lot of the wall-to-wall carpeting.

"We'll take the rug, too." Jim squatted down. "Him first. You guys each take a leg." The boys each grabbed a leg, and Jim got his arms under the priest's arms.

"Wait a sec!" Jim set the body down. He found the priest's wallet in a rear pants pocket and tossed it into the glowing coals in the fireplace. The fake leather quickly ignited, and they watched it burn for a few seconds, then bent to pick up the priest.

"Jesus fuck!" Kenny said. "He's heavy!" They lugged the body to the garage, half dragging it, and dumped it into the trunk of the Impala.

"Plenty of room," Jim said. "Let's get the rug."

Jim and Steve rolled up the rug while Kenny checked the bedroom and bathroom one more time. They were all relieved to find no stains under the small rug. Steve took the rug to the garage and shoved it into the trunk. Kenny and Jim took one last look around, turned off the lights, checked the front door, and joined Steve in the garage.

Jim slammed the trunk lid down and took the keys from Steve. He got in and started the car. Kenny walked around to the other side and hopped into the front seat next to him, while Steve climbed in the back.

"One of you dumbasses is going to have to open the door," Jim said, shaking his head. "And look out the window first. Make sure nobody's out there."

Kenny got out and peeked through the window. When he was sure no one was around, he lifted the garage door. Jim put the car into gear and pulled out. He left the lights off and stopped to wait while Kenny closed the garage door and got back in the car. Going slowly, they passed behind the church and cut across the wide parking lot that served the school and the church.

"What if the cops stop us?" Steve said, leaning forward with his arms folded across the back of the front seat.

"What cops?" Jim said with a smirk. "Bigelow's probably shacked up somewhere. And when's the last time you saw a *Dayton* cop out here at night?"

Jim found the headlight knob and turned it on. He pulled out of the schoolyard, turning left onto Belfair Avenue. No one spoke as they drove, and Jim and Kenny could hear Steve sniffling in the back seat. Not many cars were out, and Jim drove carefully, making sure not to go so slowly that they'd draw someone's attention.

The drive to the gravel pit took less than ten minutes. Jim turned off Harshman Road onto the old service lane and switched off the headlights. Kenny jumped out and lowered the chain from across the entry. They knew it was never locked, and after Jim drove over the chain, Kenny hooked it back up. Jim waited a few moments while his eyes adjusted to the dark. He pulled off the lane and wove his way through the underbrush and around some small trees. The boys could hear the underbrush and the branches scraping against the car. Finally, they pulled into the clearing that surrounded "POSITIVELY NO". Jim stopped thirty feet from the edge of the gravel pit, shifted the car into park, and turned it off.

The boys got out of the car and walked to the edge of the pit. Off to their left, they could see the lights of the Dayton skyline. The only sound was distant traffic. As they turned and walked back to the car, Jim had an idea.

"Let's take him out of the trunk and put him in the driver's seat."

"Good idea," said Kenny.

They unlocked the trunk and moved the rug. It was a huge effort getting the body out of the trunk and positioning it in the driver's seat. Jim noticed the seat belts and said, "Let's strap him in." They buckled the seat belt around Father Nelson's waist and leaned him back on the seat. When Jim removed the towels, the priest's head hung at an angle, his eyes still open wide. While they were putting the towels and the rug back into the trunk, the body slumped forward and the head hit the steering wheel. The horn gave one quick honk, startling the boys.

"Holy fuck!" Jim said, looking around.

They left the body leaning forward against the steering wheel, and closed the trunk. Jim reached in around Father Nelson and started the car.

"Ready?" he said. "I'll put it in neutral, and we'll give it a shove. I think it'll roll right in." He reached in and grabbed the shifter.

"Wait!" Kenny said, stopping them. "Maybe we should put the windows down so it'll sink faster."

"Good idea, Kenny," said Jim.

They rolled the windows down and closed the doors. But when Jim reached in and pulled the shifter into neutral, the car didn't move. "We'll have to push," he said.

They pushed together, and the car began to roll easily on its own down the slight slope of graveled earth. As the front wheels dropped over the lip of the pit, the car hesitated briefly. Its rocker panels and undercarriage scraped until the rear tires hit the lip. A last jarring thump followed as the rear of the car crashed over the edge. The Impala fell out of sight, and the front bumper split the water with a splash.

The boys moved to the edge of the pit and watched the car sink, nose first. Lit by a rising quarter-moon, the surface of the water roiled with air pouring from the open windows. They stared at the water until the surface calmed.

Walking back through the brush toward Harshman Road, no one spoke. They crossed a bridge over Mad River and could see the lights at the end of the old Wright Field runway on the other side of Springfield Street. Whenever a car passed, they ducked off the road. Steve began to cry again, and Jim put an arm around his friend's shoulders.

"C'mon, Steve, stop crying," he said. "It's gonna be okay. As long as we don't talk about it, it'll be all right."

Once they crossed over Airway Road, they kept to the smaller side roads, creeping through base housing and the surrounding neighborhoods. Steve threw up on somebody's lawn. They avoided St. Nick's, and when it was time to split up, they stopped.

"We'll never talk about this to anybody, okay? *Nobody!*" Jim declared. "Let's shake on it again."

The boys clasped their hands together for the second time that night. Kenny and Steve looked at Jim.

"Swear to God," he told them. "We've got to *say* it." They swore to God.

"Okay, that's it then," Jim said. He smiled and gave Steve another playful punch. "Don't worry, Steve. If we keep our mouths shut, nobody will ever know."

52

Kind of Weird

And now Burke knew.

"The next day we went to school like nothing happened," McGowan said, after recounting the whole story. "Poor Steve had that deer in the headlights kind of look on his face when I saw him in the morning. Kenny seemed okay. I remember we all seemed to be avoiding each other."

"Nobody said anything about Father Nelson being gone?" Burke asked.

"Not a word. I don't even know who knew at that point. I guess Mary Lou Spaulding knew, and probably Father Krueger. But nobody mentioned it in school that morning. Then – BAM!" McGowan snapped his fingers. "Kennedy got shot. And nobody gave two shits about Father Nelson. It saved my ass. Saved *our* asses, I should say."

"Yeah, I remember when we first heard about Kennedy," Burke reflected. "We were in an assembly in the cafeteria, all the seventh and eighth graders, remember that? We were watching a documentary about the Holocaust."

"I remember," said McGowan. "They stopped the movie and Sister Roberta got up in front and told us the President was dead. The nuns freaked out and started crying, and then the girls all started to cry. Even the boys were crying. They closed school and we all went home and watched TV for three or four days. Nobody could think about anything else for a week."

"Did you see Jack Ruby shoot Oswald?" Burke asked. "*Live*, on TV?"

"*I sure did!* And the funeral and all that shit – the horse with the empty saddle and the backward boots in the stirrups. *Jesus!* But nobody was talking about Father Nelson. Nobody said a word to us until later the next week when Bigelow came to the school. I thought Steve and Kenny were going to crap their pants. I was scared, too, but I managed to keep my cool. I tried to bullshit him. And that was the last we ever heard about it."

"Did you ever talk to Kenny or Steve about what happened?" asked Burke.

"Nope. Not even once. But Kenny and I talk about it now."

Burke sat up from where he'd been slouching in the chair, listening to Jim's story. "Did you think about it much? You know… about what you'd done?"

"Oh, hell yeah, I thought about it all the time. How could you not," McGowan said with a shrug. "But to tell you the truth, later on – and, God, I hope this doesn't sound too sick – later on I was actually kind of proud of what we'd done. I think what we did shaped me in some way, gave me confidence and made me stronger. I don't know, John. Can you understand that at all?"

"I think so," said Burke, admitting to himself that the way McGowan conducted himself on that night long ago was pretty impressive.

"I've always felt bad about dragging Kenny and Steve into *my* mess," McGowan said. "First of all, what Father Nelson did to them must have been pretty hard to live with. And then I think they suffered a lot of guilt over what we did that night. I know Kenny did. We talked about it."

McGowan got up and went to the window. He stood there looking out at the late summer day, with his back to Burke and his hands in his pockets.

"What about you, John?" he said, turning to Burke. "Do you think what Father Nelson did to you fucked *you* up?"

234

"Oh, yeah," said Burke with a mocking laugh. "Jesus – just ask my son. Ask my *wife*."

"But you never told them."

"Like I said, I never told anyone." Burke got out of his chair and picked up the two halves of the broken putter. He joined McGowan at the window.

"But something happened here, Jim, just now when I broke this putter. I could feel it the second I told you. Something went away, like . . . it just lifted away. Something that's been crushing me my whole goddamn life."

McGowan draped his arm around Burke's shoulders and gave him a little hug. The two men had shared each other's fifty-year-old secrets. A brotherly bond had formed.

"Sorry about your putter," Burke said.

"Don't worry about it," McGowan said, laughing. "You're a golfer. You know how it is – I've got five or six of them out in the garage."

"And I meant what I said, Jim," said Burke. "What you told me today will never leave this room."

"Thanks, John. I appreciate it."

"Are you going to tell Kenny that you told me?" Burke asked him.

"Yeah, what the hell, I'll tell him. In a lot of ways, I think it'll be a great relief to him. Just to know that somebody else knows. Can I tell Kenny what you told *me*?"

"Go ahead. I wish I'd told him myself when I was in Ithaca," Burke said. "And while you're at it, tell Kenny what I said about the prosecutor. That was on the level. If you guys *ever* want to come forward with your story, it's going to be okay. The prosecutor's a good man."

"I'll tell Kenny," McGowan said. "That'll be his choice."

Burke put the broken putter back in the corner of the room. "Let's play some golf sometime," he said.

"I'd love to. And didn't you say you liked the museum?"

"I did," said Burke. "Haven't been there lately, though. My son and I went to see Kennedy's Air Force One after they painted it."

"I should take you sometime. There's a bunch of new stuff," said McGowan. "I can get you back into the workshops – show you the areas the public doesn't get to see."

"Oh, man! I'd love that," Burke said, cheering up.

"And speaking of Kennedy's jet," said McGowan. "Don't you think it's kind of weird that it ended up half a mile away from where Father Nelson took *his* last ride?"

"Yep," Burke said, nodding. "Pretty goddamn weird."

53

Three Sisters

Driving back into Dayton from Beavercreek, Burke felt both exhausted and elated, as if he'd finished a day of hard labor and just drunk that second beer. He'd barely slept the night before, and when he got to the squad room, he called Maggie and asked if he could beg off from their dinner plans – he was whipped. Kevin patted him on the back and told him to go home.

Pulling out of the Safety Building parking lot, Burke surprised himself by turning on the car radio. He wanted to hear some music. Scanning through the stations, he paused for a moment when he heard, *"Hail Mary, full of grace . . ."* It was one of those Catholic radio stations where the Rosary is recited twenty-four hours a day, and he was about to change the station when he was suddenly seized by a vivid memory of his sister, Mary. The memory was so unexpected and strong that Burke had to pull over and park at the side of the street. He turned the radio off and let the memory play out in his head . . .

. . . a perfect spring day in late April. There had been a soaking rain, days earlier, and now it was quite warm. Burke was maybe eight or nine years old at the time, and Mary was two years older. They were with their father and grandfather, hunting for morel mushrooms – sponges and spikes – in a large woodlot out in the country, east of Dayton. It was the first time either of the kids had been allowed to come on one of these excursions. Everyone was equipped with a woven potato sack and a small knife. Burke's was a folding pocket knife that had been a birthday present.

237

This was one of their father's favorite spots for mushrooms, and had been for many years. They'd parked at the side of the road, and now it was "eyes to the ground" as they entered the woods, hunting as they walked. Their main objective was a little glade that opened up in the middle of the woods, maybe two hundred yards from the road. Burke and Mary had never been there before, but they knew that over the years this favorite spot had yielded up bushels of mushrooms. They were all hoping to find a good batch today. The men found a few morels as they walked, and said that was a good sign. When they finally reached the glade, Burke and Mary stopped and looked up in awe. An opening had been created by the over-arching branches of three enormous oak trees, forming a wide triangle. Even in early spring, with the trees not yet in full leaf, they shaded everything beneath them on the forest floor. Thin grass mixed with short weeds and little oak seedlings, may-apples, and a few delicate red and white trilliums grew there, but not much else.

The farmer who owned the woods had told Burke's father that the trees were white oaks, and for some unknown reason they'd been left alone when the rest of the area was logged off by the early settlers. The venerable trees were thought to be five hundred years old, and were now surrounded by a much younger forest.

The little party spread out and slowly moved into the glade. Almost immediately, Mary spotted the first morel — a six-inch-tall "sponge" — and the cap of the mushroom did indeed resemble a sponge. "Stand still and look around, there'll probably be more right close," their grandfather advised. As it turned out, they didn't have to look very hard. A large portion of the glade was filled *with mushrooms. "Spikes" — with a smaller, darker cap — as well as the "sponges" were everywhere. It was the "mother lode," their father exclaimed, and they set to work harvesting their find, the men grinning away, and Burke and Mary shrieking with delight. They filled all four potato sacks, and the men made two more bags out of their shirts.*

"We'll leave the rest for the fairies," said their Irish grandfather, winking.

"Do you believe in fairies, Grandpa?" Burke had asked.

"Oh, no, Johnny. I don't believe in 'em," said his grandfather, giving Burke a playful cuff on the chin. "But you know, lad, they're here anyway."

Before heading back to the car, the men sat on a log in their t-shirts, chatting and smoking cigarettes. Burke and Mary lay on the ground side by side, holding hands and gazing up into the magic canopy of the oak trees. It was one of the happiest moments of his young life . . .

Burke had remembered the oak trees once or twice over the years, the first time being when the Five Rivers Metropark system had acquired the woods. The land lay just outside the village of Bellbrook and was split by Sugar Creek. Eventually, the oak trees had been dubbed the "Three Sisters" and were now a hiking destination, part of the park trail system. Botanists agreed that the trees were over five hundred years old and had been growing already when Gutenberg invented the printing press in 1455, and Columbus landed in the Bahamas in 1492.

The last time Burke thought about the "Three Sisters" had been a few years back, when it was reported in the newspaper that one of the trees had at last fallen over. He hadn't been to the magic woods since he was a child, but now he felt an overwhelming urge to do so. Burke started the car and headed for Bellbrook. He was dead tired, but sleep could wait.

* * *

Twenty minutes later, Burke drove through Bellbrook and followed the signs to the Sugarcreek Metropark entrance on Ferry Road. He pulled into the empty parking lot, probably very near to where he had entered the woods as a boy. The hiking trails, including one leading to the "Three Sisters" were marked on a plaque. The walk in was shorter than Burke recalled, and except for the fallen tree, the glade was pretty much as he remembered it. There were no may-apples or trillium at this time of year, just grass and weeds, and another plaque explaining the history of the trees.

Burke sat on the fallen sister and gazed up into the canopy of the remaining trees. He thought again about Mary, about holding her hand and feeling so happy in this very place. *What has happened to me in the meantime?* Burke wondered. *I've lived most of my life buried alive under weight of someone else's terrible sin. Carrying on as if the awful thing had never happened. Stunted, held back, living but not really thriving. Succeeding, yes, but always on someone else's terms.* Yet somehow, despite everything, he knew that he had managed to marry a wonderful woman and raise the best son a man could hope for.

Burke was tired, and he was crying. He looked up through his tears at the ancient trees. The "Three Sisters" had been left alone, spared the axe and left to grow. *How different would my life have been if I had been left alone, able to grow, untouched? And now, where in the hell do I go from here?*

Getting up, Burke wiped his eyes, gave the fallen log a little pat, and walked out of the woods. This was a special place, and he knew he would visit it again. But now he needed sleep.

When he got to his apartment, Burke opened a beer and made himself a dinner of scrambled eggs and toast. He crawled into bed at six o'clock despite the fact that it would remain light outside for a long time yet. He fell asleep instantly and slept without dreaming for twelve hours.

54

Whistling a Tune

On Friday morning Burke was the first one in the squad room. Marco, the next to arrive, reminded Burke that over the weekend Pete Skoff would be defending his championship at the Senior Amateur golf tournament. Burke had completely forgotten about the tournament, and he hadn't seen a newspaper that morning. Tarisa arrived, and then Kevin. Kevin fist-bumped his father, then dove right into the paperwork on his desk. Marco and Tarisa soon headed out.

Burke called Maggie. It was early, but he knew she'd be up for her morning fitness class.

"Hi, Johnny," she said. "How are you? Did you get some rest?"

"I did," he said. "*Lots* of it. I feel pretty good."

"Good! So, what's up? I'm about out the door."

"Well," Burke said, "I was wondering if I could invite myself to dinner tonight. There's something I need to talk to you about."

"Sure," said Maggie. "That's fine. How about six o'clock?"

"Great," said Burke, relieved. "Is it okay if I invite Kevin, too? I want him to be there if he can make it – but just Kevin, not Becky and the girls."

"That's fine," Maggie said. "Just let me know if he's coming."

Burke hung up and called his son over. Kevin brought a small pile of paperwork with him and tossed it on Burke's desk. "You might want to check through this," he said.

"Will do," said Burke, slapping the pile and smiling. "I'm having dinner at your mother's tonight and we want you to join us. Not Becky and the girls, just you. There's something I need to talk to you and Maggie about. Do you think you can swing that?"

"Sure, I guess," said Kevin, happily noticing Burke's smile. "I'll check with Becky but I don't think it'll be a problem. What's up?"

"I'll tell you tonight," Burke said.

When Kevin walked away, Burke unlocked the top drawer of his desk. He pulled out the file he'd started on the Father Nelson case, tucked it under his arm, and walked down the hall to Major Winston's office.

"I hear Pete's playing in the final round of the Senior Amateur tomorrow," Claire said, right off the bat. "Is he working today? I'd like to wish him luck."

"Yeah, he'll be in this afternoon," said Burke. "And Kevin's working on the weekend schedule."

"Good," Claire said. "He must be doing something right. Everyone seems pretty happy."

"Claire," Burke said, getting down to business, "I just wanted to let you know that I'm closing the Father Nelson case for now. I've taken it as far as I can, and it's all dead ends. Unless something else comes up, I think we should consider it a cold case."

"Cold and *old*, I should say. I'm not surprised, John," she said. "But you got farther than I ever thought you would on a crime that old. Nothing more from the Church?"

"Stonewalled," Burke lied, shaking his head.

"Okay," said Claire. "I'm sorry it dead-ended. Keep me posted if anything pops up."

"Sure thing," said Burke.

He left Major Winston's office and went to a small, windowless room at the end of the hall. There was nothing in the room but a couple of old, seldom used photocopiers, and a shredding machine. Burke closed the door and sat in the only chair in the room. He opened the Father Nelson file and went through the contents. When he found Dr. Cara Shannon's card, he put it in his shirt pocket. The original missing persons report that Bigelow the Gigolo had written was there, and the rest of the file was mostly notes he'd made by hand – some contemporaneous, some afterthoughts – and reports he'd typed up from the interviews with Mary Lou Spaulding, Mike Donnelly, Donnelly's old friend, Father Metzger, Father Stankowski, Dr. Shannon, Steve Heckman's wife in Florida, Kenny Mason, and the general. Burke plucked out Bigelow's report – and anything else that mentioned Jim McGowan, Kenny Mason, or Steve Heckman – and unceremoniously ran them through the shredder. He checked what was left in the file one more time, then walked back to the squad room, humming softly.

"Here's the Father Nelson file," he said, dropping it on Kevin's desk. Kevin picked up the file and quickly leafed through it.

"Not much here, Pop," he said, amused by his father's humming.

"Nope, not too much," Burke said. "I'm done with it."

"*Done* with it?" Kevin said in disbelief. "You're kidding!"

"Nope. I took it as far as I'm going to take it."

Kevin threw up his hands. "Well, what should I do with it?" he asked.

"As far as I'm concerned, it's a cold case. Put it with the other cold cases," Burke told him. "Me?" he grinned, "I'm back on *short* time. Just let me know if there's anything you want me to help with." He went back to his desk.

Kevin knew better than to start asking his father a lot of questions. He was glad to see him smile – *and* hear him humming. He would leave it at that.

The squad room phone rang, and Kevin took the call. "It's for you, Pop," he called across the room. "Father Trevor Williams."

Burke flinched, and picked up the phone. There was only one likely reason that Father Stankowski's young assistant would be calling.

"Hello, Father."

"Hello, Captain," the priest said. "I'm calling to let you know that Father Stankowski died this morning. He asked me to make sure you were the first person I called."

"Thank you. I appreciate the call," said Burke. "Were you there? Were you with him when he died?"

"No, I'm afraid I wasn't," Father Williams said. "I was in my apartment downtown. He died early this morning. The hospice staff said he died in his sleep."

"I'm sorry, Father. I know you were close."

"Thanks, Captain," the priest said. "I'm going to miss him."

"What about a funeral? Do you think you could let me know when that's going to happen? I'd like to come down."

"The funeral will be a big deal," said the priest. "Dear Nicholas was greatly loved and highly regarded. I'm already making arrangements, but it probably won't happen until the archbishop returns from Rome. He's expected back at the end of the week. But yes, I can let you know."

"Thanks, Father," Burke said. "And thanks again for the call."

Burke hung up and slouched back in his chair. He laced his fingers behind his head and sat for a moment, looking up at the ceiling of the squad room. He could hear the last words the priest had spoken to him. *Would you kindly ask one o' them purdy little waitresses to come in here?* The thought made him smile.

He sat up and took Dr. Cara Shannon's card from his pocket, then dialed the number. After a moment, the doctor picked up.

"This is Cara."

"Hi, Cara. John Burke here. I was wondering if I could talk to you again."

"Sure," Cara said. "I've got to teach a class in a few minutes, but I'll be done at eleven. Could you come then?"

"Well, actually, I don't want to see you at school," said Burke. "I'd like to make an appointment to see you at your *other* office. You know, as a therapist."

"Absolutely," said Cara. "I don't have my book with me right now, but after class I'll have Jackie give you a call and you can set something up. Will that work?"

"Thanks," Burke said. "I'll be looking forward to it."

Burke watched Kevin put the Father Nelson file into the cabinet that held the other cold cases, but he knew that Father Nelson's story was just about to heat up. He called the newsroom at the *Dayton Daily News* and asked for Lisa Fowler. She picked up.

"Lisa? Hi, this is John Burke."

"Hi, J.B.," she said excitedly. "How's the Father Nelson case coming?"

"Well, that's what I'm calling about."

"Oh goody," Lisa said. "What have you got?"

"Well, nothing on the case, actually," Burke told her. "In fact, I've ended the investigation. I chased down everything I could find – not that there was much to chase."

"Shit, J.B." she said, unable to hide her disappointment. "I can't believe it."

"I'm sorry, Lisa."

"Oh well. *C'est la vie,* I guess. So much for my book."

"I do have something I think you might be interested in, however."

"Like what?" Lisa said, without much interest.

"Well, it's something someone asked me to deliver to you."

"Can you drop it off here at the newsroom?" she asked. "Or I guess I could pick it up. Are you at the Safety Building?"

"I am," Burke said. "But I don't want to bring it to you there, and I don't want you to pick it up here. I was thinking we could meet somewhere else, somewhere a little more private, out from town."

"Okay, *now* I'm curious," she said. "Where do you want to meet?"

"Hell, I don't know," said Burke. "Hey, how about where they pulled the cars out – that parking lot next to the lake? Can you meet me there, say in half an hour?"

"I'll be there." Lisa hung up.

Burke told Kevin he had to meet someone and that he wasn't sure when he would get back. He was about to go, when Tarisa and Marco came storming back into the squad room. They were in a hurry about something and Marco went straight to his desk and turned on his computer. Tarisa pulled open a file drawer and started intently flipping through the files. Burke watched them at work and thought about his own status.

I'm back on short time. He walked out of the squad room with a smile on his face, whistling a tune. Kevin, Tarisa, and Marco all looked up in amazement, and watched through the glass wall as Burke strolled down the hall. Kevin couldn't remember ever hearing his father whistle.

55

Saint Nick

Burke was sitting on the hood of his car, looking out across Eastwood Lake, when Lisa Fowler turned into the parking lot. She pulled up next to Burke's car, and he hopped down when Lisa got out. There were no other cars in the lot, and the only people around were some passing joggers and a work crew doing something at the far end of the lot.

"Thanks for coming, Lisa," Burke said, shaking her hand.

"Are you kidding?" she said. "I'm intrigued."

Burke popped open the trunk of his car. He picked up one of the file boxes, carried it to the front of his car and set it on the hood. He went back, got the other box, and set it down next to the first one.

He pulled the tape from the first box and opened the lid.

"Here's your book, Lisa," he said, smiling proudly.

"What do you mean my *book*?" She looked at Burke, arching an eyebrow.

Burke picked up Father Stankowski's letter and handed it to Lisa. She took the letter and began to read. The more she read, the wider her eyes opened in disbelief. It was exactly the reaction Burke had hoped for.

"Jesus Christ, J.B.!" she said, swallowing hard and looking up at him. "Why me? Why did he want me to have this stuff?"

"Well, apparently someone must have spoken very highly of you," Burke said, grinning.

"My God," said Lisa, looking into the open box and brushing her hand across the tops of the files. "This could be a *big deal*. I mean – it *is* a big deal!"

"I'm hoping it'll be an even bigger deal down the road," said Burke.

"What do you mean?"

"Just that the Father Nelson story may not be *completely* dead. There's a file on him in there that should interest you," he said, pointing to the other box.

"A file on Raymond Nelson?"

"Yeah," Burke said. "It's short. But it's enough. You'll see."

Burke told Lisa who Father Nicholas Stankowski was, and that he had died that morning. He explained to her what the files contained and how they were arranged, pretty much the same way the priest had explained it to him, and about his own conclusions regarding the abbreviated notations and numbers in the files.

"I'll be interested in getting your take on it," said Burke.

"Holy crap, J.B." Lisa shook her head. "I can't believe this."

"Just one thing, Lisa," Burke said, in a more serious tone. "Father Stankowski made me promise not to give you this stuff until he was dead. And now I want you to promise me you won't do anything with it until I retire in October. Don't show it to a soul until then."

"You got it, J.B."

"In the meantime, you could go through it all and get something ready for the paper," he suggested. "And you're right, I think it is going to be a big deal. In fact, you may want to make copies of everything. I imagine several prosecutors around the state are going to be pretty interested when they find out about it. They might want the originals."

"Good idea," said Lisa.

Burke helped Lisa load the boxes into the trunk of her car. He knew he could trust her to hold off on the story.

"I don't know how to thank you for this, J.B." she said, closing the trunk.

"Don't thank me," he said. "Thank Father Nicholas Stankowski. I think the man's a saint."

"Saint Nick?" said Lisa, grinning.

"Yeah," Burke laughed. "Saint Nick."

Lisa threw her arms around Burke, hugged him tightly, and thanked him again. He watched her drive away, then stepped over the low guard rail, shuffled down the slight embankment, and walked to the edge of the lake. He sat on the bank with his feet hanging over the water. In the middle of the lake a motorboat pulling a skier went past, heading toward Dayton. Burke looked up and down and across the lake.

"Positively no," he said out loud, but no one was there to hear him.

EPILOGUE

Captain John Burke officially retired from the Dayton Police Department in the middle of October. He and his wife, Maggie, who had recently retired from the Dayton Public School System, have since travelled together, spending a week in San Francisco – with a stopover in Colorado to visit his sister, Mary – and another week in New York City. Throughout the fall, they played golf together at least twice a week, several times with retired USAF Brigadier General James McGowan and his wife, Kathy.

Burke has been meeting with therapist Dr. Cara Shannon once a week since the middle of September, and citing his progress, she is planning to reduce the frequency of his visits. To Maggie's delight, Burke has started to sing again, and she and Burke are talking about having him move back into their house.

Shortly after Burke retired, the *Dayton Daily News* broke the story about the release of the material from the secret archives of the Archdiocese of Cincinnati, in a series of stories written by Lisa Fowler, framed around the mysterious death of Father Raymond Nelson. The story was picked up by all the national and international press services. Several Ohio prosecutors, including Dayton and Montgomery County prosecutor Clifford Wolfe, were indeed interested in the material.

Following the publication of Lisa Fowler's articles, Father Trevor Williams was not questioned by the archbishop about the possibility that he may have played a role in the release of the material from the archives. On the contrary, he was appointed the new Moderator of the Curia for the Archdiocese of Cincinnati, *and*, without first consulting the Vatican *or* the United States Conference of Catholic

Bishops, the archbishop himself announced that in the future, the secret archives would be made available to anyone, or the representative of anyone, with a legitimate claim to the material.

One week later, the Archbishop of Cincinnati was forced to *"retire"* due to *"the onset of dementia"* and was moved to the Vatican in Rome to live out the rest of his life. The Archbishop of Anchorage was named as the new Archbishop of Cincinnati, and his first official act was to rescind the announcement made by his predecessor. The secret archives would remain closed.

Within a month of the archive material being made public, Lisa Fowler was contacted by five different men who claimed to have been molested by Father Nelson. All five identified themselves and agreed to be interviewed. Among them was the mystery caller who had been raped by the priest in Toledo, the man who had shared his story in Father Metzger's confessional – and John Burke.

Lisa conducted interviews with all of the men, as well as with old Mike Donnelly, and their stories were published. She and Donnelly have since grown close, and she often picks him up at the Manor House in Belmont and takes him out to lunch. She even bought him a new recliner. One of Donnelly's daughters has gotten back in touch with the old man.

Mary Lou Spaulding passed away a few weeks after Father Nelson's unfathomable, perverted history was revealed in the *Dayton Daily News*. The staff at The Oakwood retirement community believes that she died from a broken heart.

In November, an ugly sex abuse scandal broke involving a nationally famous college football program. Two weeks later, inspired in part by the horrific nature of that scandal, Kenny Mason of Ithaca, New York, and retired Brigadier General Jim McGowan, came forward and confessed their involvement in the death of Father Raymond Nelson. Their confession was made at a conference that had been arranged in a room at the Dayton Safety Building. Besides McGowan and Mason, it was attended by Dayton and Montgomery County Prosecutor Clifford Wolfe, former Police Captain John Burke, his son Captain Kevin Burke (now Supervisor of the Homicide/Assault Squad for the DPD) and Major Claire Winston, Director of Special Investigations for the DPD. Also present were a police reporter, a court reporter, and Lisa Fowler from the *Dayton Daily News* – by special request from former Captain John Burke.

Lisa Fowler's article describing the conference appeared two days later in a special Thanksgiving edition of the *Dayton Daily News* (much to Lisa's delight, the owners of the DDN decided not sell the paper to the Gannett group.) Again, her story went national. A week later Lisa received a call from an editor at Random House in New York, who asked if she would be interested in writing a book, based generally on the material released from the archives, but more specifically on the stories of John Burke, Kenny Mason, and the other men abused by Father Nelson. She has since signed a six-figure book deal with Random House, and is currently working on the book. Her working title, based on a comment made by Kenny Mason during one of her interviews with him, is *Satan's Choir*.

* * *

John Burke is now a retired cop, but a man's work is never done . . .

ACKNOWLEDGEMENTS

Thanks to my wife and soul mate, Annie Campbell, and to all the members of both of our families, especially Harry, Richard, Cody, and Robin. To Emily Rhoads Johnson, for her tremendous editorial efforts. To Lamar Herrin, Cara Hoffman, Greg Dearth, Tom "Peach" Hampton, Donny Christian, Dan Matusiewicz, Jim Reidy, Jason Koski, Teri Hubbard of the Dayton Police Department, Bruce Williamson of the Southern Ohio Diving Academy, and Jim Kennard, shipwreck explorer.

Made in United States
North Haven, CT
02 December 2022

27737996R00157